The Inmost Light
and Other Tales

By Arthur Machen

ISBN: 978-1-63118-531-1

Esoteric Classics:
Occult Fiction

Other Books in this Series and Related Titles

The Devil in Love by Jacques Cazotte (978–1–63118–499–4)

With the Adepts or An Adventure Among the Rosicrucians (978-1-63118-523-6)

A Weird Tale & Other Supernatural Stories by W Q Judge (978–1–63118–518–2)

On the Cave of the Nymphs in the Odyssey by Thomas Taylor (978-1-63118-505-2)

The Comte de St. Germain: The Secret of Kings (978-1-63118-525-0)

The Janeites, The Man Who Would Be King and Other Stories of Freemasonry by Rudyard Kipling (978–1–63118–480–2)

Rosa Alchemica, The Tables of Law & The Adoration of the Magi by William Butler Yeats (978–1–63118–421–5)

The Poem of Hashish by A Crowley & C Baudelaire (978-1-63118-484-0)

The Great God Pan by Arthur Machen (978–1–63118–528–1)

The Star and the Garter by Aleister Crowley (978-1-63118-406-2)

Thirty–One Hymns to the Star Goddess by Frater Achad (978–1–63118–422–2)

A Collection of Magical Writings, Fiction, Poetry & Essays by Aleister Crowley (978–63118–424–6)

The Treasure of Atlantis by J Allan Dunn (978-1-63118-522-9)

The Sword of Welleran and Other Stories by Lord Dunsany (978-1-63118-501-4)

The Smoky God or A Voyage to the Inner World by Emerson (978-1-63118-423-9)

The Wendigo and Other Haunting Tales by A Blackwood (978–1–63118–529–8)

A Collection of Fiction and Essays by Occult Writers on Supernatural and Metaphysical Subjects by various (978–1–63118–510–6)

The A. E. Waite Reader: A Selection of Occult Essays (978–1–63118–515–1)

The Leadbeater Reader: A Selection of Occult Essays (978–1–63118–483–3)

Audio versions are also available on Audible, Amazon and Apple

Other Books in this Series and Related Titles

Paracelsus, the Four Elements and Their Spirits by M P Hall (978-1-63118-400-0)

The Magician's Heavenly Chaos by Thomas Vaughan (978-1-63118-500-7)

Confessions of an English Opium–Eater by T De Quincey (978–1–63118–485–7)

Masonic and Rosicrucian History by M P Hall & H Voorhis (978-1-63118-486-4)

Tao Te Ching & Commentary by Lao Tzu & C Johnston (978-1-63118-495-6)

The Influence of Pythagoras on Freemasonry and Other Essays (978-1-63118-404-8)

The Golden Verses of Pythagoras: Five Translations (978-1-63118-479-6)

On the Philadelphian Gold by Philochrysus & Philadelphus (978-1-63118-511-3)

The Secret Book of the Philosopher's Stone by Artephius (978-1-63118-517-5)

Aurora of the Philosophers by Paracelsus (978-1-63118-507-6)

A Collection of Early Writings on Astral Travel (978-1-63118-477-2)

Rosicrucian Rules, Secret Signs, Codes and Symbols by various (978–1–63118–488–8)

The Old Past Master by Carl H Claudy (978-1-63118-464-2)

Arcane Formulas or Mental Alchemy by W W Atkinson (978–1–63118–459–8)

The Hymns of Hermes by G. R. S. Mead (978-1-63118-405-5)

Clairvoyance and Psychic Abilities by Leadbeater & Besant (978-1-63118-403-1)

The Feminine Occult by various authors (978-1-63118-711-7)

Crystal Vision Through Crystal Gazing by Frater Achad (978–1–63118–455–0)

*A Collection of Writings Related to Occult, Esoteric, Rosicrucian and Hermetic Literature,
Including Freemasonry, the Kabbalah, the Tarot, Alchemy and Theosophy*
various authors *Volumes 1-4*
(978-1-63118-713-1) (978-1-63118-714-8)
(978-1-63118-715-5) (978-1-63118-716-2)

Audio Versions are also available on Audible, Amazon and Apple

Table of Contents

INTRODUCTION

The word "esoteric" can be difficult to define. Esotericism in general can be seen less as a system of beliefs and more as a category, which encompasses numerous, different systems of beliefs. It's a bit of juxtaposition, since the word "esoteric" indicates something that few people know about, while the term itself broadly covers numerous philosophies, practices, areas of study and belief systems.

In a greater sense, Esotericism acts as a storehouse for secret knowledge, which is often considered ancient (by *tradition, if not by fact),* passed down from generation to generation, in private. At various times in history, simply possessing the knowledge of some of these subjects, was considered illegal and a jailable offence, if discovered. This usually included such general topics as Alchemy, Pharmacology, Qabalah, Hermeticism, Occultism, Ceremonial Magic, Astrology, Divination, Rosicrucianism and so on. Collectively, these areas of study were often referred to as the esoteric sciences.

Sometimes, the outer garment of a subject isn't esoteric, while what is hidden beneath it, is. As an example, Freemasonry isn't necessarily esoteric by nature (at *least not anymore),* but certain signs, passwords and handshakes given to the candidate during their initiation, are in fact, esoteric, in the sense that they are hidden from the general public.

Today, in the twenty-first century, such topics are readily available at bookstores across the country, and numerous main-steam publishers offer beginners guides and coffee-table volumes on many of these subjects, intended for mass appeal. Books like "*The*

Secret" have turned previously arcane topics into household knowledge. All that being the case, however, it isn't to say that there still aren't buried secrets to uncover, ancient wisdom being ignored and forgotten mysteries to be explored. In fact, it is often that we are only able to further our own studies by standing on the shoulders of these disappearing giants.

Lamp of Trismegistus is doing its part to help preserve humanity's esoteric history by making some of these classics available to those students who are seeking to unearth the knowledge of these ancient colossi.

So, be sure to check other titles from our *Esoteric Classics* series, as well as our *Occult Fiction, Theosophical Classics, Foundations of Freemasonry Series, Supernatural Fiction, Paranormal Research Series, Studies in Buddhism* and our *Christian Apocrypha Series*. You can also download the audio versions of most of these titles from Amazon, Apple or Audible, for learning on the go.

THE INMOST LIGHT

I

One evening in autumn, when the deformities of London were veiled in faint blue mist, and its vistas and far-reaching streets seemed splendid, Mr. Charles Salisbury was slowly pacing down Rupert Street, drawing nearer to his favourite restaurant by slow degrees. His eyes were downcast in study of the pavement, and thus it was that as he passed in at the narrow door a man who had come up from the lower end of the street jostled against him.

'I beg your pardon—wasn't looking where I was going. Why, it's Dyson!'

'Yes, quite so. How are you, Salisbury?'

'Quite well. But where have you been, Dyson? I don't think I can have seen you for the last five years?'

'No; I dare say not. You remember I was getting rather hard up when you came to my place at Charlotte Street?'

'Perfectly. I think I remember your telling me that you owed five weeks' rent, and that you had parted with your watch for a comparatively small sum.'

'My dear Salisbury, your memory is admirable. Yes, I was hard up. But the curious thing is that soon after you saw me I became harder up. My financial state was described by a friend as "stone broke." I don't approve of slang, mind you, but such was my condition. But suppose we go in; there might be other people who would like to dine—it's a human weakness, Salisbury.'

'Certainly; come along. I was wondering as I walked down whether the corner table were taken. It has a velvet back, you know.'

'I know the spot; it's vacant. Yes, as I was saying, I became even harder up.'

'What did you do then?' asked Salisbury, disposing of his hat, and settling down in the corner of the seat, with a glance of fond anticipation at the menu.

'What did I do? Why, I sat down and reflected. I had a good classical education, and a positive distaste for business of any kind: that was the capital with which I faced the world. Do you know, I have heard people describe olives as nasty! What lamentable Philistinism! I have often thought, Salisbury, that I could write genuine poetry under the influence of olives and red wine. Let us have Chianti; it may not be very good, but the flasks are simply charming.'

'It is pretty good here. We may as well have a big flask.'

'Very good. I reflected, then, on my want of prospects, and I determined to embark in literature.'

'Really; that was strange. You seem in pretty comfortable circumstances, though.'

'Though! What a satire upon a noble profession. I am afraid, Salisbury, you haven't a proper idea of the dignity of an artist. You see me sitting at my desk—or at least you can see me if you care to call—with pen and ink, and simple nothingness before me, and if you come again in a few hours you will (in all probability) find a creation!'

'Yes, quite so. I had an idea that literature was not remunerative.'

'You are mistaken; its rewards are great. I may mention, by the way, that shortly after you saw me I succeeded to a small income. An uncle died, and proved unexpectedly generous.'

'Ah, I see. That must have been convenient.'

'It was pleasant—undeniably pleasant. I have always considered it in the light of an endowment of my researches. I told you I was a man of letters; it would, perhaps, be more correct to describe myself as a man of science.'

'Dear me, Dyson, you have really changed very much in the last few years. I had a notion, don't you know, that you were a sort of idler about town, the kind of man one might meet on the north side of Piccadilly every day from May to July.'

'Exactly. I was even then forming myself, though all unconsciously. You know my poor father could not afford to send me to the University. I used to grumble in my ignorance at not having completed my education. That was the folly of youth, Salisbury; my University was Piccadilly. There I began to study the great science which still occupies me.'

'What science do you mean?'

'The science of the great city; the physiology of London; literally and metaphysically the greatest subject that the mind of man can conceive. What an admirable salmi this is; undoubtedly the final end of the pheasant. Yet I feel sometimes positively overwhelmed with the thought of the vastness and complexity of London. Paris a man may get to understand thoroughly with a reasonable amount of study; but London is always a mystery. In Paris you may say: "Here live the actresses, here the Bohemians, and the Ratés"; but it is different in London. You may point out a street, correctly enough, as the abode of washerwomen; but, in that second floor, a man may be studying Chaldee roots, and in the garret over the way a forgotten artist is dying by inches.'

'I see you are Dyson, unchanged and unchangeable,' said Salisbury, slowly sipping his Chianti. 'I think you are misled by a too fervid imagination; the mystery of London exists only in your fancy. It seems to me a dull place enough. We seldom hear of a really artistic crime in London, whereas I believe Paris abounds in that sort of thing.'

'Give me some more wine. Thanks. You are mistaken, my dear fellow, you are really mistaken. London has nothing to be ashamed of in the way of crime. Where we fail is for want of Homers, not Agamemnons. Carent quia vate sacro, you know.'

'I recall the quotation. But I don't think I quite follow you.'

'Well, in plain language, we have no good writers in London who make a speciality of that kind of thing. Our common reporter is a dull dog; every story that he has to tell is spoilt in the telling. His idea of horror and of what excites horror is so lamentably deficient. Nothing will content the fellow but blood, vulgar red blood, and when he can get it he lays it on thick, and considers that he has produced a telling article. It's a poor notion. And, by some curious fatality, it is the most commonplace and brutal murders which always attract the most attention and get written up the most. For instance, I dare say that you never heard of the Harlesden case?'

'No; no, I don't remember anything about it.'

'Of course not. And yet the story is a curious one. I will tell it you over our coffee. Harlesden, you know, or I expect you don't know, is quite on the out-quarters of London; something curiously different from your fine old crusted suburb like Norwood or Hampstead, different as each of these is from the other. Hampstead, I mean, is where you look for the head of your great China house with his three acres of land and pine-houses, though of late there is the artistic substratum; while Norwood is the home of the prosperous middle-class family who took the house "because it was near the Palace," and sickened of the Palace six months afterwards; but Harlesden is a place of no character. It's too new to have any character as yet. There are the rows of red houses and the rows of white houses and the bright green Venetians, and the blistering doorways, and the little backyards they call gardens, and a few feeble shops, and then, just as you think you're going to grasp the physiognomy of the settlement, it all melts away.'

'How the dickens is that? the houses don't tumble down before one's eyes, I suppose!'

'Well, no, not exactly that. But Harlesden as an entity disappears. Your street turns into a quiet lane, and your staring houses into elm trees, and the back-gardens into green meadows. You pass instantly from town to country; there is no transition as in a small country town, no soft gradations of wider lawns and orchards, with houses gradually becoming less dense, but a dead stop. I believe the people who live there mostly go into the City. I have seen once or twice a laden 'bus bound thitherwards. But however that may be, I can't conceive a greater loneliness in a desert at midnight than there is there at midday. It is like a city of the dead; the streets are glaring and desolate, and as you pass it suddenly strikes you that this too is part of London. Well, a year or two ago there was a doctor living there; he had set up his brass plate and his red lamp at the very end of one of those shining streets, and from the back of the house, the fields stretched away to the north. I don't know what his reason was in settling down in such an out-of-the-way place, perhaps Dr. Black, as we will call him, was a far-seeing man and looked ahead. His relations, so it appeared afterwards, had lost sight of him for many years and didn't even know he was a doctor, much less where he lived. However, there he was settled in Harlesden, with some fragments of a practice, and an uncommonly pretty wife. People used to see them walking out together in the summer evenings soon after they came to Harlesden, and, so far as could be observed, they seemed a very affectionate couple. These walks went on through the autumn, and then ceased; but, of course, as the days grew dark and the weather cold, the lanes near Harlesden might be expected to lose many of their attractions. All through the winter nobody saw anything of Mrs. Black; the doctor used to reply to his patients' inquiries that she was a "little out of sorts, would be better, no doubt, in the spring." But the spring came, and the summer, and no Mrs. Black appeared, and at last people began to rumour and talk amongst themselves, and all sorts of queer things were said at "high teas," which you may possibly have heard are the only form of entertainment known in such suburbs. Dr. Black began to surprise some very odd looks cast in his direction, and the practice, such as it was, fell off before his eyes. In short, when the neighbours whispered about the matter, they whispered that Mrs. Black was dead, and that the doctor had made away with her. But this wasn't the case; Mrs. Black was seen alive in June. It was a Sunday afternoon, one of those few exquisite days that an English climate offers, and half London had strayed out into the fields, north, south, east, and west to smell the scent of the white May, and to see if the wild roses were yet in blossom in the hedges. I had gone out myself early in the morning, and had had a long ramble, and somehow or other as I was steering homeward I found myself in this very Harlesden we have been talking about. To be exact, I had a glass of beer in the "General Gordon," the most flourishing house in the neighbourhood, and as I was wandering rather aimlessly about, I saw an uncommonly tempting gap in a hedgerow, and resolved to explore the meadow beyond. Soft grass is very grateful to the feet after the infernal grit strewn on suburban sidewalks, and after walking about for some time I thought I should like to sit down on a bank and have a smoke. While I was getting out my pouch, I looked up in the direction of the houses, and as I looked I felt my breath caught back, and my teeth began to chatter, and the stick I had in one hand snapped in two with the grip I gave it. It was as if I had had an electric current down my spine, and yet for some moment of time which seemed long, but which must have been very short, I caught myself wondering what on earth was the matter. Then I knew what had made my very heart shudder and my bones grind together in an agony. As I glanced up I had looked straight towards the last house in the row before me, and in an upper window of that house I had seen for some short fraction of a second a face. It was the face of a woman, and yet it was not human. You and I, Salisbury, have heard in our time, as we sat in our seats in church in sober English fashion, of a lust that cannot be satiated and of a fire that is unquenchable, but few of us have any notion what these words mean. I hope you never may, for as I saw that face at the window, with the blue sky above me and the warm air playing in gusts about me, I knew I had looked into another world—looked through the window of a commonplace, brand-new house, and seen hell open before me. When the first shock was over, I thought once or twice that I should have fainted; my face streamed with a cold sweat, and my breath came and went in sobs, as if I had been half drowned. I managed to get up at last, and walked round to the street, and there I saw the name "Dr. Black" on the post by the front gate. As fate or my luck would have it, the door opened and a man came down the steps as I passed by. I had no doubt it was the doctor himself. He was of a type rather common in London; long and thin, with a pasty face and a dull black moustache. He gave me a look as we passed each other on the pavement, and though it was merely the casual glance which one foot-passenger bestows on another, I felt convinced in my mind that here was an ugly customer to deal with. As you may imagine, I went my way a good deal puzzled and horrified too by what I had seen; for I had paid another visit to the

"General Gordon," and had got together a good deal of the common gossip of the place about the Blacks. I didn't mention the fact that I had seen a woman's face in the window; but I heard that Mrs. Black had been much admired for her beautiful golden hair, and round what had struck me with such a nameless terror, there was a mist of flowing yellow hair, as it were an aureole of glory round the visage of a satyr. The whole thing bothered me in an indescribable manner; and when I got home I tried my best to think of the impression I had received as an illusion, but it was no use. I knew very well I had seen what I have tried to describe to you, and I was morally certain that I had seen Mrs. Black. And then there was the gossip of the place, the suspicion of foul play, which I knew to be false, and my own conviction that there was some deadly mischief or other going on in that bright red house at the corner of Devon Road: how to construct a theory of a reasonable kind out of these two elements. In short, I found myself in a world of mystery; I puzzled my head over it and filled up my leisure moments by gathering together odd threads of speculation, but I never moved a step towards any real solution, and as the summer days went on the matter seemed to grow misty and indistinct, shadowing some vague terror, like a nightmare of last month. I suppose it would before long have faded into the background of my brain—I should not have forgotten it, for such a thing could never be forgotten—but one morning as I was looking over the paper my eye was caught by a heading over some two dozen lines of small type. The words I had seen were simply, "The Harlesden Case," and I knew what I was going to read. Mrs. Black was dead. Black had called in another medical man to certify as to cause of death, and something or other had aroused the strange doctor's suspicions and there had been an inquest and post-mortem. And the result? That, I will confess, did astonish me considerably; it was the triumph of the unexpected. The two doctors who made the autopsy were obliged to confess that they could not discover the faintest trace of any kind of foul play; their most exquisite tests and reagents failed to detect the presence of poison in the most infinitesimal quantity. Death, they found, had been caused by a somewhat obscure and scientifically interesting form of brain disease. The tissue of the brain and the molecules of the grey matter had undergone a most extraordinary series of changes; and the younger of the two doctors, who has some reputation, I believe, as a specialist in brain trouble, made some remarks in giving his evidence which struck me deeply at the time, though I did not then grasp their full significance. He said: "At the commencement of the examination I was astonished to find appearances of a character entirely new to me, notwithstanding my somewhat large experience. I need not specify these appearances at present, it will be sufficient for me to state that as I proceeded in my task I could scarcely believe that the brain before me was that of a human being at all." There was some surprise at this statement, as you may imagine, and the coroner asked the doctor if he meant to say that the brain resembled that of an animal. "No," he replied, "I should not put it in that way. Some of the appearances I noticed seemed to point in that direction, but others, and these were the more surprising, indicated a nervous organization of a wholly different character from that either of man or the lower animals." It was a curious thing to say, but of course the jury brought in a verdict of death from natural causes, and, so far as the public was concerned, the case came to an end. But after I had read what the doctor said I made up my mind that I should like to know a good deal more, and I set to work on what seemed likely to prove an interesting investigation. I had really a good deal of trouble, but I was successful in a measure. Though why—my dear fellow, I had no notion at the time. Are you aware that we have been here nearly four hours? The waiters are staring at us. Let's have the bill and be gone.'

The two men went out in silence, and stood a moment in the cool air, watching the hurrying traffic of Coventry Street pass before them to the accompaniment of the ringing bells of hansoms and the cries of the newsboys; the deep far murmur of London surging up ever and again from beneath these louder noises.

'It is a strange case, isn't it?' said Dyson at length. 'What do you think of it?'

'My dear fellow, I haven't heard the end, so I will reserve my opinion. When will you give me the sequel?'

'Come to my rooms some evening; say next Thursday. Here's the address. Good-night; I want to get down to the Strand.' Dyson hailed a passing hansom, and Salisbury turned northward to walk home to his lodgings.

II

Mr. Salisbury, as may have been gathered from the few remarks which he had found it possible to introduce in the course of the evening, was a young gentleman of a peculiarly solid form of intellect, coy and retiring before the mysterious and the uncommon, with a constitutional dislike of paradox. During the restaurant dinner he had been forced to listen in almost absolute silence to a strange tissue of improbabilities strung together with the ingenuity of a born meddler in plots and mysteries, and it was with a feeling of weariness that he crossed Shaftesbury Avenue, and dived into the recesses of Soho, for his lodgings were in a modest neighbourhood to the north of Oxford Street. As he walked he speculated on the probable fate of Dyson, relying on literature, unbefriended by a thoughtful relative, and could not help concluding that so much subtlety united to a too vivid imagination would in all likelihood have been rewarded with a pair of sandwich-boards or a super's banner. Absorbed in this train of thought, and admiring the perverse dexterity which could transmute the face of a sickly woman and a case of brain disease into the crude elements of romance, Salisbury strayed on through the dimly-lighted streets, not noticing the gusty wind which drove sharply round corners and whirled the stray rubbish of the pavement into the air in eddies, while black clouds gathered over the sickly yellow moon. Even a stray drop or two of rain blown into his face did not rouse him from his meditations, and it was only when with a sudden rush the storm tore down upon the street that he began to consider the expediency of finding some shelter. The rain, driven by the wind, pelted down with the violence of a thunderstorm, dashing up from the stones and hissing through the air, and soon a perfect torrent of water coursed along the kennels and accumulated in pools over the choked-up drains. The few stray passengers who had been loafing rather than walking about the street had scuttered away, like frightened rabbits, to some invisible places of refuge, and though Salisbury whistled loud and long for a hansom, no hansom appeared. He looked about him, as if to discover how far he might be from the haven of Oxford Street, but strolling carelessly along, he had turned out of his way, and found himself in an unknown region, and one to all appearance devoid even of a public-house where shelter could be bought for the modest sum of twopence. The street lamps were few and at long intervals, and burned behind grimy glasses with the sickly light of oil, and by this wavering glimmer Salisbury could make out the shadowy and vast old houses of which the street was composed. As he passed along, hurrying, and shrinking from the full sweep of the rain, he noticed the innumerable bell-handles, with names that seemed about to vanish of old age graven on brass plates beneath them, and here and there a richly carved penthouse overhung the door, blackening with the grime of fifty years. The storm seemed to grow more and more furious; he was wet through, and a new hat had become a ruin, and still Oxford Street seemed as far off as ever; it was with deep relief that the dripping man caught sight of a dark archway which seemed to promise shelter from the rain if not from the wind. Salisbury took up his position in the driest corner and looked about him; he was standing in a kind of passage contrived under part of a house, and behind him stretched a narrow footway leading between blank walls to regions unknown. He had stood there for some time, vainly endeavouring to rid himself of some of his superfluous moisture, and listening for the passing wheel of a hansom, when his attention was aroused by a loud noise coming from the direction of the passage behind, and growing louder as it drew nearer. In a couple of minutes he could make out the shrill, raucous voice of a woman, threatening and renouncing, and making the very stones echo with her accents, while now and then a man grumbled and expostulated. Though to all appearance devoid of romance, Salisbury had some relish for street rows, and was, indeed, somewhat of an amateur in the more amusing phases of drunkenness; he therefore composed himself to listen and observe with something of the air of a subscriber to grand opera. To his annoyance, however, the tempest seemed suddenly to be composed, and he could hear nothing but the impatient steps of the woman and the slow lurch of the man as they came towards him. Keeping back in the shadow of the wall, he could see the two drawing nearer; the man was evidently drunk, and had much ado to avoid frequent collision with the wall as he tacked across from one side to the other, like some bark beating up against a wind. The woman was looking straight in front of her, with tears streaming from her eyes, but suddenly as they went by the flame blazed up again, and she burst forth into a torrent of abuse, facing round upon her companion.

'You low rascal, you mean, contemptible cur,' she went on, after an incoherent storm of curses, 'you think I'm to work and slave for you always, I suppose, while you're after that Green Street girl and drinking every penny you've got? But you're mistaken, Sam—indeed, I'll bear it no longer. Damn you, you dirty thief, I've done with you and your master too, so you can go your own errands, and I only hope they'll get you into trouble.'

The woman tore at the bosom of her dress, and taking something out that looked like paper, crumpled it up and flung it away. It fell at Salisbury's feet. She ran out and disappeared in the darkness, while the man lurched slowly into the street, grumbling indistinctly to himself in a perplexed tone of voice. Salisbury looked out after him and saw him maundering along the pavement, halting now and then and swaying indecisively, and then starting off at some fresh tangent. The sky had cleared, and white fleecy clouds were fleeting across the moon, high in the heaven. The light came and went by turns, as the clouds passed by, and, turning round as the clear, white rays shone into the passage, Salisbury saw the little ball of crumpled paper which the woman had cast down. Oddly curious to know what it might contain, he picked it up and put it in his pocket, and set out afresh on his journey.

III

Salisbury was a man of habit. When he got home, drenched to the skin, his clothes hanging lank about him, and a ghastly dew besmearing his hat, his only thought was of his health, of which he took studious care. So, after changing his clothes and encasing himself in a warm dressing-gown, he proceeded to prepare a sudorific in the shape of a hot gin and water, warming the latter over one of those spirit-lamps which mitigate the austerities of the modern hermit's life. By the time this preparation had been exhibited, and Salisbury's disturbed feelings had been soothed by a pipe of tobacco, he was able to get into bed in a happy state of vacancy, without a thought of his adventure in the dark archway, or of the weird fancies with which Dyson had seasoned his dinner. It was the same at breakfast the next morning, for Salisbury made a point of not thinking of any thing until that meal was over; but when the cup and saucer were cleared away, and the morning pipe was lit, he remembered the little ball of paper, and began fumbling in the pockets of his wet coat. He did not remember into which pocket he had put it, and as he dived now into one and now into another, he experienced a strange feeling of apprehension lest it should not be there at all, though he could not for the life of him have explained the importance he attached to what was in all probability mere rubbish. But he sighed with relief when his fingers touched the crumpled surface in an inside pocket, and he drew it out gently and laid it on the little desk by his easy-chair with as much care as if it had been some rare jewel. Salisbury sat smoking and staring at his find for a few minutes, an odd temptation to throw the thing in the fire and have done with it struggling with as odd a speculation as to its possible contents, and as to the reason why the infuriated woman should have flung a bit of paper from her with such vehemence. As might be expected, it was the latter feeling that conquered in the end, and yet it was with something like repugnance that he at last took the paper and unrolled it, and laid it out before him. It was a piece of common dirty paper, to all appearance torn out of a cheap exercise-book, and in the middle were a few lines written in a queer cramped hand. Salisbury bent his head and stared eagerly at it for a moment, drawing a long breath, and then fell back in his chair gazing blankly before him, till at last with a sudden revulsion he burst into a peal of laughter, so long and loud and uproarious that the landlady's baby on the floor below awoke from sleep and echoed his mirth with hideous yells. But he laughed again and again, and took the paper up to read a second time what seemed such meaningless nonsense.

'Q. has had to go and see his friends in Paris,' it began. 'Traverse Handle S. "Once around the grass, and twice around the lass, and thrice around the maple tree."'

Salisbury took up the paper and crumpled it as the angry woman had done, and aimed it at the fire. He did not throw it there, however, but tossed it carelessly into the well of the desk, and laughed again. The sheer folly of the thing offended him, and he was ashamed of his own eager speculation, as one who pores over the high-sounding announcements in the agony column of the daily paper, and finds nothing but advertisement and triviality. He walked to the window, and stared out at the languid morning life of his quarter; the maids in slatternly print dresses washing door-steps, the fish-monger and the butcher on their rounds, and the tradesmen standing at the doors of their small shops, drooping for lack of trade and excitement. In the distance a blue haze gave some grandeur to the prospect, but the view as a whole was depressing, and would only have interested a student of the life of London, who finds something rare and choice in its very aspect. Salisbury turned away in disgust, and settled himself in the easy-chair, upholstered in a bright shade of green, and decked with yellow gimp, which was the pride and attraction of the apartments. Here he composed himself to his morning's occupation—the perusal of a novel that dealt with sport and love in a manner that suggested the collaboration of a stud-groom and a ladies' college. In an ordinary way, however, Salisbury would have been carried on by the interest of the story up to lunch-time, but this morning he fidgeted in and out of his chair, took the book up and laid it down again, and swore at last to himself and at himself in mere irritation. In point of fact the jingle of the paper found in the archway had 'got into his head,' and do what he would he could not help muttering over and over, 'Once around the grass, and twice around the lass, and thrice around the maple tree.' It became a positive pain, like the foolish burden of a music-hall song, everlastingly quoted, and sung at all hours of the day and night, and treasured by the street-boys as an unfailing resource for six months together. He went out into the streets, and tried to forget his enemy in the jostling of the crowds and the roar and clatter of the traffic, but presently he would find himself stealing quietly aside, and pacing some deserted byway, vainly puzzling his brains, and trying to fix some meaning to phrases that were meaningless. It was a positive relief when Thursday came, and he remembered that he had made an appointment to go and see Dyson; the flimsy reveries of the self-styled man of letters appeared entertaining when compared with this ceaseless iteration, this maze of thought from which there seemed no possibility of escape. Dyson's abode was in one of the quietest of the quiet streets that led down from the Strand to the river, and when Salisbury passed from the narrow stairway into his friend's room, he saw that the uncle had been beneficent indeed. The floor glowed and flamed with all the colours of the East; it was, as Dyson pompously remarked, 'a sunset in a dream,' and the lamplight, the twilight of London streets, was shut out with strangely worked curtains, glittering here and there with threads of gold. In the shelves of an oak armoire stood jars and plates of old French china, and the black and white of etchings not to be found in the Haymarket or in Bond Street, stood out against the splendour of a Japanese paper. Salisbury sat down on the settle by the hearth, and sniffed the mingled fumes of incense and tobacco, wondering and dumb before all this splendour after the green rep and the oleographs, the gilt-framed mirror, and the lustres of his own apartment.

'I am glad you have come,' said Dyson. 'Comfortable little room, isn't it? But you don't look very well, Salisbury. Nothing disagreed with you, has it?'

'No; but I have been a good deal bothered for the last few days. The fact is I had an odd kind of—of—adventure, I suppose I may call it, that night I saw you, and it has worried me a good deal. And the provoking part of it is that it's the merest nonsense—but, however, I will tell you all about it, by and by. You were going to let me have the rest of that odd story you began at the restaurant.'

'Yes. But I am afraid, Salisbury, you are incorrigible. You are a slave to what you call matter of fact. You know perfectly well that in your heart you think the oddness in that case is of my making, and that it is all really as plain as the police reports. However, as I have begun, I will go on. But first we will have something to drink, and you may as well light your pipe.'

Dyson went up to the oak cupboard, and drew from its depths a rotund bottle and two little glasses, quaintly gilded.

'It's Benedictine,' he said. 'You'll have some, won't you?'

Salisbury assented, and the two men sat sipping and smoking reflectively for some minutes before Dyson began.

'Let me see,' he said at last, 'we were at the inquest, weren't we? No, we had done with that. Ah, I remember. I was telling you that on the whole I had been successful in my inquiries, investigation, or whatever you like to call it, into the matter. Wasn't that where I left off?'

'Yes, that was it. To be precise, I think "though" was the last word you said on the matter.'

'Exactly. I have been thinking it all over since the other night, and I have come to the conclusion that that "though" is a very big "though" indeed. Not to put too fine a point on it, I have had to confess that what I found out, or thought I found out, amounts in reality to nothing. I am as far away from the heart of the case as ever. However, I may as well tell you what I do know. You may remember my saying that I was impressed a good deal by some remarks of one of the doctors who gave evidence at the inquest. Well, I determined that my first step must be to try if I could get something more definite and intelligible out of that doctor. Somehow or other I managed to get an introduction to the man, and he gave me an appointment to come and see him. He turned out to be a pleasant, genial fellow; rather young and not in the least like the typical medical man, and he began the conference by offering me whisky and cigars. I didn't think it worth while to beat about the bush, so I began by saying that part of his evidence at the Harlesden Inquest struck me as very peculiar, and I gave him the printed report, with the sentences in question underlined. He just glanced at the slip, and gave me a queer look. "It struck you as peculiar, did it?" said he. "Well, you must remember that the Harlesden case was very peculiar. In fact, I think I may safely say that in some features it was unique—quite unique." "Quite so," I replied, "and that's exactly why it interests me, and why I want to know more about it. And I thought that if anybody could give me any information it would be you. What is your opinion of the matter?"

'It was a pretty downright sort of question, and my doctor looked rather taken aback.

'"Well," he said, "as I fancy your motive in inquiring into the question must be mere curiosity, I think I may tell you my opinion with tolerable freedom. So, Mr., Mr. Dyson? if you want to know my theory, it is this: I believe that Dr. Black killed his wife."

'"But the verdict," I answered, "the verdict was given from your own evidence."

'"Quite so; the verdict was given in accordance with the evidence of my colleague and myself, and, under the circumstances, I think the jury acted very sensibly. In fact, I don't see what else they could have done. But I stick to my opinion, mind you, and I say this also. I don't wonder at Black's doing what I firmly believe he did. I think he was justified."

'"Justified! How could that be?" I asked. I was astonished, as you may imagine, at the answer I had got. The doctor wheeled round his chair and looked steadily at me for a moment before he answered.

"'I suppose you are not a man of science yourself? No; then it would be of no use my going into detail. I have always been firmly opposed myself to any partnership between physiology and psychology. I believe that both are bound to suffer. No one recognizes more decidedly than I do the impassable gulf, the fathomless abyss that separates the world of consciousness from the sphere of matter. We know that every change of consciousness is accompanied by a rearrangement of the molecules in the grey matter; and that is all. What the link between them is, or why they occur together, we do not know, and most authorities believe that we never can know. Yet, I will tell you that as I did my work, the knife in my hand, I felt convinced, in spite of all theories, that what lay before me was not the brain of a dead woman—not the brain of a human being at all. Of course I saw the face; but it was quite placid, devoid of all expression. It must have been a beautiful face, no doubt, but I can honestly say that I would not have looked in that face when there was life behind it for a thousand guineas, no, nor for twice that sum."

"'My dear sir,' I said, "you surprise me extremely. You say that it was not the brain of a human being. What was it then?"

"'The brain of a devil.' He spoke quite coolly, and never moved a muscle. "The brain of a devil," he repeated, "and I have no doubt that Black found some way of putting an end to it. I don't blame him if he did. Whatever Mrs. Black was, she was not fit to stay in this world. Will you have anything more? No? Good-night, good-night."

'It was a queer sort of opinion to get from a man of science, wasn't it? When he was saying that he would not have looked on that face when alive for a thousand guineas, or two thousand guineas, I was thinking of the face I had seen, but I said nothing. I went again to Harlesden, and passed from one shop to another, making small purchases, and trying to find out whether there was anything about the Blacks which was not already common property, but there was very little to hear. One of the tradesmen to whom I spoke said he had known the dead woman well; she used to buy of him such quantities of grocery as were required for their small household, for they never kept a servant, but had a charwoman in occasionally, and she had not seen Mrs. Black for months before she died. According to this man Mrs. Black was "a nice lady," always kind and considerate, and so fond of her husband and he of her, as every one thought. And yet, to put the doctor's opinion on one side, I knew what I had seen. And then after thinking it all over, and putting one thing with another, it seemed to me that the only person likely to give me much assistance would be Black himself, and I made up my mind to find him.

Of course he wasn't to be found in Harlesden; he had left, I was told, directly after the funeral. Everything in the house had been sold, and one fine day Black got into the train with a small portmanteau, and went, nobody knew where. It was a chance if he were ever heard of again, and it was by a mere chance that I came across him at last. I was walking one day along Gray's Inn Road, not bound for anywhere in particular, but looking about me, as usual, and holding on to my hat, for it was a gusty day in early March, and the wind was making the treetops in the Inn rock and quiver. I had come up from the Holborn end, and I had almost got to Theobald's Road when I noticed a man walking in front of me, leaning on a stick, and to all appearance very feeble. There was something about his look that made me curious, I don't know why, and I began to walk briskly with the idea of overtaking him, when of a sudden his hat blew off and came bounding along the pavement to my feet. Of course I rescued the hat, and gave it a glance as I went towards its owner. It was a biography in itself; a Piccadilly maker's name in the inside, but I don't think a beggar would have picked it out of the gutter. Then I looked up and saw Dr. Black of Harlesden waiting for me. A queer thing, wasn't it? But, Salisbury, what a change! When I saw Dr. Black come down the steps of his house at Harlesden he was an upright man, walking firmly with well-built limbs; a man, I should say, in the prime of his life. And now before me there crouched this wretched creature, bent and feeble, with shrunken cheeks, and hair that was whitening fast, and limbs that trembled and shook together, and misery in his eyes. He thanked me for bringing him his hat, saying, "I don't think I should ever have got it, I can't run much now. A gusty day, sir, isn't it?" and with this he was turning away, but by little and little I contrived to draw him into the current of conversation, and we walked together eastward. I think the man would have been glad to get rid of me; but I didn't intend to let him go, and he stopped at last in front of a miserable house in a miserable street. It was, I verily believe, one of the most wretched quarters I have ever seen: houses that must have been sordid and hideous enough when new, that had gathered foulness with every year, and now seemed to lean and totter to their fall. "I live up there," said Black, pointing to the tiles, "not in the front—in the back. I am very quiet there. I won't ask you to come in now, but perhaps some other day——" I caught him up at that, and told him I should be only too glad to come and see him. He gave me an odd sort of glance, as if he were wondering what on earth I or anybody else could care about him, and I left him fumbling with his latch-key. I think you will say I did pretty well when I tell you that within a few weeks I had made myself an intimate friend of Black's. I shall never forget the first time I went to his room; I hope I shall never see such abject, squalid misery again. The foul paper, from which all pattern or trace of a pattern had long vanished, subdued and penetrated with the grime of the evil street, was hanging in mouldering pennons from the wall. Only at the end of the room was it possible to stand upright, and the sight of the wretched bed and the odour of corruption that pervaded the place made me turn faint and sick. Here I found him munching a piece of bread; he seemed surprised to find that I had kept my promise, but he gave me his chair and sat on the bed while we talked. I used to go to see him often, and we had long conversations together, but he never mentioned Harlesden or his wife. I fancy that he supposed me ignorant of the matter, or thought that if I had heard of it, I should never connect the respectable Dr. Black of Harlesden with a poor garreteer in the backwoods of London. He was a strange man, and as we sat together smoking, I often wondered whether he were mad or sane, for I think the wildest dreams of Paracelsus and the Rosicrucians would appear plain and sober fact compared with the theories I have heard him earnestly advance in that grimy den of his. I once ventured to hint something of the sort to him. I suggested that something he had said was in flat contradiction to all science and all experience. "No," he answered, "not all experience, for mine counts for something. I am no dealer in unproved theories; what I say I have proved for myself, and at a terrible cost. There is a region of knowledge which you will never know, which wise men seeing from afar off shun like the plague, as well they may, but into that region I have gone. If you knew, if you could even dream of what may be done, of what one or two men have done in this quiet world of ours, your very soul would shudder and faint within you. What you have heard from me has been but the merest husk and outer covering of true science—that science which means death, and that which is more awful than death, to those who gain it. No, when men say that there are strange things in the world, they little know the awe and the terror that dwell always with them and about them." There was a sort of fascination about the man that drew me to him, and I was quite sorry to have to leave London for a month or two; I missed his odd talk. A few days after I came back to town I thought I would look him up, but when I gave the two rings at the bell that used to summon him, there was no answer. I rang and rang again, and was just turning to go away, when the door opened and a dirty woman asked me what I wanted. From her look I fancy she took me for a plain-clothes officer after one of her lodgers, but when I inquired if Mr. Black were in, she gave me a stare of another kind. "There's no Mr. Black lives here," she said. "He's gone. He's dead this six weeks. I always thought he was a bit queer in his head, or else had been and got into some trouble or other. He used to go out every morning from ten till one, and one Monday morning we heard him come in, and go into his room and shut the door, and a few minutes after, just as we was a-sitting down to our dinner, there was such a scream that I thought I should have gone right off. And then we heard a stamping, and down he came, raging and cursing most dreadful, swearing he had been robbed of something that was worth millions. And then he just dropped down in the passage, and we thought he was dead. We got him up to his room, and put him on his bed, and I just sat there and waited, while my 'usband he went for the doctor. And there was the winder wide open, and a little tin box he had lying on the floor open and empty, but of course nobody could possible have got in at the winder, and as for him having anything that was worth anything, it's nonsense, for he was often weeks and weeks behind with his rent, and my 'usband he threatened often and often to turn him into the street, for, as he said, we've got a living to myke like other people—and, of course, that's true; but, somehow, I didn't like to do it, though he was an odd kind of a man, and I fancy had been better off. And then the doctor came and looked at him, and said as he couldn't do nothing, and that night he died as I was a-sitting by his bed; and I can tell you that, with one thing and another, we lost money by him, for the few bits of clothes as he had were worth next to nothing when they came to be sold." I gave the woman half a sovereign for her trouble, and went home thinking of Dr. Black and the epitaph she had made him, and wondering at his strange fancy that he had been robbed. I take it that he had very little to fear on that score, poor fellow; but I suppose that he was really mad, and died in a sudden access of his mania. His landlady said that once or twice when she had had occasion to go into his room (to dun the poor wretch for his rent, most likely), he would keep her at the door for about a minute, and that when she came in she would find him putting away his tin box in the corner by the window; I suppose he had become possessed with the idea of some great treasure, and fancied himself a wealthy man in the midst of all his misery. Explicit, my tale is ended, and you see that though I knew Black, I know nothing of his wife or of the history of her death.—That's the Harlesden case, Salisbury, and I think it interests me all the more deeply because there does not seem the shadow of a possibility that I or any one else will ever know more about it. What do you think of it?'

'Well, Dyson, I must say that I think you have contrived to surround the whole thing with a mystery of your own making. I go for the doctor's solution: Black murdered his wife, being himself in all probability an undeveloped lunatic.'

'What? Do you believe, then, that this woman was something too awful, too terrible to be allowed to remain on the earth? You will remember that the doctor said it was the brain of a devil?'

'Yes, yes, but he was speaking, of course, metaphorically. It's really quite a simple matter if you only look at it like that.'

'Ah, well, you may be right; but yet I am sure you are not. Well, well, it's no good discussing it any more. A little more Benedictine? That's right; try some of this tobacco. Didn't you say that you had been bothered by something—something which happened that night we dined together?'

'Yes, I have been worried, Dyson, worried a great deal. I——But it's such a trivial matter—indeed, such an absurdity—that I feel ashamed to trouble you with it.'

'Never mind, let's have it, absurd or not.'

With many hesitations, and with much inward resentment of the folly of the thing, Salisbury told his tale, and repeated reluctantly the absurd intelligence and the absurder doggerel of the scrap of paper, expecting to hear Dyson burst out into a roar of laughter.

'Isn't it too bad that I should let myself be bothered by such stuff as that?' he asked, when he had stuttered out the jingle of once, and twice, and thrice.

Dyson listened to it all gravely, even to the end, and meditated for a few minutes in silence.

'Yes,' he said at length, 'it was a curious chance, your taking shelter in that archway just as those two went by. But I don't know that I should call what was written on the paper nonsense; it is bizarre certainly, but I expect it has a meaning for somebody. Just repeat it again, will you, and I will write it down. Perhaps we might find a cipher of some sort, though I hardly think we shall.'

Again had the reluctant lips of Salisbury slowly to stammer out the rubbish that he abhorred, while Dyson jotted it down on a slip of paper.

'Look over it, will you?' he said, when it was done; 'it may be important that I should have every word in its place. Is that all right?'

'Yes; that is an accurate copy. But I don't think you will get much out of it. Depend upon it, it is mere nonsense, a wanton scribble. I must be going now, Dyson. No, no more; that stuff of yours is pretty strong. Good-night.'

'I suppose you would like to hear from me, if I did find out anything?'

'No, not I; I don't want to hear about the thing again. You may regard the discovery, if it is one, as your own.'

'Very well. Good-night.'

IV

A good many hours after Salisbury had returned to the company of the green rep chairs, Dyson still sat at his desk, itself a Japanese romance, smoking many pipes, and meditating over his friend's story. The bizarre quality of the inscription which had annoyed Salisbury was to him an attraction, and now and again he took it up and scanned thoughtfully what he had written, especially the quaint jingle at the end. It was a token, a symbol, he decided, and not a cipher, and the woman who had flung it away was in all probability entirely ignorant of its meaning; she was but the agent of the 'Sam' she had abused and discarded, and he too was again the agent of some one unknown, possibly of the individual styled Q, who had been forced to visit his French friends. But what to make of 'Traverse Handle S.' Here was the root and source of the enigma, and not all the tobacco of Virginia seemed likely to suggest any clue here. It seemed almost hopeless, but Dyson regarded himself as the Wellington of mysteries, and went to bed feeling assured that sooner or later he would hit upon the right track For the next few days he was deeply engaged in his literary labours, labours which were a profound mystery even to the most intimate of his friends, who searched the railway bookstalls in vain for the result of so many hours spent at the Japanese bureau in company with strong tobacco and black tea. On this occasion Dyson confined himself to his room for four days, and it was with genuine relief that he laid down his pen and went out into the streets in quest of relaxation and fresh air. The gas-lamps were being lighted, and the fifth edition of the evening papers was being howled through the streets, and Dyson, feeling that he wanted quiet, turned away from the clamorous Strand, and began to trend away to the north-west. Soon he found himself in streets that echoed to his footsteps, and crossing a broad new thoroughfare, and verging still to the west, Dyson discovered that he had penetrated to the depths of Soho. Here again was life; rare vintages of France and Italy, at prices which seemed contemptibly small, allured the passer-by; here were cheeses, vast and rich, here olive oil, and here a grove of Rabelaisian sausages; while in a neighbouring shop the whole Press of Paris appeared to be on sale. In the middle of the roadway a strange miscellany of nations sauntered to and fro, for there cab and hansom rarely ventured; and from window over window the inhabitants looked forth in pleased contemplation of the scene. Dyson made his way slowly along, mingling with the crowd on the cobble-stones, listening to the queer babel of French and German, and Italian and English, glancing now and again at the shop-windows with their levelled batteries of bottles, and had almost gained the end of the street, when his attention was arrested by a small shop at the corner, a vivid contrast to its neighbours. It was the typical shop of the poor quarter; a shop entirely English. Here were vended tobacco and sweets, cheap pipes of clay and cherry-wood; penny exercise-books and penholders jostled for precedence with comic songs, and story papers with appalling cuts showed that romance claimed its place beside the actualities of the evening paper, the bills of which fluttered at the doorway. Dyson glanced up at the name above the door, and stood by the kennel trembling, for a sharp pang, the pang of one who has made a discovery, had for a moment left him incapable of motion. The name over the shop was Travers. Dyson looked up again, this time at the corner of the wall above the lamp-post, and read in white letters on a blue ground the words 'Handel Street, W. C.,' and the legend was repeated in fainter letters just below. He gave a little sigh of satisfaction, and without more ado walked boldly into the shop, and stared full in the face the fat man who was sitting behind the counter. The fellow rose to his feet, and returned the stare a little curiously, and then began in stereotyped phrase—

'What can I do for you, sir?'

Dyson enjoyed the situation and a dawning perplexity on the man's face. He propped his stick carefully against the counter and leaning over it, said slowly and impressively—

'Once around the grass, and twice around the lass, and thrice around the maple-tree.'

Dyson had calculated on his words producing an effect, and he was not disappointed. The vendor of miscellanies gasped, open-mouthed like a fish, and steadied himself against the counter. When he spoke, after a short interval, it was in a hoarse mutter, tremulous and unsteady.

'Would you mind saying that again, sir? I didn't quite catch it.'

'My good man, I shall most certainly do nothing of the kind. You heard what I said perfectly well. You have got a clock in your shop, I see; an admirable timekeeper, I have no doubt. Well, I give you a minute by your own clock.'

The man looked about him in a perplexed indecision, and Dyson felt that it was time to be bold.

'Look here, Travers, the time is nearly up. You have heard of Q, I think. Remember, I hold your life in my hands. Now!'

Dyson was shocked at the result of his own audacity. The man shrank and shrivelled in terror, the sweat poured down a face of ashy white, and he held up his hands before him.

'Mr. Davies, Mr. Davies, don't say that—don't for Heaven's sake. I didn't know you at first, I didn't indeed. Good God! Mr. Davies, you wouldn't ruin me? I'll get it in a moment.'

'You had better not lose any more time.'

The man slunk piteously out of his own shop, and went into a back parlour. Dyson heard his trembling fingers fumbling with a bunch of keys, and the creak of an opening box. He came back presently with a small package neatly tied up in brown paper in his hands, and, still full of terror, handed it to Dyson.

'I'm glad to be rid of it,' he said. 'I'll take no more jobs of this sort.'

Dyson took the parcel and his stick, and walked out of the shop with a nod, turning round as he passed the door. Travers had sunk into his seat, his face still white with terror, with one hand over his eyes, and Dyson speculated a good deal as he walked rapidly away as to what queer chords those could be on which he had played so roughly. He hailed the first hansom he could see and drove home, and when he had lit his hanging lamp, and laid his parcel on the table, he paused for a moment, wondering on what strange thing the lamplight would soon shine. He locked his door, and cut the strings, and unfolded the paper layer after layer, and came at last to a small wooden box, simply but solidly made. There was no lock, and Dyson had simply to raise the lid, and as he did so he drew a long breath and started back. The lamp seemed to glimmer feebly like a single candle, but the whole room blazed with light—and not with light alone, but with a thousand colours, with all the glories of some painted window; and upon the walls of his room and on the familiar furniture, the glow flamed back and seemed to flow again to its source, the little wooden box. For there upon a bed of soft wool lay the most splendid jewel, a jewel such as Dyson had never dreamed of, and within it shone the blue of far skies, and the green of the sea by the shore, and the red of the ruby, and deep violet rays, and in the middle of all it seemed aflame as if a fountain of fire rose up, and fell, and rose again with sparks like stars for drops. Dyson gave a long deep sigh, and dropped into his chair, and put his hands over his eyes to think. The jewel was like an opal, but from a long experience of the shop-windows he knew there was no such thing as an opal one-quarter or one-eighth of its size. He looked at the stone again, with a feeling that was almost awe, and placed it gently on the table under the lamp, and watched the wonderful flame that shone and sparkled in its centre, and then turned to the box, curious to know whether it might contain other marvels. He lifted the bed of wool on which the opal had reclined, and saw beneath, no more jewels, but a little old pocket-book, worn and shabby with use. Dyson opened it at the first leaf, and dropped the book again appalled. He had read the name of the owner, neatly written in blue ink:

Steven Black, m. d.,
    Oranmore,
        Devon Road,
            Harlesden.

It was several minutes before Dyson could bring himself to open the book a second time; he remembered the wretched exile in his garret; and his strange talk, and the memory too of the face he had seen at the window, and of what the specialist had said, surged up in his mind, and as he held his finger on the cover, he shivered, dreading what might be written within. When at last he held it in his hand, and turned the pages, he found that the first two leaves were blank, but the third was covered with clear, minute writing, and Dyson began to read with the light of the opal flaming in his eyes.

V

'Ever since I was a young man'—the record began—'I devoted all my leisure and a good deal of time that ought to have been given to other studies to the investigation of curious and obscure branches of knowledge. What are commonly called the pleasures of life had never any attractions for me, and I lived alone in London, avoiding my fellow-students, and in my turn avoided by them as a man self-absorbed and unsympathetic. So long as I could gratify my desire of knowledge of a peculiar kind, knowledge of which the very existence is a profound secret to most men, I was intensely happy, and I have often spent whole nights sitting in the darkness of my room, and thinking of the strange world on the brink of which I trod. My professional studies, however, and the necessity of obtaining a degree, for some time forced my more obscure employment into the background, and soon after I had qualified I met Agnes, who became my wife. We took a new house in this remote suburb, and I began the regular routine of a sober practice, and for some months lived happily enough, sharing in the life about me, and only thinking at odd intervals of that occult science which had once fascinated my whole being. I had learnt enough of the paths I had begun to tread to know that they were beyond all expression difficult and dangerous, that to persevere meant in all probability the wreck of a life, and that they led to regions so terrible, that the mind of man shrinks appalled at the very thought. Moreover, the quiet and the peace I had enjoyed since my marriage had wiled me away to a great extent from places where I knew no peace could dwell. But suddenly—I think indeed it was the work of a single night, as I lay awake on my bed gazing into the darkness—suddenly, I say, the old desire, the former longing, returned, and returned with a force that had been intensified ten times by its absence; and when the day dawned and I looked out of the window, and saw with haggard eyes the sunrise in the east, I knew that my doom had been pronounced; that as I had gone far, so now I must go farther with unfaltering steps. I turned to the bed where my wife was sleeping peacefully, and lay down again, weeping bitter tears, for the sun had set on our happy life and had risen with a dawn of terror to us both. I will not set down here in minute detail what followed; outwardly I went about the day's labour as before, saying nothing to my wife. But she soon saw that I had changed; I spent my spare time in a room which I had fitted up as a laboratory, and often I crept upstairs in the grey dawn of the morning, when the light of many lamps still glowed over London; and each night I had stolen a step nearer to that great abyss which I was to bridge over, the gulf between the world of consciousness and the world of matter. My experiments were many and complicated in their nature, and it was some months before I realized whither they all pointed, and when this was borne in upon me in a moment's time, I felt my face whiten and my heart still within me. But the power to draw back, the power to stand before the doors that now opened wide before me and not to enter in, had long ago been absent; the way was closed, and I could only pass onward. My position was as utterly hopeless as that of the prisoner in an utter dungeon, whose only light is that of the dungeon above him; the doors were shut and escape was impossible. Experiment after experiment gave the same result, and I knew, and shrank even as the thought passed through my mind, that in the work I had to do there must be elements which no laboratory could furnish, which no scales could ever measure. In that work, from which even I doubted to escape with life, life itself must enter; from some human being there must be drawn that essence which men call the soul, and in its place (for in the scheme of the world there is no vacant chamber)—in its place would enter in what the lips can hardly utter, what the mind cannot conceive without a horror more awful than the horror of death itself. And when I knew this, I knew also on whom this fate would fall; I looked into my wife's eyes. Even at that hour, if I had gone out and taken a rope and hanged myself, I might have escaped, and she also, but in no other way. At last I told her all. She shuddered, and wept, and called on her dead mother for help, and asked me if I had no mercy, and I could only sigh. I concealed nothing from her; I told her what she would become, and what would enter in where her life had been; I told her of all the shame and of all the horror. You who will read this when I am dead—if indeed I allow this record to survive,—you who have opened the box and have seen what lies there, if you could understand what lies hidden in that opal! For one night my wife consented to what I asked of her, consented with the tears running down her beautiful face, and hot shame flushing red over her neck and breast, consented to undergo this for me. I threw open the window, and we looked together at the sky and the dark earth for the last time; it was a fine star-light night, and there was a pleasant breeze blowing, and I kissed her on her lips, and her tears ran down upon my face. That night she came down to my laboratory, and there, with shutters bolted and barred down, with curtains drawn thick and close, so that the very stars might be shut out from the sight of that room, while the crucible hissed and boiled over the lamp, I did what had to be done, and led out what was no longer a woman. But on the table the opal flamed and sparkled with such light as no eyes of man have ever gazed on, and the rays of the flame that was within it flashed and glittered, and shone even to my heart. My wife had only asked one thing of me; that when there came at last what I had told her, I would kill her. I have kept that promise.'

There was nothing more. Dyson let the little pocket-book fall, and turned and looked again at the opal with its flaming inmost light, and then with unutterable irresistible horror surging up in his heart, grasped the jewel, and flung it on the ground, and trampled it beneath his heel. His face was white with terror as he turned away, and for a moment stood sick and trembling, and then with a start he leapt across the room and steadied himself against the door. There was an angry hiss, as of steam escaping under great pressure, and as he gazed, motionless, a volume of heavy yellow smoke was slowly issuing from the very centre of the jewel, and wreathing itself in snake-like coils above it. And then a thin white flame burst forth from the smoke, and shot up into the air and vanished; and on the ground there lay a thing like a cinder, black and crumbling to the touch.

A FRAGMENT OF LIFE

I

Edward Darnell awoke from a dream of an ancient wood, and of a clear well rising into grey film and vapour beneath a misty, glimmering heat; and as his eyes opened he saw the sunlight bright in the room, sparkling on the varnish of the new furniture. He turned and found his wife's place vacant, and with some confusion and wonder of the dream still lingering in his mind, he rose also, and began hurriedly to set about his dressing, for he had overslept a little, and the 'bus passed the corner at 9.15. He was a tall, thin man, dark-haired and dark-eyed, and in spite of the routine of the City, the counting of coupons, and all the mechanical drudgery that had lasted for ten years, there still remained about him the curious hint of a wild grace, as if he had been born a creature of the antique wood, and had seen the fountain rising from the green moss and the grey rocks.

The breakfast was laid in the room on the ground floor, the back room with the French windows looking on the garden, and before he sat down to his fried bacon he kissed his wife seriously and dutifully. She had brown hair and brown eyes, and though her lovely face was grave and quiet, one would have said that she might have awaited her husband under the old trees, and bathed in the pool hollowed out of the rocks.

They had a good deal to talk over while the coffee was poured out and the bacon eaten, and Darnell's egg brought in by the stupid, staring servant-girl of the dusty face. They had been married for a year, and they had got on excellently, rarely sitting silent for more than an hour, but for the past few weeks Aunt Marian's present had afforded a subject for conversation which seemed inexhaustible. Mrs. Darnell had been Miss Mary Reynolds, the daughter of an auctioneer and estate agent in Notting Hill, and Aunt Marian was her mother's sister, who was supposed rather to have lowered herself by marrying a coal merchant, in a small way, at Turnham Green.

Marian had felt the family attitude a good deal, and the Reynoldses were sorry for many things that had been said, when the coal merchant saved money and took up land on building leases in the neighbourhood of Crouch End, greatly to his advantage, as it appeared. Nobody had thought that Nixon could ever do very much; but he and his wife had been living for years in a beautiful house at Barnet, with bow-windows, shrubs, and a paddock, and the two families saw but little of each other, for Mr. Reynolds was not very prosperous. Of course, Aunt Marian and her husband had been asked to Mary's wedding, but they had sent excuses with a nice little set of silver apostle spoons, and it was feared that nothing more was to be looked for. However, on Mary's birthday her aunt had written a most affectionate letter, enclosing a cheque for a hundred pounds from 'Robert' and herself, and ever since the receipt of the money the Darnells had discussed the question of its judicious disposal. Mrs. Darnell had wished to invest the whole sum in Government securities, but Mr. Darnell had pointed out that the rate of interest was absurdly low, and after a good deal of talk he had persuaded his wife to put ninety pounds of the money in a safe mine, which was paying five per cent. This was very well, but the remaining ten pounds, which Mrs. Darnell had insisted on reserving, gave rise to legends and discourses as interminable as the disputes of the schools.

At first Mr. Darnell had proposed that they should furnish the 'spare' room. There were four bedrooms in the house: their own room, the small one for the servant, and two others overlooking the garden, one of which had been used for storing boxes, ends of rope, and odd numbers of 'Quiet Days' and 'Sunday Evenings,' besides some worn suits belonging to Mr. Darnell which had been carefully wrapped up and laid by, as he scarcely knew what to do with them. The other room was frankly waste and vacant, and one Saturday afternoon, as he was coming home in the 'bus, and while he revolved that difficult question of the ten pounds, the unseemly emptiness of the spare room suddenly came into his mind, and he glowed with the idea that now, thanks to Aunt Marian, it could be furnished. He was busied with this delightful thought all the way home, but when he let himself in, he said nothing to his wife, since he felt that his idea must be matured. He told Mrs. Darnell that, having important business, he was obliged to go out again directly, but that he should be back without fail for tea at half-past six; and Mary, on her side, was not sorry to be alone, as she was a little behind-hand with the household books. The fact was, that Darnell, full of the design of furnishing the spare bedroom, wished to consult his friend Wilson, who lived at Fulham, and had often given him judicious advice as to the laying out of money to the very best advantage. Wilson was connected with the Bordeaux wine trade, and Darnell's only anxiety was lest he should not be at home.

However, it was all right; Darnell took a tram along the Goldhawk Road, and walked the rest of the way, and was delighted to see Wilson in the front garden of his house, busy amongst his flower-beds.

'Haven't seen you for an age,' he said cheerily, when he heard Darnell's hand on the gate; 'come in. Oh, I forgot,' he added, as Darnell still fumbled with the handle, and vainly attempted to enter. 'Of course you can't get in; I haven't shown it you.'

It was a hot day in June, and Wilson appeared in a costume which he had put on in haste as soon as he arrived from the City. He wore a straw hat with a neat pugaree protecting the back of his neck, and his dress was a Norfolk jacket and knickers in heather mixture.

'See,' he said, as he let Darnell in; 'see the dodge. You don't turn the handle at all. First of all push hard, and then pull. It's a trick of my own, and I shall have it patented. You see, it keeps undesirable characters at a distance—such a great thing in the suburbs. I feel I can leave Mrs. Wilson alone now; and, formerly, you have no idea how she used to be pestered.'

'But how about visitors?' said Darnell. 'How do they get in?'

'Oh, we put them up to it. Besides,' he said vaguely, 'there is sure to be somebody looking out. Mrs. Wilson is nearly always at the window. She's out now; gone to call on some friends. The Bennetts' At Home day, I think it is. This is the first Saturday, isn't it? You know J. W. Bennett, don't you? Ah, he's in the House; doing very well, I believe. He put me on to a very good thing the other day.'

'But, I say,' said Wilson, as they turned and strolled towards the front door, 'what do you wear those black things for? You look hot. Look at me. Well, I've been gardening, you know, but I feel as cool as a cucumber. I dare say you don't know where to get these things? Very few men do. Where do you suppose I got 'em?'

'In the West End, I suppose,' said Darnell, wishing to be polite.

'Yes, that's what everybody says. And it is a good cut. Well, I'll tell you, but you needn't pass it on to everybody. I got the tip from Jameson—you know him, "Jim-Jams," in the China trade, 39 Eastbrook—and he said he didn't want everybody in the City to know about it. But just go to Jennings, in Old Wall, and mention my name, and you'll be all right. And what d'you think they cost?'

'I haven't a notion,' said Darnell, who had never bought such a suit in his life.

'Well, have a guess.'

Darnell regarded Wilson gravely. The jacket hung about his body like a sack, the knickerbockers drooped lamentably over his calves, and in prominent positions the bloom of the heather seemed about to fade and disappear.

'Three pounds, I suppose, at least,' he said at length.

'Well, I asked Dench, in our place, the other day, and he guessed four ten, and his father's got something to do with a big business in Conduit Street. But I only gave thirty-five and six. To measure? Of course; look at the cut, man.'

Darnell was astonished at so low a price.

'And, by the way,' Wilson went on, pointing to his new brown boots, 'you know where to go for shoe-leather? Oh, I thought everybody was up to that! There's only one place. "Mr. Bill," in Gunning Street,— nine and six.

They were walking round and round the garden, and Wilson pointed out the flowers in the beds and borders. There were hardly any blossoms, but everything was neatly arranged.

'Here are the tuberous-rooted Glasgownias,' he said, showing a rigid row of stunted plants; 'those are Squintaceæ; this is a new introduction, Moldavia Semperflorida Andersonii; and this is Prattsia'

'When do they come out?' said Darnell.

'Most of them in the end of August or beginning of September,' said Wilson briefly. He was slightly annoyed with himself for having talked so much about his plants, since he saw that Darnell cared nothing for flowers; and, indeed, the visitor could hardly dissemble vague recollections that came to him; thoughts of an old, wild garden, full of odours, beneath grey walls, of the fragrance of the meadowsweet beside the brook.

'I wanted to consult you about some furniture,' Darnell said at last. 'You know we've got a spare room, and I'm thinking of putting a few things into it. I haven't exactly made up my mind, but I thought you might advise me.'

'Come into my den,' said Wilson. 'No; this way, by the back'; and he showed Darnell another ingenious arrangement at the side door whereby a violent high-toned bell was set pealing in the house if one did but touch the latch. Indeed, Wilson handled it so briskly that the bell rang a wild alarm, and the servant, who was trying on her mistress's things in the bedroom, jumped madly to the window and then danced a hysteric dance. There was plaster found on the drawing-room table on Sunday afternoon, and Wilson wrote a letter to the 'Fulham Chronicle,' ascribing the phenomenon 'to some disturbance of a seismic nature.'

For the moment he knew nothing of the great results of his contrivance, and solemnly led the way towards the back of the house. Here there was a patch of turf, beginning to look a little brown, with a background of shrubs. In the middle of the turf, a boy of nine or ten was standing all alone, with something of an air.

'The eldest,' said Wilson. 'Havelock. Well, Lockie, what are ye doing now? And where are your brother and sister?'

The boy was not at all shy. Indeed, he seemed eager to explain the course of events.

'I'm playing at being Gawd,' he said, with an engaging frankness. 'And I've sent Fergus and Janet to the bad place. That's in the shrubbery. And they're never to come out any more. And they're burning for ever and ever.'

'What d'you think of that?' said Wilson admiringly. 'Not bad for a youngster of nine, is it? They think a lot of him at the Sunday-school. But come into my den.'

The den was an apartment projecting from the back of the house. It had been designed as a back kitchen and washhouse, but Wilson had draped the 'copper' in art muslin and had boarded over the sink, so that it served as a workman's bench.

'Snug, isn't it?' he said, as he pushed forward one of the two wicker chairs. 'I think out things here, you know; it's quiet. And what about this furnishing? Do you want to do the thing on a grand scale?'

'Oh, not at all. Quite the reverse. In fact, I don't know whether the sum at our disposal will be sufficient. You see the spare room is ten feet by twelve, with a western exposure, and I thought if we could manage it, that it would seem more cheerful furnished. Besides, it's pleasant to be able to ask a visitor; our aunt, Mrs. Nixon, for example. But she is accustomed to have everything very nice.'

'And how much do you want to spend?'

'Well, I hardly think we should be justified in going much beyond ten pounds. That isn't enough, eh?'

Wilson got up and shut the door of the back kitchen impressively.

'Look here,' he said, 'I'm glad you came to me in the first place. Now you'll just tell me where you thought of going yourself.'

'Well, I had thought of the Hampstead Road,' said Darnell in a hesitating manner.

'I just thought you'd say that. But I'll ask you, what is the good of going to those expensive shops in the West End? You don't get a better article for your money. You're merely paying for fashion.'

'I've seen some nice things in Samuel's, though. They get a brilliant polish on their goods in those superior shops. We went there when we were married.'

'Exactly, and paid ten per cent more than you need have paid. It's throwing money away. And how much did you say you had to spend? Ten pounds. Well, I can tell you where to get a beautiful bedroom suite, in the very highest finish, for six pound ten. What d'you think of that? China included, mind you; and a square of carpet, brilliant colours, will only cost you fifteen and six. Look here, go any Saturday afternoon to Dick's, in the Seven Sisters Road, mention my name, and ask for Mr. Johnston. The suite's in ash, "Elizabethan" they call it. Six pound ten, including the china, with one of their "Orient" carpets, nine by nine, for fifteen and six. Dick's.'

Wilson spoke with some eloquence on the subject of furnishing. He pointed out that the times were changed, and that the old heavy style was quite out of date.

'You know,' he said, 'it isn't like it was in the old days, when people used to buy things to last hundreds of years. Why, just before the wife and I were married, an uncle of mine died up in the North and left me his furniture. I was thinking of furnishing at the time, and I thought the things might come in handy; but I assure you there wasn't a single article that I cared to give house-room to. All dingy, old mahogany; big bookcases and bureaus, and claw-legged chairs and tables. As I said to the wife (as she was soon afterwards), "We don't exactly want to set up a chamber of horrors, do we?" So I sold off the lot for what I could get. I must confess I like a cheerful room.'

Darnell said he had heard that artists liked the old-fashioned furniture.

'Oh, I dare say. The "unclean cult of the sunflower," eh? You saw that piece in the "Daily Post"? I hate all that rot myself. It isn't healthy, you know, and I don't believe the English people will stand it. But talking of curiosities, I've got something here that's worth a bit of money.'

He dived into some dusty receptacle in a corner of the room, and showed Darnell a small, worm-eaten Bible, wanting the first five chapters of Genesis and the last leaf of the Apocalypse.

It bore the date of 1753.

'It's my belief that's worth a lot,' said Wilson. 'Look at the worm-holes. And you see it's "imperfect," as they call it. You've noticed that some of the most valuable books are "imperfect" at the sales?'

The interview came to an end soon after, and Darnell went home to his tea. He thought seriously of taking Wilson's advice, and after tea he told Mary of his idea and of what Wilson had said about Dick's.

Mary was a good deal taken by the plan when she had heard all the details. The prices struck her as very moderate. They were sitting one on each side of the grate (which was concealed by a pretty cardboard screen, painted with landscapes), and she rested her cheek on her hand, and her beautiful dark eyes seemed to dream and behold strange visions. In reality she was thinking of Darnell's plan.

'It would be very nice in some ways,' she said at last. 'But we must talk it over. What I am afraid of is that it will come to much more than ten pounds in the long run. There are so many things to be considered. There's the bed. It would look shabby if we got a common bed without brass mounts. Then the bedding, the mattress, and blankets, and sheets, and counterpane would all cost something.'

She dreamed again, calculating the cost of all the necessaries, and Darnell stared anxiously; reckoning with her, and wondering what her conclusion would be. For a moment the delicate colouring of her face, the grace of her form, and the brown hair, drooping over her ears and clustering in little curls about her neck, seemed to hint at a language which he had not yet learned; but she spoke again.

'The bedding would come to a great deal, I am afraid. Even if Dicks are considerably cheaper than Boons or Samuels. And, my dear, we must have some ornaments on the mantelpiece. I saw some very nice vases at eleven-three the other day at Wilkin and Dodd's. We should want six at least, and there ought to be a centre-piece. You see how it mounts up.'

Darnell was silent. He saw that his wife was summing up against his scheme, and though he had set his heart on it, he could not resist her arguments.

'It would be nearer twelve pounds than ten,' she said.

'The floor would have to be stained round the carpet (nine by nine, you said?), and we should want a piece of linoleum to go under the washstand. And the walls would look very bare without any pictures.'

'I thought about the pictures,' said Darnell; and he spoke quite eagerly. He felt that here, at least, he was unassailable. 'You know there's the "Derby Day" and the "Railway Station," ready framed, standing in the corner of the box-room already. They're a bit old-fashioned, perhaps, but that doesn't matter in a bedroom. And couldn't we use some photographs? I saw a very neat frame in natural oak in the City, to hold half a dozen, for one and six. We might put in your father, and your brother James, and Aunt Marian, and your grandmother, in her widow's cap— and any of the others in the album. And then there's that old family picture in the hair-trunk— that might do over the mantelpiece.'

'You mean your great-grandfather in the gilt frame? But that's very old-fashioned, isn't it? He looks so queer in his wig. I don't think it would quite go with the room, somehow.'

Darnell thought a moment. The portrait was a 'kitcat' of a young gentleman, bravely dressed in the fashion of 1750, and he very faintly remembered some old tales that his father had told him about this ancestor—tales of the woods and fields, of the deep sunken lanes, and the forgotten country in the west.

'No,' he said, 'I suppose it is rather out of date. But I saw some very nice prints in the City, framed and quite cheap.'

'Yes, but everything counts. Well, we will talk it over, as you say. You know we must be careful.'

The servant came in with the supper, a tin of biscuits, a glass of milk for the mistress, and a modest pint of beer for the master, with a little cheese and butter. Afterwards Edward smoked two pipes of honeydew, and they went quietly to bed; Mary going first, and her husband following a quarter of an hour later, according to the ritual established from the first days of their marriage. Front and back doors were locked, the gas was turned off at the meter, and when Darnell got upstairs he found his wife already in bed, her face turned round on the pillow.

She spoke softly to him as he came into the room.

'It would be impossible to buy a presentable bed at anything under one pound eleven, and good sheets are dear, anywhere.'

He slipped off his clothes and slid gently into bed, putting out the candle on the table. The blinds were all evenly and duly drawn, but it was a June night, and beyond the walls, beyond that desolate world and wilderness of grey Shepherd's Bush, a great golden moon had floated up through magic films of cloud, above the hill, and the earth was filled with a wonderful light between red sunset lingering over the mountain and that marvellous glory that shone into the woods from the summit of the hill. Darnell seemed to see some reflection of that wizard brightness in the room; the pale walls and the white bed and his wife's face lying amidst brown hair upon the pillow were illuminated, and listening he could almost hear the corncrake in the fields, the fern-owl sounding his strange note from the quiet of the rugged place where the bracken grew, and, like the echo of a magic song, the melody of the nightingale that sang all night in the alder by the little brook. There was nothing that he could say, but he slowly stole his arm under his wife's neck, and played with the ringlets of brown hair. She never moved, she lay there gently breathing, looking up to the blank ceiling of the room with her beautiful eyes, thinking also, no doubt, thoughts that she could not utter, kissing her husband obediently when he asked her to do so, and he stammered and hesitated as he spoke.

They were nearly asleep, indeed Darnell was on the very eve of dreaming, when she said very softly— 'I am afraid, darling, that we could never afford it.' And he heard her words through the murmur of the water, dripping from the grey rock, and falling into the clear pool beneath.

Sunday morning was always an occasion of idleness. Indeed, they would never have got breakfast if Mrs. Darnell, who had the instincts of the housewife, had not awoke and seen the bright sunshine, and felt that the house was too still. She lay quiet for five minutes, while her husband slept beside her, and listened intently, waiting for the sound of Alice stirring down below. A golden tube of sunlight shone through some opening in the Venetian blinds, and it shone on the brown hair that lay about her head on the pillow, and she looked steadily into the room at the 'duchesse' toilet-table, the coloured ware of the washstand, and the two photogravures in oak frames, 'The Meeting' and 'The Parting,' that hung upon the wall. She was half dreaming as she listened for the servant's footsteps, and the faint shadow of a shade of a thought came over her, and she imagined dimly, for the quick moment of a dream, another world where rapture was wine, where one wandered in a deep and happy valley, and the moon was always rising red above the trees. She was thinking of Hampstead, which represented to her the vision of the world beyond the walls, and the thought of the heath led her away to Bank Holidays, and then to Alice. There was not a sound in the house; it might have been midnight for the stillness if the drawling cry of the Sunday paper had not suddenly echoed round the corner of Edna Road, and with it came the warning clank and shriek of the milkman with his pails.

Mrs. Darnell sat up, and wide awake, listened more intently. The girl was evidently fast asleep, and must be roused, or all the work of the day would be out of joint, and she remembered how Edward hated any fuss or discussion about household matters, more especially on a Sunday, after his long week's work in the City. She gave her husband an affectionate glance as he slept on, for she was very fond of him, and so she gently rose from the bed and went in her nightgown to call the maid.

The servant's room was small and stuffy, the night had been very hot, and Mrs. Darnell paused for a moment at the door, wondering whether the girl on the bed was really the dusty-faced servant who bustled day by day about the house, or even the strangely bedizened creature, dressed in purple, with a shiny face, who would appear on the Sunday afternoon, bringing in an early tea, because it was her 'evening out.' Alice's hair was black and her skin was pale, almost of the olive tinge, and she lay asleep, her head resting on one arm, reminding Mrs. Darnell of a queer print of a 'Tired Bacchante' that she had seen long ago in a shop window in Upper Street, Islington. And a cracked bell was ringing; that meant five minutes to eight, and nothing done.

She touched the girl gently on the shoulder, and only smiled when her eyes opened, and, waking with a start, she got up in sudden confusion. Mrs. Darnell went back to her room and dressed slowly while her husband still slept, and it was only at the last moment, as she fastened her cherry-coloured bodice, that she roused him, telling him that the bacon would be overdone unless he hurried over his dressing.

Over the breakfast they discussed the question of the spare room all over again. Mrs. Darnell still admitted that the plan of furnishing it attracted her, but she could not see how it could be done for the ten pounds, and as they were prudent people they did not care to encroach on their swings. Edward was highly paid, having (with allowances for extra work in busy weeks) a hundred and forty pounds a year, and Mary had inherited from an old uncle, her godfather, three hundred pounds, which had been judiciously laid out in mortgage at 4½ per cent. Their total income, then, counting in Aunt Marian's present, was a hundred and fifty-eight pounds a year and they were clear of debt, since Darnell had bought the furniture for the house out of money which he had saved for five or six years before. In the first few years of his life in the City his income had, of course, been smaller, and at first he had lived very freely, without a thought of laying by. The theatres and music-halls had attracted him, and scarcely a week passed without his going (in the pit) to one or the other; and he had occasionally bought photographs of actresses who pleased him. These he had solemnly burnt when he became engaged to Mary; he remembered the evening well; his heart had been so full of joy and wonder, and the landlady had complained bitterly of the mess in the grate when he came home from the City the next night.

Still, the money was lost, as far as he could recollect, ten or twelve shillings; and it annoyed him all the more to reflect that if he had put it by, it would have gone far towards the purchase of an 'Orient' carpet in brilliant colours. Then there had been other expenses of his youth: he had purchased threepenny and even fourpenny cigars, the latter rarely, but the former frequently, sometimes singly, and sometimes in bundles of twelve for half-a-crown. Once a meerschaum pipe had haunted him for six weeks; the tobacconist had drawn it out of a drawer with some air of secrecy as be was buying a packet of 'Lone Star.' Here was another useless expense, these American-manufactured tobaccos: his 'Lone Star,' 'Long Judge,' 'Old Hank,' 'Sultry Clime,' and the rest of them cost from a shilling to one and six the two-ounce packet; whereas now he got excellent loose honeydew for threepence halfpenny an ounce. But the crafty tradesman, who had marked him down as a buyer of expensive fancy goods, nodded with his air of mystery, and, snapping open the case, displayed the meerschaum before the dazzled eyes of Darnell. The bowl was carved in the likeness of a female figure, showing the head and torso, and the mouthpiece was of the very best amber—only twelve and six, the man said, and the amber alone, he declared, was worth more than that. He explained that he felt some delicacy about showing the pipe to any but a regular customer, and was willing to take a little under cost price and 'cut the loss.' Darnell resisted for the time, but the pipe troubled him, and at last he bought it. He was pleased to show it to the younger men in the office for a while, but it never smoked very well, and he gave it away just before his marriage, as from the nature of the carving it would have been impossible to use it in his wife's presence. Once, while he was taking his holidays at Hastings, he had purchased a malacca cane—a useless thing that had cost seven shillings—and he reflected with sorrow on the innumerable evenings on which he had rejected his landlady's plain fried chop, and had gone out to flaner among the Italian restaurants in Upper Street, Islington (he lodged in Holloway), pampering himself with expensive delicacies: cutlets and green peas, braised beef with tomato sauce, fillet steak and chipped potatoes, ending the banquet very often with a small wedge of Gruyère, which cost twopence. One night, after receiving a rise in his salary, he had actually drunk a quarter-flask of Chianti and had added the enormities of Benedictine, coffee, and cigarettes to an expenditure already disgraceful, and sixpence to the waiter made the bill amount to four shillings instead of the shilling that would have provided him with a wholesome and sufficient repast at home. Oh, there were many other items in this account of extravagance, and Darnell had often regretted his way of life, thinking that if he had been more careful, five or six pounds a year might have been added to their income.

And the question of the spare room brought back these regrets in an exaggerated degree. He persuaded himself that the extra five pounds would have given a sufficient margin for the outlay that he desired to make; though this was, no doubt, a mistake on his part. But he saw quite clearly that, under the present conditions, there must be no levies made on the very small sum of money that they had saved. The rent of the house was thirty-five, and rates and taxes added another ten pounds—nearly a quarter of their income for houseroom. Mary kept down the housekeeping bills to the very best of her ability, but meat was always dear, and she suspected the maid of cutting surreptitious slices from the joint and eating them in her bedroom with bread and treacle in the dead of night, for the girl had disordered and eccentric appetites. Mr. Darnell thought no more of restaurants, cheap or dear; he took his lunch with him to the City, and joined his wife in the evening at high tea—chops, a bit of steak, or cold meat from the Sunday's dinner.

Mrs. Darnell ate bread and jam and drank a little milk in the middle of the day; but, with the utmost economy, the effort to live within their means and to save for future contingencies was a very hard one. They had determined to do without change of air for at least three years, as the honeymoon at Walton-on-the-Naze had cost a good deal; and it was on this ground that they had, somewhat illogically, reserved the ten pounds, declaring that as they were not to have any holiday they would spend the money on something useful.

And it was this consideration of utility that was finally fatal to Darnell's scheme. They had calculated and recalculated the expense of the bed and bedding, the linoleum, and the ornaments, and by a great deal of exertion the total expenditure had been made to assume the shape of 'something very little over ten pounds,' when Mary said quite suddenly— 'But, after all, Edward, we don't really want to furnish the room at all. I mean it isn't necessary. And if we did so it might lead to no end of expense. People would hear of it and be sure to fish for invitations. You know we have relatives in the country, and they would be almost certain, the Mallings, at any rate, to give hints.'

Darnell saw the force of the argument and gave way. But he was bitterly disappointed.

'It would have been very nice, wouldn't it?' he said with a sigh.

'Never mind, dear,' said Mary, who saw that he was a good deal cast down. 'We must think of some other plan that will be nice and useful too.'

She often spoke to him in that tone of a kind mother, though she was by three years the younger.

'And now,' she said, 'I must get ready for church. Are you coming?'

Darnell said that he thought not. He usually accompanied his wife to morning service, but that day he felt some bitterness in his heart, and preferred to lounge under the shade of the big mulberry tree that stood in the middle of their patch of garden—relic of the spacious lawns that had once lain smooth and green and sweet, where the dismal streets now swarmed in a hopeless labyrinth.

So Mary went quietly and alone to church. St. Paul's stood in a neighbouring street, and its Gothic design would have interested a curious inquirer into the history of a strange revival.

Obviously, mechanically, there was nothing amiss. The style chosen was 'geometrical decorated,' and the tracery of the windows seemed correct. The nave, the aisles, the spacious chancel, were reasonably proportioned; and, to be quite serious, the only feature obviously wrong was the substitution of a low 'chancel wall' with iron gates for the rood screen with the loft and rood. But this, it might plausibly be contended, was merely an adaptation of the old idea to modern requirements, and it would have been quite difficult to explain why the whole building, from the mere mortar setting between the stones to the Gothic gas standards, was a mysterious and elaborate blasphemy. The canticles were sung to Joll in B flat, the chants were 'Anglican,' and the sermon was the gospel for the day, amplified and rendered into the more modern and graceful English of the preacher. And Mary came away.

After their dinner (an excellent piece of Australian mutton, bought in the 'World Wide' Stores, in Hammersmith), they sat for some time in the garden, partly sheltered by the big mulberry tree from the observation of their neighbours. Edward smoked his honeydew, and Mary looked at him with placid affection.

'You never tell me about the men in your office,' she said at length. 'Some of them are nice fellows, aren't they?'

'Oh, yes, they're very decent. I must bring some of them round, one of these days.'

He remembered with a pang that it would be necessary to provide whisky. One couldn't ask the guest to drink table beer at tenpence the gallon.

'Who are they, though?' said Mary. 'I think they might have given you a wedding present.'

'Well, I don't know. We never have gone in for that sort of thing. But they're very decent chaps. Well, there's Harvey; "Sauce" they call him behind his back. He's mad on bicycling. He went in last year for the Two Miles Amateur Record. He'd have made it, too, if he could have got into better training.

'Then there's James, a sporting man. You wouldn't care for him. I always think he smells of the stable.'

'How horrid!' said Mrs. Darnell, finding her husband a little frank, lowering her eyes as she spoke.

'Dickenson might amuse you,' Darnell went on. 'He's always got a joke. A terrible liar, though. When he tells a tale we never know how much to believe. He swore the other day he'd seen one of the governors buying cockles off a barrow near London Bridge, and Jones, who's just come, believed every word of it.'

Darnell laughed at the humorous recollection of the jest.

'And that wasn't a bad yarn about Salter's wife,' he went on. 'Salter is the manager, you know.

Dickenson lives close by, in Notting Hill, and he said one morning that he had seen Mrs. Salter, in the Portobello Road, in red stockings, dancing to a piano organ.'

'He's a little coarse, isn't he?' said Mrs. Darnell. 'I don't see much fun in that.'

'Well, you know, amongst men it's different. You might like Wallis; he's a tremendous photographer. He often shows us photos he's taken of his children—one, a little girl of three, in her bath. I asked him how he thought she'd like it when she was twenty-three.'

Mrs. Darnell looked down and made no answer.

There was silence for some minutes while Darnell smoked his pipe. 'I say, Mary,' he said at length, 'what do you say to our taking a paying guest?'

'A paying guest! I never thought of it. Where should we put him?'

'Why, I was thinking of the spare room. The plan would obviate your objection, wouldn't it? Lots of men in the City take them, and make money of it too. I dare say it would add ten pounds a year to our income. Redgrave, the cashier, finds it worth his while to take a large house on purpose. They have a regular lawn for tennis and a billiard-room.'

Mary considered gravely, always with the dream in her eyes. 'I don't think we could manage it, Edward,' she said; 'it would be inconvenient in many ways. She hesitated for a moment. 'And I don't think I should care to have a young man in the house. It is so very small, and our accommodation, as you know, is so limited.'

She blushed slightly, and Edward, a little disappointed as he was, looked at her with a singular longing, as if he were a scholar confronted with a doubtful hieroglyph, either wholly wonderful or altogether commonplace. Next door children were playing in the garden, playing shrilly, laughing crying, quarrelling, racing to and fro. Suddenly a dear, pleasant voice sounded from an upper window.

'Enid! Charles! Come up to my room at once!'

There was an instant sudden hush. The children's voices died away.

'Mrs. Parker is supposed to keep her children in great order,' said Mary. 'Alice was telling me about it the other day. She had been talking to Mrs. Parker's servant. I listened to her without any remark, as I don't think it right to encourage servants' gossip; they always exaggerate everything. And I dare say children often require to be corrected.'

The children were struck silent as if some ghastly terror had seized them.

Darnell fancied that he heard a queer sort of cry from the house, but could not be quite sure. He turned to the other side, where an elderly, ordinary man with a grey moustache was strolling up and down on the further side of his garden. He caught Darnell's eye, and Mrs. Darnell looking towards him at the same moment, he very politely raised his tweed cap. Darnell was surprised to see his wife blushing fiercely.

'Sayce and I often go into the City by the same 'bus,' he said, 'and as it happens we've sat next to each other two or three times lately. I believe he's a traveller for a leather firm in Bermondsey. He struck me as a pleasant man. Haven't they got rather a good-looking servant?'

'Alice has spoken to me about her—and the Sayces,' said Mrs. Darnell. 'I understand that they are not very well thought of in the neighbourhood. But I must go in and see whether the tea is ready. Alice will be wanting to go out directly.' Darnell looked after his wife as she walked quickly away. He only dimly understood, but he could see the charm of her figure, the delight of the brown curls clustering about her neck, and he again felt that sense of the scholar confronted by the hieroglyphic. He could not have expressed his emotion, but he wondered whether he would ever find the key, and something told him that before she could speak to him his own lips must be unclosed. She had gone into the house by the back kitchen door, leaving it open, and he heard her speaking to the girl about the water being 'really boiling.' He was amazed, almost indignant with himself; but the sound of the words came to his ears as strange, heart-piercing music, tones from another, wonderful sphere. And yet he was her husband, and they had been married nearly a year; and yet, whenever she spoke, he had to listen to the sense of what she said, constraining himself, lest he should believe she was a magic creature, knowing the secrets of immeasurable delight.

He looked out through the leaves of the mulberry tree. Mr. Sayce had disappeared from his view, but he saw the light-blue fume of the cigar that he was smoking floating slowly across the shadowed air. He was wondering at his wife's manner when Sayce's name was mentioned, puzzling his head as to what could be amiss in the household of a most respectable personage, when his wife appeared at the dining-room window and called him in to tea. She smiled as he looked up, and he rose hastily and walked in, wondering whether he were not a little 'queer,' so strange were the dim emotions and the dimmer impulses that rose within him.

Alice was all shining purple and strong scent, as she brought in the teapot and the jug of hot water. It seemed that a visit to the kitchen had inspired Mrs. Darnell in her turn with a novel plan for disposing of the famous ten pounds. The range had always been a trouble to her, and when sometimes she went into the kitchen, and found, as she said, the fire 'roaring halfway up the chimney,' it was in vain that she reproved the maid on the ground of extravagance and waste of coal. Alice was ready to admit the absurdity of making up such an enormous fire merely to bake (they called it 'roast') a bit of beef or mutton, and to boil the potatoes and the cabbage; but she was able to show Mrs. Darnell that the fault lay in the defective contrivance of the range, in an oven which 'would not get hot.' Even with a chop or a steak it was almost as bad; the heat seemed to escape up the chimney or into the room, and Mary had spoken several times to her husband on the shocking waste of coal, and the cheapest coal procurable was never less than eighteen shillings the ton. Mr. Darnell had written to the landlord, a builder, who had replied in an illiterate but offensive communication, maintaining the excellence of the stove and charging all the faults to the account of 'your good lady,' which really implied that the Darnells kept no servant, and that Mrs. Darnell did everything. The range, then, remained, a standing annoyance and expense. Every morning, Alice said, she had the greatest difficulty in getting the fire to light at all, and once lighted it 'seemed as if it fled right up the chimney.' Only a few nights before Mrs. Darnell had spoken seriously to her husband about it; she had got Alice to weigh the coals expended in cooking a cottage pie, the dish of the evening, and deducting what remained in the scuttle after the pie was done, it appeared that the wretched thing had consumed nearly twice the proper quantity of fuel.

'You remember what I said the other night about the range?' said Mrs. Darnell, as she poured out the tea and watered the leaves. She thought the introduction a good one, for though her husband was a most amiable man, she guessed that he had been just a little hurt by her decision against his furnishing scheme.

'The range?' said Darnell. He paused as he helped himself to the marmalade and considered for a moment. 'No, I don't recollect. What night was it?'

'Tuesday. Don't you remember? You had "overtime," and didn't get home till quite late.' She paused for a moment, blushing slightly; and then began to recapitulate the misdeeds of the range, and the outrageous outlay of coal in the preparation of the cottage pie.

'Oh, I recollect now. That was the night I thought I heard the nightingale (people say there are nightingales in Bedford Park), and the sky was such a wonderful deep blue.'

He remembered how he had walked from Uxbridge Road Station, where the green 'bus stopped, and in spite of the fuming kilns under Acton, a delicate odour of the woods and summer fields was mysteriously in the air, and he had fancied that he smelt the red wild roses, drooping from the hedge. As he came to his gate he saw his wife standing in the doorway, with a light in her hand, and he threw his arms violently about her as she welcomed him, and whispered something in her ear, kissing her scented hair. He had felt quite abashed a moment afterwards, and he was afraid that he had frightened her by his nonsense; she seemed trembling and confused. And then she had told him how they had weighed the coal.

'Yes, I remember now,' he said. 'It is a great nuisance, isn't it? I hate to throw away money like that.'

'Well, what do you think? Suppose we bought a really good range with aunt's money? It would save us a lot, and I expect the things would taste much nicer.'

Darnell passed the marmalade, and confessed that the idea was brilliant.

'It's much better than mine, Mary,' he said quite frankly. 'I am so glad you thought of it. But we must talk it over; it doesn't do to buy in a hurry. There are so many makes.'

Each had seen ranges which looked miraculous inventions; he in the neighbourhood of the City; she in Oxford Street and Regent Street, on visits to the dentist. They discussed the matter at tea, and afterwards they discussed it walking round and round the garden, in the sweet cool of the evening.

'They say the "Newcastle" will burn anything, coke even,' said Mary.

'But the "Glow" got the gold medal at the Paris Exhibition,' said Edward.

'But what about the "Eutopia" Kitchener? Have you seen it at work in Oxford Street?' said Mary. 'They say their plan of ventilating the oven is quite unique.'

'I was in Fleet Street the other day,' answered Edward, 'and I was looking at the "Bliss" Patent Stoves. They burn less fuel than any in the market—so the makers declare.'

He put his arm gently round her waist. She did not repel him; she whispered quite softly—'I think Mrs. Parker is at her window,' and he drew his arm back slowly.

'But we will talk it over,' he said. 'There is no hurry. I might call at some of the places near the City, and you might do the same thing in Oxford Street and Regent Street and Piccadilly, and we could compare notes.'

Mary was quite pleased with her husband's good temper. It was so nice of him not to find fault with her plan; 'He's so good to me,' she thought, and that was what she often said to her brother, who did not care much for Darnell. They sat down on the seat under the mulberry, close together, and she let Darnell take her hand, and as she felt his shy, hesitating fingers touch her in the shadow, she pressed them ever so softly, and as he fondled her hand, his breath was on her neck, and she heard his passionate, hesitating voice whisper, 'My dear, my dear,' as his lips touched her cheek. She trembled a little, and waited. Darnell kissed her gently on the cheek and drew away his hand, and when he spoke he was almost breathless.

'We had better go in now,' he said. 'There is a heavy dew, and you might catch cold.'

A warm, scented gale came to them from beyond the walls. He longed to ask her to stay out with him all night beneath the tree, that they might whisper to one another, that the scent of her hair might inebriate him, that he might feel her dress still brushing against his ankles. But he could not find the words, and it was absurd, and she was so gentle that she would do whatever he asked, however foolish it might be, just because he asked her. He was not worthy to kiss her lips; he bent down and kissed her silk bodice, and again he felt that she trembled, and he was ashamed, fearing that he had frightened her.

They went slowly into the house, side by side, and Darnell lit the gas in the drawing-room, where they always sat on Sunday evenings. Mrs. Darnell felt a little tired and lay down on the sofa, and Darnell took the arm-chair opposite. For a while they were silent, and then Darnell said suddenly—'What's wrong with the Sayces? You seemed to think there was something a little strange about them. Their maid looks quite quiet.'

'Oh, I don't know that one ought to pay any attention to servants' gossip. They're not always very truthful.'

'It was Alice told you, wasn't it?'

'Yes. She was speaking to me the other day, when I was in the kitchen in the afternoon.'

'But what was it?'

'Oh, I'd rather not tell you, Edward. It's not pleasant. I scolded Alice for repeating it to me.'

Darnell got up and took a small, frail chair near the sofa.

'Tell me,' he said again, with an odd perversity. He did not really care to hear about the household next door, but he remembered how his wife's cheeks flushed in the afternoon, and now he was looking at her eyes.

'Oh, I really couldn't tell you, dear. I should feel ashamed.'

'But you're my wife.'

'Yes, but it doesn't make any difference. A woman doesn't like to talk about such things.'

Darnell bent his head down. His heart was beating; he put his ear to her mouth and said, 'Whisper.'

Mary drew his head down still lower with her gentle hand, and her cheeks burned as she whispered—'Alice says that—upstairs—they have only—one room furnished. The maid told her—herself.' With an unconscious gesture she pressed his head to her breast, and he in turn was bending her red lips to his own, when a violent jangle clamoured through the silent house. They sat up, and Mrs. Darnell went hurriedly to the door.

'That's Alice,' she said. 'She is always in in time. It has only just struck ten.'

Darnell shivered with annoyance. His lips, he knew, had almost been opened. Mary's pretty handkerchief, delicately scented from a little flagon that a school friend had given her, lay on the floor, and he picked it up, and kissed it, and hid it away.

The question of the range occupied them all through June and far into July. Mrs. Darnell took every opportunity of going to the West End and investigating the capacity of the latest makes, gravely viewing the new improvements and hearing what the shopmen had to say; while Darnell, as he said, 'kept his eyes open' about the City. They accumulated quite a literature of the subject, bringing away illustrated pamphlets, and in the evenings it was an amusement to look at the pictures. They viewed with reverence and interest the drawings of great ranges for hotels and public institutions, mighty contrivances furnished with a series of ovens each for a different use, with wonderful apparatus for grilling, with batteries of accessories which seemed to invest the cook almost with the dignity of a chief engineer. But when, in one of the lists, they encountered the images of little toy 'cottage' ranges, for four pounds, and even for three pounds ten, they grew scornful, on the strength of the eight or ten pound article which they meant to purchase— when the merits of the divers patents had been thoroughly thrashed out.

The 'Raven' was for a long time Mary's favourite. It promised the utmost economy with the highest efficiency, and many times they were on the point of giving the order. But the 'Glow' seemed equally seductive, and it was only £8. 5s. as compared with £9. 7s. 6d., and though the 'Raven' was supplied to the Royal Kitchen, the 'Glow' could show more fervent testimonials from continental potentates.

It seemed a debate without end, and it endured day after day till that morning, when Darnell woke from the dream of the ancient wood, of the fountains rising into grey vapour beneath the heat of the sun. As he dressed, an idea struck him, and he brought it as a shock to the hurried breakfast, disturbed by the thought of the City 'bus which passed the corner of the street at 9.15.

'I've got an improvement on your plan, Mary,' he said, with triumph. 'Look at that,' and he flung a little book on the table.

He laughed. 'It beats your notion all to fits. After all, the great expense is the coal. It's not the stove—at least that's not the real mischief. It's the coal is so dear. And here you are. Look at those oil stoves. They don't burn any coal, but the cheapest fuel in the world—oil; and for two pounds ten you can get a range that will do everything you want.'

'Give me the book,' said Mary, 'and we will talk it over in the evening, when you come home.

'Must you be going?'

Darnell cast an anxious glance at the clock.

'Good-bye,' and they kissed each other seriously and dutifully, and Mary's eyes made Darnell think of those lonely water-pools, hidden in the shadow of the ancient woods.

So, day after day, he lived in the grey phantasmal world, akin to death, that has, somehow, with most of us, made good its claim to be called life. To Darnell the true life would have seemed madness, and when, now and again, the shadows and vague images reflected from its splendour fell across his path, he was afraid, and took refuge in what he would have called the sane 'reality' of common and usual incidents and interests. His absurdity was, perhaps, the more evident, inasmuch as 'reality' for him was a matter of kitchen ranges, of saving a few shillings; but in truth the folly would have been greater if it had been concerned with racing stables, steam yachts, and the spending of many thousand pounds.

But so went forth Darnell, day by day, strangely mistaking death for life, madness for sanity, and purposeless and wandering phantoms for true beings. He was sincerely of opinion that he was a City clerk, living in Shepherd's Bush—having forgotten the mysteries and the far-shining glories of the kingdom which was his by legitimate inheritance.

II

All day long a fierce and heavy heat had brooded over the City, and as Darnell neared home he saw the mist lying on all the damp lowlands, wreathed in coils about Bedford Park to the south, and mounting to the West, so that the tower of Acton Church loomed out of a grey lake. The grass in the squares and on the lawns which he overlooked as the 'bus lumbered wearily along was burnt to the colour of dust. Shepherd's Bush Green was a wretched desert, trampled brown, bordered with monotonous poplars, whose leaves hung motionless in air that was still, hot smoke. The foot passengers struggled wearily along the pavements, and the reek of the summer's end mingled with the breath of the brickfields made Darnell gasp, as if he were inhaling the poison of some foul sick-room.

He made but a slight inroad into the cold mutton that adorned the tea-table, and confessed that he felt rather 'done up' by the weather and the day's work.

'I have had a trying day, too,' said Mary. 'Alice has been very queer and troublesome all day, and I have had to speak to her quite seriously. You know I think her Sunday evenings out have a rather unsettling influence on the girl. But what is one to do?'

'Has she got a young man?'

'Of course: a grocer's assistant from the Goldhawk Road—Wilkin's, you know. I tried them when we settled here, but they were not very satisfactory.'

'What do they do with themselves all the evening? They have from five to ten, haven't they?'

'Yes; five, or sometimes half-past, when the water won't boil. Well, I believe they go for walks usually. Once or twice he has taken her to the City Temple, and the Sunday before last they walked up and down Oxford Street, and then sat in the Park. But it seems that last Sunday they went to tea with his mother at Putney. I should like to tell the old woman what I really think of her.'

'Why? What happened? Was she nasty to the girl?'

'No; that's just it. Before this, she has been very unpleasant on several occasions. When the young man first took Alice to see her—that was in March—the girl came away crying; she told me so herself. Indeed, she said she never wanted to see old Mrs. Murry again; and I told Alice that, if she had not exaggerated things, I could hardly blame her for feeling like that.'

'Why? What did she cry for?'

'Well, it seems that the old lady—she lives in quite a small cottage in some Putney back street—was so stately that she would hardly speak. She had borrowed a little girl from some neighbour's family, and had managed to dress her up to imitate a servant, and Alice said nothing could be sillier than to see that mite opening the door, with her black dress and her white cap and apron, and she hardly able to turn the handle, as Alice said. George (that's the young man's name) had told Alice that it was a little bit of a house; but he said the kitchen was comfortable, though very plain and old-fashioned. But, instead of going straight to the back, and sitting by a big fire on the old settle that they had brought up from the country, that child asked for their names (did you ever hear such nonsense?) and showed them into a little poky parlour, where old Mrs. Murry was sitting "like a duchess," by a fireplace full of coloured paper, and the room as cold as ice. And she was so grand that she would hardly speak to Alice.'

'That must have been very unpleasant.'

'Oh, the poor girl had a dreadful time. She began with: "Very pleased to make your acquaintance, Miss Dill. I know so very few persons in service." Alice imitates her mincing way of talking, but I can't do it. And then she went on to talk about her family, how they had farmed their own land for five hundred years—such stuff! George had told Alice all about it: they had had an old cottage with a good strip of garden and two fields somewhere in Essex, and that old woman talked almost as if they had been country gentry, and boasted about the Rector, Dr. Somebody, coming to see them so often, and of Squire Somebody Else always looking them up, as if they didn't visit them out of kindness. Alice told me it was as much as she could do to keep from laughing in Mrs. Murry's face, her young man having told her all about the place, and how small it was, and how the Squire had been so kind about buying it when old Murry died and George was a little boy, and his mother not able to keep things going. However, that silly old woman "laid it on thick," as you say, and the young man got more and more uncomfortable, especially when she went on to speak about marrying in one's own class, and how unhappy she had known young men to be who had married beneath them, giving some very pointed looks at Alice as she talked. And then such an amusing thing happened: Alice had noticed George looking about him in a puzzled sort of way, as if he couldn't make out something or other, and at last he burst out and asked his mother if she had been buying up the neighbours' ornaments, as he remembered the two green cut-glass vases on the mantelpiece at Mrs. Ellis's, and the wax flowers at Miss Turvey's. He was going on, but his mother scowled at him, and upset some books, which he had to pick up; but Alice quite understood she had been borrowing things from her neighbours, just as she had borrowed the little girl, so as to look grander. And then they had tea—water bewitched, Alice calls it—and very thin bread and butter, and rubbishy foreign pastry from the Swiss shop in the High Street—all sour froth and rancid fat, Alice declares. And then Mrs. Murry began boasting again about her family, and snubbing Alice and talking at her, till the girl came away quite furious, and very unhappy, too. I don't wonder at it, do you?'

'It doesn't sound very enjoyable, certainly,' said Darnell, looking dreamily at his wife. He had not been attending very carefully to the subject-matter of her story, but he loved to hear a voice that was incantation in his ears, tones that summoned before him the vision of a magic world.

'And has the young man's mother always been like this?' he said after a long pause, desiring that the music should continue.

'Always, till quite lately, till last Sunday in fact. Of course Alice spoke to George Murry at once, and said, like a sensible girl, that she didn't think it ever answered for a married couple to live with the man's mother, "especially," she went on, "as I can see your mother hasn't taken much of a fancy to me." He told her, in the usual style, it was only his mother's way, that she didn't really mean anything, and so on; but Alice kept away for a long time, and rather hinted, I think, that it might come to having to choose between her and his mother. And so affairs went on all through the spring and summer, and then, just before the August Bank Holiday, George spoke to Alice again about it, and told her how sorry the thought of any unpleasantness made him, and how he wanted his mother and her to get on with each other, and how she was only a bit old-fashioned and queer in her ways, and had spoken very nicely to him about her when there was nobody by. So the long and the short of it was that Alice said she might come with them on the Monday, when they had settled to go to Hampton Court—the girl was always talking about Hampton Court, and wanting to see it. You remember what a beautiful day it was, don't you?'

'Let me see,' said Darnell dreamily. 'Oh yes, of course—I sat out under the mulberry tree all day, and we had our meals there: it was quite a picnic. The caterpillars were a nuisance, but I enjoyed the day very much.' His ears were charmed, ravished with the grave, supernal melody, as of antique song, rather of the first made world in which all speech was descant, and all words were sacraments of might, speaking not to the mind but to the soul. He lay back in his chair, and said—'Well, what happened to them?'

'My dear, would you believe it; but that wretched old woman behaved worse than ever. They met as had been arranged, at Kew Bridge, and got places, with a good deal of difficulty, in one of those char-à-banc things, and Alice thought she was going to enjoy herself tremendously.

Nothing of the kind. They had hardly said "Good morning," when old Mrs. Murry began to talk about Kew Gardens, and how beautiful it must be there, and how much more convenient it was than Hampton, and no expense at all; just the trouble of walking over the bridge. Then she went on to say, as they were waiting for the char-à-banc, that she had always heard there was nothing to see at Hampton, except a lot of nasty, grimy old pictures, and some of them not fit for any decent woman, let alone girl, to look at, and she wondered why the Queen allowed such things to be shown, putting all kinds of notions into girls' heads that were light enough already; and as she said that she looked at Alice so nastily— horrid old thing—that, as she told me afterwards, Alice would have slapped her face if she hadn't been an elderly woman, and George's mother. Then she talked about Kew again, saying how wonderful the hot-houses were, with palms and all sorts of wonderful things, and a lily as big as a parlour table, and the view over the river. George was very good, Alice told me. He was quite taken aback at first, as the old woman had promised faithfully to be as nice as ever she could be; but then he said, gently but firmly, "Well, mother, we must go to Kew some other day, as Alice has set her heart on Hampton for to-day, and I want to see it myself!" All Mrs. Murry did was to snort, and look at the girl like vinegar, and just then the char-à-banc came up, and they had to scramble for their seats. Mrs. Mummy grumbled to herself in an indistinct sort of voice all the way to Hampton Court. Alice couldn't very well make out what she said, but now and then she seemed to hear bits of sentences, like: Pity to grow old, if Sons grow bold; and Honour thy father and mother; and Lie on the shelf, said the housewife to the old shoe, and the wicked son to his mother; and I gave you milk and you give me the go-by.

Alice thought they must be proverbs (except the Commandment, of course), as George was always saying how old-fashioned his mother is; but she says there were so many of them, and all pointed at her and George, that she thinks now Mrs. Murry must have made them up as they drove along. She says it would be just like her to do it, being old-fashioned, and ill-natured too, and fuller of talk than a butcher on Saturday night.

60

Well, they got to Hampton at last, and Alice thought the place would please her, perhaps, and they might have some enjoyment. But she did nothing but grumble, and out loud too, so that people looked at them, and a woman said, so that they could hear, "Ah well, they'll be old themselves some day," which made Alice very angry, for, as she said, they weren't doing anything. When they showed her the chestnut avenue in Bushey Park, she said it was so long and straight that it made her quite dull to look at it, and she thought the deer (you know how pretty they are, really) looked thin and miserable, as if they would be all the better for a good feed of hog-wash, with plenty of meal in it. She said she knew they weren't happy by the look in their eyes, which seemed to tell hem that their keepers beat them. It was the same with everything; she said she remembered market-gardens in Hammersmith and Gunnersbury that had a better show of flowers, and when they took her to the place where the water is, under the trees, she burst out with its being rather hard to tramp her off her legs to show her a common canal, with not so much as a barge on it to liven it up a bit. She went on like that the whole day, and Alice told me she was only too thankful to get home and get rid of her. Wasn't it wretched for the girl?'

'It must have been, indeed. But what happened last Sunday?'

'That's the most extraordinary thing of all. I noticed that Alice was rather queer in her manner this morning; she was a longer time washing up the breakfast things, and she answered me quite sharply when I called to her to ask when she would be ready to help me with the wash; and when I went into the kitchen to see about something, I noticed that she was going about her work in a sulky sort of way. So I asked her what was the matter, and then it all came out. I could scarcely believe my own ears when she mumbled out something about Mrs. Murry thinking she could do very much better for herself; but I asked her one question after another till I had it all out of her.

It just shows one how foolish and empty-headed these girls are. I told her she was no better than a weather-cock. If you will believe me, that horrid old woman was quite another person when Alice went to see her the other night. Why, I can't think, but so she was. She told the girl how pretty she was; what a neat figure she had; how well she walked; and how she'd known many a girl not half so clever or well-looking earning her twenty-five or thirty pounds a year, and with good families. She seems to have gone into all sorts of details, and made elaborate calculations as to what she would be able to save, "with decent folks, who don't screw, and pinch, and lock up everything in the house," and then she went off into a lot of hypocritical nonsense about how fond she was of Alice, and how she could go to her grave in peace, knowing how happy her dear George would be with such a good wife, and about her savings from good wages helping to set up a little home, ending up with "And, if you take an old woman's advice, deary, it won't be long before you hear the marriage bells."

'I see,' said Darnell; 'and the upshot of it all is, I suppose, that the girl is thoroughly dissatisfied?'

'Yes, she is so young and silly. I talked to her, and reminded her of how nasty old Mrs. Murry had been, and told her that she might change her place and change for the worse. I think I have persuaded her to think it over quietly, at all events. Do you know what it is, Edward? I have an idea. I believe that wicked old woman is trying to get Alice to leave us, that she may tell her son how changeable she is; and I suppose she would make up some of her stupid old proverbs:

"A changeable wife, a troublesome life," or some nonsense of the kind. Horrid old thing!'

'Well, well,' said Darnell, 'I hope she won't go, for your sake. It would be such a bother for you, hunting for a fresh servant.'

He refilled his pipe and smoked placidly, refreshed somewhat after the emptiness and the burden of the day. The French window was wide open, and now at last there came a breath of quickening air, distilled by the night from such trees as still wore green in that arid valley. The song to which Darnell had listened in rapture, and now the breeze, which even in that dry, grim suburb still bore the word of the woodland, had summoned the dream to his eyes, and he meditated over matters that his lips could not express.

'She must, indeed, be a villainous old woman,' he said at length.

'Old Mrs. Murry? Of course she is; the mischievous old thing! Trying to take the girl from a comfortable place where she is happy.'

'Yes; and not to like Hampton Court! That shows how bad she must be, more than anything.'

'It is beautiful, isn't it?'

'I shall never forget the first time I saw it. It was soon after I went into the City; the first year. I had my holidays in July, and I was getting such a small salary that I couldn't think of going away to the seaside, or anything like that. I remember one of the other men wanted me to come with him on a walking tour in Kent. I should have liked that, but the money wouldn't run to it. And do you know what I did? I lived in Great College Street then, and the first day I was off, I stayed in bed till past dinner-time, and lounged about in an arm-chair with a pipe all the afternoon. I had got a new kind of tobacco—one and four for the two-ounce packet—much dearer than I could afford to smoke, and I was enjoying it immensely. It was awfully hot, and when I shut the window and drew down the red blind it grew hotter; at five o'clock the room was like an oven.

But I was so pleased at not having to go into the City, that I didn't mind anything, and now and again I read bits from a queer old book that had belonged to my poor dad. I couldn't make out what a lot of it meant, but it fitted in somehow, and I read and smoked till tea-time. Then I went out for a walk, thinking I should be better for a little fresh air before I went to bed; and I went wandering away, not much noticing where I was going, turning here and there as the fancy took me. I must have gone miles and miles, and a good many of them mound and round, as they say they do in Australia if they lose their way in the bush; and I am sure I couldn't have gone exactly the same way all over again for any money. Anyhow, I was still in the streets when the twilight came on, and the lamp-lighters were trotting round from one lamp to another. It was a wonderful night: I wish you had been there, my dear.'

'I was quite a little girl then.'

'Yes, I suppose you were. Well, it was a wonderful night. I remember, I was walking in a little street of little grey houses all alike, with stucco copings and stucco door-posts; there were brass plates on a lot of the doors, and one had "Maker of Shell Boxes" on it, and I was quite pleased, as I had often wondered where those boxes and things that you buy at the seaside came from. A few children were playing about in the road with some rubbish or other, and men were singing in a small public-house at the corner, and I happened to look up, and I noticed what a wonderful colour the sky had turned. I have seen it since, but I don't think it has ever been quite what it was that night, a dark blue, glowing like a violet, just as they say the sky looks in foreign countries. I don't know why, but the sky or something made me feel quite queer; everything seemed changed in a way I couldn't understand. I remember, I told an old gentleman I knew then—a friend of my poor father's, he's been dead for five years, if not more—about how I felt, and he looked at me and said something about fairyland; I don't know what he meant, and I dare say I didn't explain myself properly. But, do you know, for a moment or two I felt as if that little back street was beautiful, and the noise of the children and the men in the public-house seemed to fit in with the sky and become part of it. You know that old saying about "treading on air" when one is glad!

'Well, I really felt like that as I walked, not exactly like air, you know, but as if the pavement was velvet or some very soft carpet. And then—I suppose it was all my fancy—the air seemed to smell sweet, like the incense in Catholic churches, and my breath came queer and catchy, as it does when one gets very excited about anything. I felt altogether stranger than I've ever felt before or since.'

Darnell stopped suddenly and looked up at his wife. She was watching him with parted lips, with eager, wondering eyes.

'I hope I'm not tiring you, dear, with all this story about nothing. You have had a worrying day with that stupid girl; hadn't you better go to bed?'

'Oh, no, please, Edward. I'm not a bit tired now. I love to hear you talk like that. Please go on.'

'Well, after I had walked a bit further, that queer sort of feeling seemed to fade away. I said a bit further, and I really thought I had been walking about five minutes, but I had looked at my watch just before I got into that little street, and when I looked at it again it was eleven o'clock. I must have done about eight miles. I could scarcely believe my own eyes, and I thought my watch must have gone mad; but I found out afterwards it was perfectly right. I couldn't make it out, and I can't now; I assure you the time passed as if I walked up one side of Edna Road and down the other. But there I was, right in the open country, with a cool wind blowing on me from a wood, and the air full of soft rustling sounds, and notes of birds from the bushes, and the singing noise of a little brook that ran under the road. I was standing on the bridge when I took out my watch and struck a wax light to see the time; and it came upon me suddenly what a strange evening it had been. It was all so different, you see, to what I had been doing all my life, particularly for the year before, and it almost seemed as if I couldn't be the man who had been going into the City every day in the morning and coming back from it every evening after writing a lot of uninteresting letters. It was like being pitched all of a sudden from one world into another. Well, I found my way back somehow or other, and as I went along I made up my mind how I'd spend my holiday. I said to myself, "I'll have a walking tour as well as Ferrars, only mine is to be a tour of London and its environs," and I had got it all settled when I let myself into the house about four o'clock in the morning, and the sun was shining, and the street almost as still as the wood at midnight!'

'I think that was a capital idea of yours. Did you have your tour? Did you buy a map of London?'

'I had the tour all right. I didn't buy a map; that would have spoilt it, somehow; to see everything plotted out, and named, and measured. What I wanted was to feel that I was going where nobody had been before. That's nonsense, isn't it? as if there could be any such places in London, or England either, for the matter of that.'

'I know what you mean; you wanted to feel as if you were going on a sort of voyage of discovery. Isn't that it?'

'Exactly, that's what I was trying to tell you. Besides, I didn't want to buy a map. I made a map.'

'How do you mean? Did you make a map out of your head?'

'I'll tell you about it afterwards. But do you really want to hear about my grand tour?'

'Of course I do; it must have been delightful. I call it a most original idea.'

'Well, I was quite full of it, and what you said just now about a voyage of discovery reminds me of how I felt then. When I was a boy I was awfully fond of reading of great travellers—I suppose all boys are—and of sailors who were driven out of their course and found themselves in latitudes where no ship had ever sailed before, and of people. who discovered wonderful cities in strange countries; and all the second day of my holidays I was feeling just as I used to when I read these books. I didn't get up till pretty late. I was tired to death after all those miles I had walked; but when I had finished my breakfast and filled my pipe, I had a grand time of it. It was such nonsense, you know; as if there could be anything strange or wonderful in London.'

'Why shouldn't there be?'

'Well, I don't know; but I have thought afterwards what a silly lad I must have been. Anyhow, I had a great day of it, planning what I would do, half making-believe—just like a kid—that I didn't know where I might find myself, or what might happen to me. And I was enormously pleased to think it was all my secret, that nobody else knew anything about it, and that, whatever I might see, I would keep to myself. I had always felt like that about the books. Of course, I loved reading them, but it seemed to me that, if I had been a discoverer, I would have kept my discoveries a secret. If I had been Columbus, and, if it could possibly have been managed, I would have found America all by myself, and never have said a word about it to anybody.

Fancy! how beautiful it would be to be walking about in one's own town, and talking to people, and all the while to have the thought that one knew of a great world beyond the seas, that nobody else dreamed of. I should have loved that!

'And that is exactly what I felt about the tour I was going to make. I made up my mind that nobody should know; and so, from that day to this, nobody has heard a word of it.'

'But you are going to tell me?'

'You are different. But I don't think even you will hear everything; not because I won't, but because I can't tell many of the things I saw.'

'Things you saw? Then you really did see wonderful, strange things in London?'

'Well, I did and I didn't. Everything, or pretty nearly everything, that I saw is standing still, and hundreds of thousands of people have looked at the same sights—there were many places that the fellows in the office knew quite well, I found out afterwards. And then I read a book called "London and its Surroundings." But (I don't know how it is) neither the men at the office nor the writers of the book seem to have seen the things that I did. That's why I stopped reading the book; it seemed to take the life, the real heart, out of everything, making it as dry and stupid as the stuffed birds in a museum.

'I thought about what I was going to do all that day, and went to bed early, so as to be fresh. I knew wonderfully little about London, really; though, except for an odd week now and then, I had spent all my life in town. Of course I knew the main streets—the Strand, Regent Street, Oxford Street, and so on—and I knew the way to the school I used to go to when I was a boy, and the way into the City. But I had just kept to a few tracks, as they say the sheep do on the mountains; and that made it all the easier for me to imagine that I was going to discover a new world.'

Darnell paused in the stream of his talk. He looked keenly at his wife to see if he were wearying her, but her eyes gazed at him with unabated interest—one would have almost said that they were the eyes of one who longed and half expected to be initiated into the mysteries, who knew not what great wonder was to be revealed. She sat with her back to the open window, framed in the sweet dusk of the night, as if a painter had made a curtain of heavy velvet behind her; and the work that she had been doing had fallen to the floor. She supported her head with her two hands placed on each side of her brow, and her eyes were as the wells in the wood of which Darnell dreamed in the night-time and in the day.

'And all the strange tales I had ever heard were in my head that morning,' he went on, as if continuing the thoughts that had filled his mind while his lips were silent. 'I had gone to bed early, as I told you, to get a thorough rest, and I had set my alarum clock to wake me at three, so that I might set out at an hour that was quite strange for the beginning of a journey. There was a hush in the world when I awoke, before the clock had rung to arouse me, and then a bird began to sing and twitter in the elm tree that grew in the next garden, and I looked out of the window, and everything was still, and the morning air breathed in pure and sweet, as I had never known it before. My room was at the back of the house, and most of the gardens had trees in them, and beyond these trees I could see the backs of the houses of the next street rising like the wall of an old city; and as I looked the sun rose, and the great light came in at my window, and the day began.

'And I found that when I was once out of the streets just about me that I knew, some of the queer feeling that had come to me two days before came back again. It was not nearly so strong, the streets no longer smelt of incense, but still there was enough of it to show me what a strange world I passed by. There were things that one may see again and again in many London streets: a vine or a fig tree on a wall, a lark singing in a cage, a curious shrub blossoming in a garden, an odd shape of a roof, or a balcony with an uncommon-looking trellis-work in iron. There's scarcely a street, perhaps, where you won't see one or other of such things as these; but that morning they rose to my eyes in a new light, as if I had on the magic spectacles in the fairy tale, and just like the man in the fairy tale, I went on and on in the new light. I remember going through wild land on a high place; there were pools of water shining in the sun, and great white houses in the middle of dark, rocking pines, and then on the turn of the height I came to a little lane that went aside from the main road, a lane that led to a wood, and in the lane was a little old shadowed house, with a bell turret in the roof, and a porch of trellis-work all dim and faded into the colour of the sea; and in the garden there were growing tall, white lilies, just as we saw them that day we went to look at the old pictures; they were shining like silver, and they filled the air with their sweet scent. It was from near that house I saw the valley and high places far away in the sun. So, as I say, I went "on and on," by woods and fields, till I came to a little town on the top of a hill, a town full of old houses bowing to the ground beneath their years, and the morning was so still that the blue smoke rose up straight into the sky from all the roof-tops, so still that I heard far down in the valley the song of a boy who was singing an old song through the streets as he went to school, and as I passed through the awakening town, beneath the old, grave houses, the church bells began to ring.

'It was soon after I had left this town behind me that I found the Strange Road. I saw it branching off from the dusty high road, and it looked so green that I turned aside into it, and soon I felt as if I had really come into a new country. I don't know whether it was one of the roads the old Romans made that my father used to tell me about; but it was covered with deep, soft turf, and the great tall hedges on each side looked as if they had not been touched for a hundred years; they had grown so broad and high and wild that they met overhead, and I could only get glimpses here and there of the country through which I was passing, as one passes in a dream. The Strange Road led me on and on, up and down hill; sometimes the rose bushes had grown so thick that I could scarcely make my way between them, and sometimes the road broadened out into a green, and in one valley a brook, spanned by an old wooden bridge, ran across it. I was tired, and I found a soft and shady place beneath an ash tree, where I must have slept for many hours, for when I woke up it was late in the afternoon. So I went on again, and at last the green road came out into the highway, and I looked up and saw another town on a high place with a great church in the middle of it, and when I went up to it there was a great organ sounding from within, and the choir was singing.'

There was a rapture in Darnell's voice as he spoke, that made his story well-nigh swell into a song, and he drew a long breath as the words ended, filled with the thought of that far-off summer day, when some enchantment had informed all common things, transmuting them into a great sacrament, causing earthly works to glow with the fire and the glory of the everlasting light.

And some splendour of that light shone on the face of Mary as she sat still against the sweet gloom of the night, her dark hair making her face more radiant. She was silent for a little while, and then she spoke— 'Oh, my dear, why have you waited so long to tell me these wonderful things? I think it is beautiful. Please go on.'

'I have always been afraid it was all nonsense,' said Darnell. 'And I don't know how to explain what I feel. I didn't think I could say so much as I have to-night.'

'And did you find it the same day after day?'

'All through the tour? Yes, I think every journey was a success. Of course, I didn't go so far afield every day; I was too tired. Often I rested all day long, and went out in the evening, after the lamps were lit, and then only for a mile or two. I would roam about old, dim squares, and hear the wind from the hills whispering in the trees; and when I knew I was within call of some great glittering street, I was sunk in the silence of ways where I was almost the only passenger, and the lamps were so few and faint that they seemed to give out shadows instead of light. And I would walk slowly, to and fro, perhaps for an hour at a time, in such dark streets, and all the time I felt what I told you about its being my secret—that the shadow, and the dim lights, and the cool of the evening, and trees that were like dark low clouds were all mine, and mine alone, that I was living in a world that nobody else knew of, into which no one could enter.

'I remembered one night I had gone farther. It was somewhere in the far west, where there are orchards and gardens, and great broad lawns that slope down to trees by the river. A great red moon rose that night through mists of sunset, and thin, filmy clouds, and I wandered by a road that passed through the orchards, till I came to a little hill, with the moon showing above it glowing like a great rose. Then I saw figures pass between me and the moon, one by one, in a long line, each bent double, with great packs upon their shoulders. One of them was singing, and then in the middle of the song I heard a horrible shrill laugh, in the thin cracked voice of a very old woman, and they disappeared into the shadow of the trees. I suppose they were people going to work, or coming from work in the gardens; but how like it was to a nightmare! I can't tell you about Hampton; I should never finish talking. I was there one evening, not long before they closed the gates, and there were very few people about. But the grey-red, silent, echoing courts, and the flowers falling into dreamland as the night came on, and the dark yews and shadowy-looking statues, and the far, still stretches of water beneath the avenues; and all melting into a blue mist, all being hidden from one's eyes, slowly, surely, as if veils were dropped, one by one, on a great ceremony! Oh! my dear, what could it mean? Far away, across the river, I heard a soft bell ring three times, and three times, and again three times, and I turned away, and my eyes were full of tears.

'I didn't know what it was when I came to it; I only found out afterwards that it must have been Hampton Court. One of the men in the office told me he had taken an A. B. C. girl there, and they had great fun. They got into the maze and couldn't get out again, and then they went on the river and were nearly drowned. He told me there were some spicy pictures in the galleries; his girl shrieked with laughter, so he said.'

Mary quite disregarded this interlude.

'But you told me you had made a map. What was it like?'

'I'll show it you some day, if you want to see it. I marked down all the places I had gone to, and made signs—things like queer letters—to remind me of what I had seen. Nobody but myself could understand it. I wanted to draw pictures, but I never learnt how to draw, so when I tried nothing was like what I wanted it to be. I tried to draw a picture of that town on the hill that I came to on the evening of the first day; I wanted to make a steep hill with houses on top, and in the middle, but high above them, the great church, all spires and pinnacles, and above it, in the air, a cup with rays coming from it. But it wasn't a success. I made a very strange sign for Hampton Court, and gave it a name that I made up out of my head.'

The Darnells avoided one another's eyes as they sat at breakfast the next morning. The air had lightened in the night, for rain had fallen at dawn; and there was a bright blue sky, with vast white clouds rolling across it from the south-west, and a fresh and joyous wind blew in at the open window; the mists had vanished. And with the mists there seemed to have vanished also the sense of strange things that had possessed Mary and her husband the night before; and as they looked out into the clear light they could scarcely believe that the one had spoken and the other had listened a few hours before to histories very far removed from the usual current of their thoughts and of their lives. They glanced shyly at one another, and spoke of common things, of the question whether Alice would be corrupted by the insidious Mrs. Murry, or whether Mrs. Darnell would be able to persuade the girl that the old woman must be actuated by the worst motives.

'And I think, if I were you,' said Darnell, as he went out, 'I should step over to the stores and complain of their meat. That last piece of beef was very far from being up to the mark—full of sinew.'

III

It might have been different in the evening, and Darnell had matured a plan by which he hoped to gain much. He intended to ask his wife if she would mind having only one gas, and that a good deal lowered, on the pretext that his eyes were tired with work; he thought many things might happen if the room were dimly lit, and the window opened, so that they could sit and watch the night, and listen to the rustling murmur of the tree on the lawn. But his plans were made in vain, for when he got to the garden gate his wife, in tears, came forth to meet him.

'Oh, Edward,' she began, 'such a dreadful thing has happened! I never liked him much, but I didn't think he would ever do such awful things.'

'What do you mean? Who are you talking about? What has happened? Is it Alice's young man?'

'No, no. But come in, dear. I can see that woman opposite watching us: she's always on the look out.'

'Now, what is it?' said Darnell, as they sat down to tea. 'Tell me, quick! you've quite frightened me.'

'I don't know how to begin, or where to start. Aunt Marian has thought that there was something queer for weeks. And then she found— oh, well, the long and short of it is that Uncle Robert has been carrying on dreadfully with some horrid girl, and aunt has found out everything!'

'Lord! you don't say so! The old rascal! Why, he must be nearer seventy than sixty!'

'He's just sixty-five; and the money he has given her—'

The first shock of surprise over, Darnell turned resolutely to his mince.

'We'll have it all out after tea,' he said; 'I am not going to have my meals spoilt by that old fool of a Nixon. Fill up my cup, will you, dear?'

'Excellent mince this,' he went on, calmly. 'A little lemon juice and a bit of ham in it? I thought there was something extra. Alice all right to-day? That's good. I expect she's getting over all that nonsense.'

He went on calmly chattering in a manner that astonished Mrs. Darnell, who felt that by the fall of Uncle Robert the natural order had been inverted, and had scarcely touched food since the intelligence had arrived by the second post. She had started out to keep the appointment her aunt had made early in the morning, and had spent most of the day in a first-class waiting-room at Victoria Station, where she had heard all the story.

'Now,' said Darnell, when the table had been cleared, 'tell us all about it. How long has it been going on?'

'Aunt thinks now, from little things she remembers, that it must have been going on for a year at least. She says there has been a horrid kind of mystery about uncle's behaviour for a long time, and her nerves were quite shaken, as she thought he must be involved with Anarchists, or something dreadful of the sort.'

'What on earth made her think that?'

"Well, you see, once or twice when she was out walking with her husband, she has been startled by whistles, which seemed to follow them everywhere. You know there are some nice country walks at Barnet, and one in particular, in the fields near Totteridge, that uncle and aunt rather made a point of going to on fine Sunday evenings. Of course, this was not the first thing she noticed, but, at the time, it made a great impression on her mind; she could hardly get a wink of sleep for weeks and weeks.'

'Whistling?' said Darnell. 'I don't quite understand. Why should she be frightened by whistling?'

'I'll tell you. The first time it happened was one Sunday in last May. Aunt had a fancy they were being followed a Sunday or two before, but she didn't see or hear anything, except a sort of crackling noise in the hedge. But this particular Sunday they had hardly got through the stile into the fields, when she heard a peculiar kind of low whistle. She took no notice, thinking it was no concern of hers or her husband's, but as they went on she heard it again, and then again, and it followed them the whole walk, and it made her so uncomfortable, because she didn't know where it was coming from or who was doing it, or why. Then, just as they got out of the fields into the lane, uncle said he felt quite faint, and he thought he would try a little brandy at the "Turpin's Head," a small public-house there is there. And she looked at him and saw his face was quite purple— more like apoplexy, as she says, than fainting fits, which make people look a sort of greenish-white. But she said nothing, and thought perhaps uncle had a peculiar way of fainting of his own, as he always was a man to have his own way of doing everything. So she just waited in the road, and he went ahead and slipped into the public, and aunt says she thought she saw a little figure rise out of the dusk and slip in after him, but she couldn't be sure. And when uncle came out he looked red instead of purple, and said he felt much better; and so they went home quietly together, and nothing more was said. You see, uncle had said nothing about the whistling, and aunt had been so frightened that she didn't dare speak, for fear they might be both shot.

'She wasn't thinking anything more about it, when two Sundays afterwards the very same thing happened just as it had before. This time aunt plucked up a spirit, and asked uncle what it could be. And what do you think he said? "Birds, my dear, birds." Of course aunt said to him that no bird that ever flew with wings made a noise like that: sly, and low, with pauses in between; and then he said that many rare sorts of birds lived in North Middlesex and Hertfordshire. "Nonsense, Robert," said aunt, "how can you talk so, considering it has followed us all the way, for a mile or more?" And then uncle told her that some birds were so attached to man that they would follow one about for miles sometimes; he said he had just been reading about a bird like that in a book of travels. And do you know that when they got home he actually showed her a piece in the "Hertfordshire Naturalist" which they took in to oblige a friend of theirs, all about rare birds found in the neighbourhood, all the most outlandish names, aunt says, that she had never heard or thought of, and uncle had the impudence to say that it must have been a Purple Sandpiper, which, the paper said, had "a low shrill note, constantly repeated." And then he took down a book of Siberian Travels from the bookcase and showed her a page which told how a man was followed by a bird all day long through a forest. And that's what Aunt Marian says vexes her more than anything almost; to think that he should be so artful and ready with those books, twisting them to his own wicked ends. But, at the time, when she was out walking, she simply couldn't make out what he meant by talking about birds in that random, silly sort of way, so unlike him, and they went on, that horrible whistling following them, she looking straight ahead and walking fast, really feeling more huffy and put out than frightened. And when they got to the next stile, she got over and turned round, and "lo and behold," as she says, there was no Uncle Robert to be seen! She felt herself go quite white with alarm, thinking of that whistle, and making sure he'd been spirited away or snatched in some way or another, and she had just screamed out "Robert" like a mad woman, when he came quite slowly round the corner, as cool as a cucumber, holding something in his hand. He said there were some flowers he could never pass, and when aunt saw that he had got a dandelion torn up by the roots, she felt as if her head were going round.'

Mary's story was suddenly interrupted. For ten minutes Darnell had been writhing in his chair, suffering tortures in his anxiety to avoid wounding his wife's feelings, but the episode of the dandelion was too much for him, and he burst into a long, wild shriek of laughter, aggravated by suppression into the semblance of a Red Indian's war-whoop. Alice,

73

who was washing-up in the scullery, dropped some three shillings' worth of china, and the neighbours ran out into their gardens wondering if it were murder. Mary gazed reproachfully at her husband.

'How can you be so unfeeling, Edward?' she said, at length, when Darnell had passed into the feebleness of exhaustion. 'If you had seen the tears rolling down poor Aunt Marian's cheeks as she told me, I don't think you would have laughed. I didn't think you were so hard-hearted.'

'My dear Mary,' said Darnell, faintly, through sobs and catching of the breath, 'I am awfully sorry. I know it's very sad, really, and I'm not unfeeling; but it is such an odd tale, now, isn't it? The Sandpiper, you know, and then the dandelion!'

His face twitched and he ground his teeth together. Mary looked gravely at him for a moment, and then she put her hands to her face, and Darnell could see that she also shook with merriment.

'I am as bad as you,' she said, at last. 'I never thought of it in that way. I'm glad I didn't, or I should have laughed in Aunt Marian's face, and I wouldn't have done that for the world. Poor old thing; she cried as if her heart would break. I met her at Victoria, as she asked me, and we had some soup at a confectioner's. I could scarcely touch it; her tears kept dropping into the plate all the time; and then we went to the waiting-room at the station, and she cried there terribly.'

'Well,' said Darnell, 'what happened next? I won't laugh any more.'

'No, we mustn't; it's much too horrible for a joke. Well, of course aunt went home and wondered and wondered what could be the matter, and tried to think it out, but, as she says, she could make nothing of it. She began to be afraid that uncle's brain was giving way through overwork, as he had stopped in the City (as he said) up to all hours lately, and he had to go to Yorkshire (wicked old story-teller!), about some very tiresome business connected with his leases. But then she reflected that however queer he might be getting, even his queerness couldn't make whistles in the air, though, as she said, he was always a wonderful man. So she had to give that up; and then she wondered if there were anything the matter with her, as she had read about people who heard noises when there was really nothing at all. But that wouldn't do either, because though it might account for the whistling, it wouldn't account for the dandelion or the Sandpiper, or for fainting fits that turned purple, or any of uncle's queerness. So aunt said she could think of nothing but to read the Bible every day from the beginning, and by the time she got into Chronicles she felt rather better, especially as nothing had happened for three or four Sundays. She noticed uncle seemed absent-minded, and not as nice to her as he might be, but she put that down to too much work, as he never came home before the last train, and had a hansom twice all the way, getting there between three and four in the morning. Still, she felt it was no good bothering her head over what couldn't be made out or explained anyway, and she was just settling down, when one Sunday evening it began all over again, and worse things happened. The whistling followed them just as it did before, and poor aunt set her teeth and said nothing to uncle, as she knew he would only tell her stories, and they were walking on, not saying a word, when something made her look back, and there was a horrible boy with red hair, peeping through the hedge just behind, and grinning. She said it was a dreadful face, with something unnatural about it, as if it had been a dwarf, and before she had time to have a good look, it popped back like lightning, and aunt all but fainted away.'

'A red-headed boy?' said Darnell. 'I thought—What an extraordinary story this is. I've never heard of anything so queer. Who was the boy?'

'You will know in good time,' said Mrs. Darnell. 'It is very strange, isn't it?'

'Strange!' Darnell ruminated for a while.

'I know what I think, Mary,' he said at length. 'I don't believe a word of it. I believe your aunt is going mad, or has gone mad, and that she has delusions. The whole thing sounds to me like the invention of a lunatic.'

'You are quite wrong. Every word is true, and if you will let me go on, you will understand how it all happened.'

'Very good, go ahead.'

'Let me see, where was I? Oh, I know, aunt saw the boy grinning in the hedge. Yes, well, she was dreadfully frightened for a minute or two; there was something so queer about the face, but then she plucked up a spirit and said to herself, "After all, better a boy with red hair than a big man with a gun," and she made up her mind to watch Uncle Robert closely, as she could see by his look he knew all about it; he seemed as if he were thinking hard and puzzling over something, as if he didn't know what to do next, and his mouth kept opening and shutting, like a fish's. So she kept her face straight, and didn't say a word, and when he said something to her about the fine sunset, she took no notice. "Don't you hear what I say, Marian?" he said, speaking quite crossly, and bellowing as if it were to somebody in the next field. So aunt said she was very sorry, but her cold made her so deaf, she couldn't hear much. She noticed uncle looked quite pleased, and relieved too, and she knew he thought she hadn't heard the whistling. Suddenly uncle pretended to see a beautiful spray of honeysuckle high up in the hedge, and he said he must get it for aunt, only she must go on ahead, as it made him nervous to be watched. She said she would, but she just stepped aside behind a bush where there was a sort of cover in the hedge, and found she could see him quite well, though she scratched her face terribly with poking it into a rose bush. And in a minute or two out came the boy from behind the hedge, and she saw uncle and him talking, and she knew it was the same boy, as it wasn't dark enough to hide his flaming red head. And uncle put out his hand as if to catch him, but he just darted into the bushes and vanished. Aunt never said a word at the time, but that night when they got home she charged uncle with what she'd seen and asked him what it all meant. He was quite taken aback at first, and stammered and stuttered and said a spy wasn't his notion of a good wife, but at last he made her swear secrecy, and told her that he was a very high Freemason, and that the boy was an emissary of the order who brought him messages of the greatest importance. But aunt didn't believe a word of it, as an uncle of hers was a mason, and he never behaved like that. It was then she began to be afraid that it was really Anarchists, or something of the kind, and every time the bell rang she thought that uncle had been found out, and the police had come for him.'

'What nonsense! As if a man with house property would be an Anarchist.'

'Well, she could see there must be some horrible secret, and she didn't know what else to think. And then she began to have the things through the post.'

'Things through the post! What do you mean by that?'

'All sorts of things; bits of broken bottle-glass, packed carefully as if it were jewellery; parcels that unrolled and unrolled worse than Chinese boxes, and then had "cat" in large letters when you came to the middle; old artificial teeth, a cake of red paint, and at last cockroaches.'

'Cockroaches by post! Stuff and nonsense; your aunt's mad.'

'Edward, she showed me the box; it was made to hold cigarettes, and there were three dead cockroaches inside. And when she found a box of exactly the same kind, half-full of cigarettes, in uncle's great-coat pocket, then her head began to turn again.'

Darnell groaned, and stirred uneasily in his chair, feeling that the tale of Aunt Marian's domestic troubles was putting on the semblance of an evil dream.

'Anything else?' he asked.

'My dear, I haven't repeated half the things poor aunt told me this afternoon. There was the night she thought she saw a ghost in the shrubbery. She was anxious about some chickens that were just due to hatch out, so she went out after dark with some egg and bread-crumbs, in case they might be out. And just before her she saw a figure gliding by the rhododendrons. It looked like a short, slim man dressed as they used to be hundreds of years ago; she saw the sword by his side, and the feather in his cap. She thought she should have died, she said, and though it was gone in a minute, and she tried to make out it was all her fancy, she fainted when she got into the house. Uncle was at home that night, and when she came to and told him he ran out, and stayed out for half-an-hour or more, and then came in and said he could find nothing; and the next minute aunt heard that low whistle just outside the window, and uncle ran out again.'

'My dear Mary, do let us come to the point. What on earth does it all lead to?'

'Haven't you guessed? Why, of course it was that girl all the time.

'Girl? I thought you said it was a boy with a red head?'

'Don't you see? She's an actress, and she dressed up. She won't leave uncle alone. It wasn't enough that he was with her nearly every evening in the week, but she must be after him on Sundays too. Aunt found a letter the horrid thing had written, and so it has all come out. Enid Vivian she calls herself, though I don't suppose she has any right to one name or the other. And the question is, what is to be done?'

'Let us talk of that again. I'll have a pipe, and then we'll go to bed.'

They were almost asleep when Mary said suddenly—'Doesn't it seem queer, Edward? Last night you were telling me such beautiful things, and to-night I have been talking about that disgraceful old man and his goings on.'

'I don't know,' answered Darnell, dreamily. 'On the walls of that great church upon the hill I saw all kinds of strange grinning monsters, carved in stone.'

The misdemeanours of Mr. Robert Nixon brought in their train consequences strange beyond imagination. It was not that they continued to develop on the somewhat fantastic lines of these first adventures which Mrs. Darnell had related; indeed, when 'Aunt Marian' came over to Shepherd's Bush, one Sunday afternoon, Darnell wondered how he had had the heart to laugh at the misfortunes of a broken-hearted woman.

He had never seen his wife's aunt before, and he was strangely surprised when Alice showed her into the garden where they were sitting on the warm and misty Sunday in September. To him, save during these latter days, she had always been associated with ideas of splendour and success: his wife had always mentioned the Nixons with a tinge of reverence; he had heard, many times, the epic of Mr. Nixon's struggles and of his slow but triumphant rise. Mary had told the story as she had received it from her parents, beginning with the flight to London from some small, dull, and unprosperous town in the flattest of the Midlands, long ago, when a young man from the country had great chances of fortune. Robert Nixon's father had been a grocer in the High Street, and in after days the successful coal merchant and builder loved to tell of that dull provincial life, and while he glorified his own victories, he gave his hearers to understand that he came of a race which had also known how to achieve. That had been long ago, he would explain: in the days when that rare citizen who desired to go to London or to York was forced to rise in the dead of night, and make his way, somehow or other, by ten miles of quagmirish, wandering lanes to the Great North Road, there to meet the 'Lightning' coach, a vehicle which stood to all the countryside as the visible and tangible embodiment of tremendous speed—'and indeed,' as Nixon would add, 'it was always up to time, which is more than can be said of the Dunham Branch Line nowadays!' It was in this ancient Dunham that the Nixons had waged successful trade for perhaps a hundred years, in a shop with bulging bay windows looking on the market-place.

There was no competition, and the townsfolk, and well-to-do farmers, the clergy and the country families, looked upon the house of Nixon as an institution fixed as the town hall (which stood on Roman pillars) and the parish church. But the change came: the railway crept nearer and nearer, the farmers and the country gentry became less well-to-do; the tanning, which was the local industry, suffered from a great business which had been established in a larger town, some twenty miles away, and the profits of the Nixons grew less and less. Hence the hegira of Robert, and he would dilate on the poorness of his beginnings, how he saved, by little and little, from his sorry wage of City clerk, and how he and a fellow clerk, 'who had come into a hundred pounds,' saw an opening in the coal trade—and filled it. It was at this stage of Robert's fortunes, still far from magnificent, that Miss Marian Reynolds had encountered him, she being on a visit to friends in Gunnersbury. Afterwards, victory followed victory; Nixon's wharf became a landmark to bargemen; his power stretched abroad, his dusky fleets went outwards to the sea, and inward by all the far reaches of canals. Lime, cement, and bricks were added to his merchandise, and at last be hit upon the great stroke—that extensive taking up of land in the north of London. Nixon himself ascribed this coup to native sagacity, and the possession of capital; and there were also obscure rumours to the effect that some one or other had been 'done' in the course of the transaction. However that might be, the Nixons grew wealthy to excess, and Mary had often told her husband of the state in which they dwelt, of their liveried servants, of the glories of their drawing-room, of their broad lawn, shadowed by a splendid and ancient cedar.

And so Darnell had somehow been led into conceiving the lady of this demesne as a personage of no small pomp. He saw her, tall, of dignified port and presence, inclining, it might be, to some measure of obesity, such a measure as was not unbefitting in an elderly lady of position, who lived well and lived at ease. He even imagined a slight ruddiness of complexion, which went very well with hair that was beginning to turn grey, and when he heard the door-bell ring, as he sat under the mulberry on the Sunday afternoon, he bent forward to catch sight of this stately figure, clad, of course, in the richest, blackest silk, girt about with heavy chains of gold.

He started with amazement when he saw the strange presence that followed the servant into the garden. Mrs. Nixon was a little, thin old woman, who bent as she feebly trotted after Alice; her eyes were on the ground, and she did not lift them when the Darnells rose to greet her. She glanced to the right, uneasily, as she shook hands with Darnell, to the left when Mary kissed her, and when she was placed on the garden seat with a cushion at her back, she looked away at the back of the houses in the next street. She was dressed in black, it was true, but even Darnell could see that her gown was old and shabby, that the fur trimming of her cape and the fur boa which was twisted about her neck were dingy and disconsolate, and had all the melancholy air which fur wears when it is seen in a second-hand clothes-shop in a back street. And her gloves— they were black kid, wrinkled with much wear, faded to a bluish hue at the finger-tips, which showed signs of painful mending. Her hair, plastered over her forehead, looked dull and colourless, though some greasy matter had evidently been used with a view of producing a becoming gloss, and on it perched an antique bonnet, adorned with black pendants that rattled paralytically one against the other.

And there was nothing in Mrs. Nixon's face to correspond with the imaginary picture that Darnell had made of her. She was sallow, wrinkled, pinched; her nose ran to a sharp point, and her red-rimmed eyes were a queer water-grey, that seemed to shrink alike from the light and from encounter with the eyes of others. As she sat beside his wife on the green garden-seat, Darnell, who occupied a wicker-chair brought out from the drawing-room, could not help feeling that this shadowy and evasive figure, muttering replies to Mary's polite questions, was almost impossibly remote from his conceptions of the rich and powerful aunt, who could give away a hundred pounds as a mere birthday gift. She would say little at first; yes, she was feeling rather tired, it had been so hot all the way, and she had been afraid to put on lighter things as one never knew at this time of year what it might be like in the evenings; there were apt to be cold mists when the sun went down, and she didn't care to risk bronchitis.

'I thought I should never get here,' she went on, raising her voice to an odd querulous pipe.

'I'd no notion it was such an out-of-the-way place, it's so many years since I was in this neighbourhood.'

She wiped her eyes, no doubt thinking of the early days at Turnham Green, when she married Nixon; and when the pocket-handkerchief had done its office she replaced it in a shabby black bag which she clutched rather than carried. Darnell noticed, as he watched her, that the bag seemed full, almost to bursting, and he speculated idly as to the nature of its contents: correspondence, perhaps, he thought, further proofs of Uncle Robert's treacherous and wicked dealings. He grew quite uncomfortable, as he sat and saw her glancing all the while furtively away from his wife and himself, and presently he got up and strolled away to the other end of the garden, where he lit his pipe and walked to and fro on the gravel walk, still astounded at the gulf between the real and the imagined woman.

Presently he heard a hissing whisper, and he saw Mrs. Nixon's head inclining to his wife's.

Mary rose and came towards him.

'Would you mind sitting in the drawing-room, Edward?' she murmured. 'Aunt says she can't bring herself to discuss such a delicate matter before you. I dare say it's quite natural.'

'Very well, but I don't thing I'll go into the drawing-room. I feel as if a walk would do me good. You mustn't be frightened if I am a little late,' he said; 'if I don't get back before your aunt goes, say good-bye to her for me.'

He strolled into the main road, where the trains were humming to and fro. He was still confused and perplexed, and he tried to account for a certain relief he felt in removing himself from the presence of Mrs.

Nixon. He told himself that her grief at her husband's ruffianly conduct was worthy of all pitiful respect, but at the same time, to his shame, he had felt a certain physical aversion from her as she sat in his garden in her dingy black, dabbing her red-rimmed eyes with a damp pocket-handkerchief. He had been to the Zoo when he was a lad, and he still remembered how he had shrunk with horror at the sight of certain reptiles slowly crawling over one another in their slimy pond. But he was enraged at the similarity between the two sensations, and he walked briskly on that level and monotonous road, looking about him at the unhandsome spectacle of suburban London keeping Sunday.

There was something in the tinge of antiquity which still exists in Acton that soothed his mind and drew it away from those unpleasant contemplations, and when at last he had penetrated rampant after rampart of brick, and heard no more the harsh shrieks and laughter of the people who were enjoying themselves, he found a way into a little sheltered field, and sat down in peace beneath a tree, whence he could look out on a pleasant valley. The sun sank down beneath the hills, the clouds changed into the likeness of blossoming rose-gardens; and he still sat there in the gathering darkness till a cool breeze blew upon him, and he rose with a sigh, and turned back to the brick ramparts and the glimmering streets, and the noisy idlers sauntering to and fro in the procession of their dismal festival. But he was murmuring to himself some words that seemed a magic song, and it was with uplifted heart that he let himself into his house.

Mrs. Nixon had gone an hour and a half before his return, Mary told him. Darnell sighed with relief, and he and his wife strolled out into the garden and sat down side by side.

They kept silence for a time, and at last Mary spoke, not without a nervous tremor in her voice.

'I must tell you, Edward,' she began, 'that aunt has made a proposal which you ought to hear. I think we should consider it.'

'A proposal? But how about the whole affair? Is it still going on?'

'Oh, yes! She told me all about it. Uncle is quite unrepentant. It seems he has taken a flat somewhere in town for that woman, and furnished it in the most costly manner. He simply laughs at aunt's reproaches, and says he means to have some fun at last. You saw how broken she was?'

'Yes; very sad. But won't he give her any money? Wasn't she very badly dressed for a woman in her position?'

'Aunt has no end of beautiful things, but I fancy she likes to hoard them; she has a horror of spoiling her dresses. It isn't for want of money, I assure you, as uncle settled a very large sum on her two years ago, when he was everything that could be desired as a husband. And that brings me to what I want to say. Aunt would like to live with us. She would pay very liberally. What do you say?'

'Would like to live with us?' exclaimed Darnell, and his pipe dropped from his hand on to the grass. He was stupefied by the thought of Aunt Marian as a boarder, and sat staring vacantly before him, wondering what new monster the night would next produce.

'I knew you wouldn't much like the idea,' his wife went on. 'But I do think, dearest, that we ought not to refuse without very serious consideration. I am afraid you did not take to poor aunt very much.'

Darnell shook his head dumbly.

'I thought you didn't; she was so upset, poor thing, and you didn't see her at her best. She is really so good. But listen to me, dear. Do you think we have the right to refuse her offer? I told you she has money of her own, and I am sure she would be dreadfully offended if we said we wouldn't have her. And what would become of me if anything happened to you? You know we have very little saved.'

Darnell groaned.

'It seems to me,' he said, 'that it would spoil everything. We are so happy, Mary dear, by ourselves. Of course I am extremely sorry for your aunt. I think she is very much to be pitied.

'But when it comes to having her always here—'

'I know, dear. Don't think I am looking forward to the prospect; you know I don't want anybody but you. Still, we ought to think of the future, and besides we shall be able to live so very much better. I shall be able to give you all sorts of nice things that I know you ought to have after all that hard work in the City. Our income would be doubled.'

'Do you mean she would pay us £150 a year?'

'Certainly. And she would pay for the spare room being furnished, and any extra she might want. She told me, specially, that if a friend or two came now and again to see her, she would gladly bear the cost of a fire in the drawing-room, and give something towards the gas bill, with a few shillings for the girl for any additional trouble. We should certainly be more than twice as well off as we are now. You see, Edward, dear, it's not the sort of offer we are likely to have again. Besides, we must think of the future, as I said. Do you know aunt took a great fancy to you?'

He shuddered and said nothing, and his wife went on with her argument.

'And, you see, it isn't as if we should see so very much of her. She will have her breakfast in bed, and she told me she would often go up to her room in the evening directly after dinner. I thought that very nice and considerate. She quite understands that we shouldn't like to have a third person always with us. Don't you think, Edward, that, considering everything, we ought to say we will have her?'

'Oh, I suppose so,' he groaned. 'As you say, it's a very good offer, financially, and I am afraid it would be very imprudent to refuse. But I don't like the notion, I confess.'

'I am so glad you agree with me, dear. Depend upon it, it won't be half so bad as you think.

'And putting our own advantage on one side, we shall really be doing poor aunt a very great kindness. Poor old dear, she cried bitterly after you were gone; she said she had made up her mind not to stay any longer in Uncle Robert's house, and she didn't know where to go, or what would become of her, if we refused to take her in. She quite broke down.'

'Well, well; we will try it for a year, anyhow. It may be as you say; we shan't find it quite so bad as it seems now. Shall we go in?'

He stooped for his pipe, which lay as it had fallen, on the grass. He could not find it, and lit a wax match which showed him the pipe, and close beside it, under the seat, something that looked like a page torn from a book. He wondered what it could be, and picked it up.

The gas was lit in the drawing-room, and Mrs. Darnell, who was arranging some notepaper, wished to write at once to Mrs. Nixon, cordially accepting her proposal, when she was startled by an exclamation from her husband.

'What is the matter?' she said, startled by the tone of his voice. 'You haven't hurt yourself?'

'Look at this,' he replied, handing her a small leaflet; 'I found it under the garden seat just now.'

Mary glanced with bewilderment at her husband and read as follows.

THE NEW AND CHOSEN SEED OF ABRAHAM
PROPHECIES TO BE FULFILLED IN THE PRESENT YEAR
1. The Sailing of a Fleet of One hundred and Forty and Four Vessels for Tarshish and the Isles.

2. Destruction of the Power of the Dog, including all the instruments of anti-Abrahamic legislation.

3. Return of the Fleet from Tarshish, bearing with it the gold of Arabia, destined to be the Foundation of the New City of Abraham.

4. The Search for the Bride, and the bestowing of the Seals on the Seventy and Seven.

5. The Countenance of FATHER to become luminous, but with a greater glory than the face of Moses.

6. The Pope of Rome to be stoned with stones in the valley called Berek-Zittor.

7. FATHER to be acknowledged by Three Great Rulers. Two Great Rulers will deny FATHER, and will immediately perish in the Effluvia of FATHER'S Indignation.

8. Binding of the Beast with the Little Horn, and all Judges cast down.

9. Finding of the Bride in the Land of Egypt, which has been revealed to FATHER as now existing in the western part of London.

10. Bestowal of the New Tongue on the Seventy and Seven, and on the One Hundred and Forty and Four. FATHER proceeds to the Bridal Chamber.

11. Destruction of London and rebuilding of the City called No, which is the New City of Abraham.

12. FATHER united to the Bride, and the present Earth removed to the Sun for the space of half an hour.

Mrs. Darnell's brow cleared as she read matter which seemed to her harmless if incoherent.

From her husband's voice she had been led to fear something more tangibly unpleasant than a vague catena of prophecies.

'Well,' she said, 'what about it?'

'What about it? Don't you see that your aunt dropped it, and that she must be a raging lunatic?'

'Oh, Edward! don't say that. In the first place, how do you know that aunt dropped it at all? It might easily have blown over from any of the other gardens.

And, if it were hers, I don't think you should call her a lunatic. I don't believe, myself, that there are any real prophets now; but there are many good people who think quite differently. I knew an old lady once who, I am sure, was very good, and she took in a paper every week that was full of prophecies and things very like this. Nobody called her mad, and I have heard father say that she had one of the sharpest heads for business he had ever come across.'

'Very good; have it as you like. But I believe we shall both be sorry.'

They sat in silence for some time. Alice came in after her 'evening out,' and they sat on, till Mrs. Darnell said she was tired and wanted to go to bed.

Her husband kissed her. 'I don't think I will come up just yet,' he said; 'you go to sleep, dearest. I want to think things over. No, no; I am not going to change my mind: your aunt shall come, as I said. But there are one or two things I should like to get settled in my mind.'

He meditated for a long while, pacing up and down the room. Light after light was extinguished in Edna Road, and the people of the suburb slept all around him, but still the gas was alight in Darnell's drawing-room, and he walked softly up and down the floor. He was thinking that about the life of Mary and himself, which had been so quiet, there seemed to be gathering on all sides grotesque and fantastic shapes, omens of confusion and disorder, threats of madness; a strange company from another world. It was as if into the quiet, sleeping streets of some little ancient town among the hills there had come from afar the sound of drum and pipe, snatches of wild song, and there had burst into the market-place the mad company of the players, strangely bedizened, dancing a furious measure to their hurrying music, drawing forth the citizens from their sheltered homes and peaceful lives, and alluring them to mingle in the significant figures of their dance.

Yet afar and near (for it was hidden in his heart) he beheld the glimmer of a sure and constant star. Beneath, darkness came on, and mists and shadows closed about the town. The red, flickering flame of torches was kindled in the midst of it. The song grew louder, with more insistent, magical tones, surging and falling in unearthly modulations, the very speech of incantation; and the drum beat madly, and the pipe shrilled to a scream, summoning all to issue forth, to leave their peaceful hearths; for a strange rite was preconized in their midst. The streets that were wont to be so still, so hushed with the cool and tranquil veils of darkness, asleep beneath the patronage of the evening star, now danced with glimmering lanterns, resounded with the cries of those who hurried forth, drawn as by a magistral spell; and the songs swelled and triumphed, the reverberant beating of the drum grew louder, and in the midst of the awakened town the players, fantastically arrayed, performed their interlude under the red blaze of torches.

He knew not whether they were players, men that would vanish suddenly as they came, disappearing by the track that climbed the hill; or whether they were indeed magicians, workers of great and efficacious spells, who knew the secret word by which the earth may be transformed into the hall of Gehenna, so that they that gazed and listened, as at a passing spectacle, should be entrapped by the sound and the sight presented to them, should be drawn into the elaborated figures of that mystic dance, and so should be whirled away into those unending mazes on the wild hills that were abhorred, there to wander for evermore.

But Darnell was not afraid, because of the Daystar that had risen in his heart. It had dwelt there all his life, and had slowly shone forth with clearer and clearer light, and he began to see that though his earthly steps might be in the ways of the ancient town that was beset by the Enchanters, and resounded with their songs and their processions, yet he dwelt also in that serene and secure world of brightness, and from a great and unutterable height looked on the confusion of the mortal pageant, beholding mysteries in which he was no true actor, hearing magic songs that could by no means draw him down from the battlements of the high and holy city.

His heart was filled with a great joy and a great peace as he lay down beside his wife and fell asleep, and in the morning, when he woke up, he was glad.

IV

In a haze as of a dream Darnell's thoughts seemed to move through the opening days of the next week. Perhaps nature had not intended that he should be practical or much given to that which is usually called 'sound common sense,' but his training had made him desirous of good, plain qualities of the mind, and he uneasily strove to account to himself for his strange mood of the Sunday night, as he had often endeavoured to interpret the fancies of his boyhood and early man-hood.

At first he was annoyed by his want of success; the morning paper, which he always secured as the 'bus delayed at Uxbridge Road Station, fell from his hands unread, while he vainly reasoned, assuring himself that the threatened incursion of a whimsical old woman, though tiresome enough, was no rational excuse for those curious hours of meditation in which his thoughts seemed to have dressed themselves in unfamiliar, fantastic habits, and to parley with him in a strange speech, and yet a speech that he had understood.

With such arguments he perplexed his mind on the long, accustomed ride up the steep ascent of Holland Park, past the incongruous hustle of Notting Hill Gate, where in one direction a road shows the way to the snug, somewhat faded bowers and retreats of Bayswater, and in another one sees the portal of the murky region of the slums. The customary companions of his morning's journey were in the seats about him; he heard the hum of their talk, as they disputed concerning politics, and the man next to him, who came from Acton, asked him what he thought of the Government now. There was a discussion, and a loud and excited one, just in front, as to whether rhubarb was a fruit or vegetable, and in his ear he heard Redman, who was a near neighbour, praising the economy of 'the wife.'

'I don't know how she does it. Look here; what do you think we had yesterday? Breakfast: fish-cakes, beautifully fried—rich, you know, lots of herbs, it's a receipt of her aunt's; you should just taste 'em. Coffee, bread, butter, marmalade, and, of course, all the usual etceteras.

Dinner: roast beef, Yorkshire, potatoes, greens, and horse-radish sauce, plum tart, cheese. And where will you get a better dinner than that? Well, I call it wonderful, I really do.'

But in spite of these distractions he fell into a dream as the 'bus rolled and tossed on its way Citywards, and still he strove to solve the enigma of his vigil of the night before, and as the shapes of trees and green lawns and houses passed before his eyes, and as he saw the procession moving on the pavement, and while the murmur of the streets sounded in his ears, all was to him strange and unaccustomed, as if he moved through the avenues of some city in a foreign land. It was, perhaps, on these mornings, as he rode to his mechanical work, that vague and floating fancies that must have long haunted his brain began to shape themselves, and to put on the form of definite conclusions, from which he could no longer escape, even if he had wished it. Darnell had received what is called a sound commercial education, and would therefore have found very great difficulty in putting into articulate speech any thought that was worth thinking; but he grew certain on these mornings that the 'common sense' which he had always heard exalted as man's supremest faculty was, in all probability, the smallest and least-considered item in the equipment of an ant of average intelligence. And with this, as an almost necessary corollary, came a firm belief that the whole fabric of life in which he moved was sunken, past all thinking, in the grossest absurdity; that he and all his friends and acquaintances and fellow-workers were interested in matters in which men were never meant to be interested, were pursuing aims which they were never meant to pursue, were, indeed, much like fair stones of an altar serving as a pigsty wall. Life, it seemed to him, was a great search for—he knew not what; and in the process of the ages one by one the true marks upon the ways had been shattered, or buried, or the meaning of the words had been slowly forgotten; one by one the signs had been turned awry, the true entrances had been thickly overgrown, the very way itself had been diverted from the heights to the depths, till at last the race of pilgrims had become hereditary stone-breakers and ditch-scourers on a track that led to destruction—if it led anywhere at all. Darnell's heart thrilled with a strange and trembling joy, with a sense that was all new, when it came to his mind that this great loss might not be a hopeless one, that perhaps the difficulties were by no means insuperable.

It might be, he considered, that the stonebreaker had merely to throw down his hammer and set out, and the way would be plain before him; and a single step would free the delver in rubbish from the foul slime of the ditch.

It was, of course, with difficulty and slowly that these things became clear to him. He was an English City clerk, 'flourishing' towards the end of the nineteenth century, and the rubbish heap that had been accumulating for some centuries could not be cleared away in an instant. Again and again the spirit of nonsense that had been implanted in him as in his fellows assured him that the true world was the visible and tangible world, the world in which good and faithful letter-copying was exchangeable for a certain quantum of bread, beef, and house-room, and that the man who copied letters well, did not beat his wife, nor lose money foolishly, was a good man, fulfilling the end for which he had been made. But in spite of these arguments, in spite of their acceptance by all who were about him, he had the grace to perceive the utter falsity and absurdity of the whole position. He was fortunate in his entire ignorance of sixpenny 'science,' but if the whole library had been projected into his brain it would not have moved him to 'deny in the darkness that which he had known in the light.' Darnell knew by experience that man is made a mystery for mysteries and visions, for the realization in his consciousness of ineffable bliss, for a great joy that transmutes the whole world, for a joy that surpasses all joys and overcomes all sorrows. He knew this certainly, though he knew it dimly; and he was apart from other men, preparing himself for a great experiment.

With such thoughts as these for his secret and concealed treasure, he was able to bear the threatened invasion of Mrs. Nixon with something approaching indifference. He knew, indeed, that her presence between his wife and himself would be unwelcome to him, and he was not without grave doubts as to the woman's sanity; but after all, what did it matter? Besides, already a faint glimmering light had risen within him that showed the profit of self-negation, and in this matter he had preferred his wife's will to his own. Et non sua pomo; to his astonishment he found a delight in denying himself his own wish, a process that he had always regarded as thoroughly detestable. This was a state of things which he could not in the least understand; but, again, though a member of a most hopeless class, living in the most hopeless surroundings that the world has ever seen, though he knew as much of the askesis as of Chinese metaphysics; again, he had the grace not to deny the light that had begun to glimmer in his soul.

And he found a present reward in the eyes of Mary, when she welcomed him home after his foolish labours in the cool of the evening. They sat together, hand in hand, under the mulberry tree, at the coming of the dusk, and as the ugly walls about them became obscure and vanished into the formless world of shadows, they seemed to be freed from the bondage of Shepherd's Bush, freed to wander in that undisfigured, undefiled world that lies beyond the walls. Of this region Mary knew little or nothing by experience, since her relations had always been of one mind with the modern world, which has for the true country an instinctive and most significant horror and dread. Mr. Reynolds had also shared in another odd superstition of these later days— that it is necessary to leave London at least once a year; consequently Mary had some knowledge of various seaside resorts on the south and east coasts, where Londoners gather in hordes, turn the sands into one vast, bad music-hall, and derive, as they say, enormous benefit from the change. But experiences such as these give but little knowledge of the country in its true and occult sense; and yet Mary, as she sat in the dusk beneath the whispering tree, knew something of the secret of the wood, of the valley shut in by high hills, where the sound of pouring water always echoes from the clear brook. And to Darnell these were nights of great dreams; for it was the hour of the work, the time of transmutation, and he who could not understand the miracle, who could scarcely believe in it, yet knew, secretly and half consciously, that the water was being changed into the wine of a new life. This was ever the inner music of his dreams, and to it he added on these still and sacred nights the far-off memory of that time long ago when, a child, before the world had overwhelmed him, he journeyed down to the old grey house in the west, and for a whole month heard the murmur of the forest through his bedroom window, and when the wind was hushed, the washing of the tides about the reeds; and sometimes awaking very early he had heard the strange cry of a bird as it rose from its nest among the reeds, and had looked out and had seen the valley whiten to the dawn, and the winding river whiten as it swam down to the sea. The memory of all this had faded and become shadowy as he grew older and the chains of common life were riveted firmly about his soul; all the atmosphere by which he was surrounded was well-nigh fatal to such thoughts, and only now and again in half-conscious moments or in sleep he had revisited that valley in the far-off west, where the breath of wind was an incantation, and every leaf and stream and hill spoke of great and ineffable mysteries. But now the broken vision was in great part restored to him, and looking with love in his wife's eyes he saw the gleam of water-pools in the still forest, saw the mists rising in the evening, and heard the music of the winding river.

They were sitting thus together on the Friday evening of the week that had begun with that odd and half-forgotten visit of Mrs. Nixon, when, to Darnell's annoyance, the door-bell gave a discordant peal, and Alice with some disturbance of manner came out and announced that a gentleman wished to see the master. Darnell went into the drawing-room, where Alice had lit one gas so that it flared and burnt with a rushing sound, and in this distorting light there waited a stout, elderly gentleman, whose countenance was altogether unknown to him. He stared blankly, and hesitated, about to speak, but the visitor began.

'You don't know who I am, but I expect you'll know my name. It's Nixon.' He did not wait to be interrupted. He sat down and plunged into narrative, and after the first few words, Darnell, whose mind was not altogether unprepared, listened without much astonishment.

'And the long and the short of it is,' Mr. Nixon said at last, 'she's gone stark, staring mad, and we had to put her away to-day—poor thing.'

His voice broke a little, and he wiped his eyes hastily, for though stout and successful he was not unfeeling, and he was fond of his wife. He had spoken quickly, and had gone lightly over many details which might have interested specialists in certain kinds of mania, and Darnell was sorry for his evident distress. 'I came here,' he went on after a brief pause, 'because I found out she had been to see you last Sunday, and I knew the sort of story she must have told.'

Darnell showed him the prophetic leaflet which Mrs. Nixon had dropped in the garden. 'Did you know about this?' he said.

'Oh, him,' said the old man, with some approach to cheerfulness; 'oh yes, I thrashed him black and blue the day before yesterday.'

'Isn't he mad? Who is the man?'

'He's not mad, he's bad. He's a little Welsh skunk named Richards. He's been running some sort of chapel over at New Barnet for the last few years, and my poor wife—she never could find the parish church good enough for her—had been going to his damned schism shop for the last twelve-month. It was all that finished her off. Yes; I thrashed him the day before yesterday, and I'm not afraid of a summons either. I know him, and he knows I know him.'

Old Nixon whispered something in Darnell's ear, and chuckled faintly as he repeated for the third time his formula—'I thrashed him black and blue the day before yesterday.'

Darnell could only murmur condolences and express his hope that Mrs. Nixon might recover.

The old man shook his head.

'I'm afraid there's no hope of that,' he said. 'I've had the best advice, but they couldn't do anything, and told me so.'

Presently he asked to see his niece, and Darnell went out and prepared Mary as well as he could. She could scarcely take in the news that her aunt was a hopeless maniac, for Mrs. Nixon, having been extremely stupid all her days, had naturally succeeded in passing with her relations as typically sensible. With the Reynolds family, as with the great majority of us, want of imagination is always equated with sanity, and though many of us have never heard of Lombroso we are his ready-made converts. We have always believed that poets are mad, and if statistics unfortunately show that few poets have really been inhabitants of lunatic asylums, it is soothing to learn that nearly all poets have had whooping-cough, which is doubtless, like intoxication, a minor madness.

'But is it really true?' she asked at length. 'Are you certain uncle is not deceiving you? Aunt seemed so sensible always.'

She was helped at last by recollecting that Aunt Marian used to get up very early of mornings, and then they went into the drawing-room and talked to the old man. His evident kindliness and honesty grew upon Mary, in spite of a lingering belief in her aunt's fables, and when he left, it was with a promise to come to see them again.

Mrs. Darnell said she felt tired, and went to bed; and Darnell returned to the garden and began to pace to and fro, collecting his thoughts. His immeasurable relief at the intelligence that, after all, Mrs. Nixon was not coming to live with them taught him that, despite his submission, his dread of the event had been very great. The weight was removed, and now he was free to consider his life without reference to the grotesque intrusion that he had feared. He sighed for joy, and as he paced to and fro he savoured the scent of the night, which, though it came faintly to him in that brick-bound suburb, summoned to his mind across many years the odour of the world at night as he had known it in that short sojourn of his boyhood; the odour that rose from the earth when the flame of the sun had gone down beyond the mountain, and the afterglow had paled in the sky and on the fields. And as he recovered as best he could these lost dreams of an enchanted land, there came to him other images of his childhood, forgotten and yet not forgotten, dwelling unheeded in dark places of the memory, but ready to be summoned forth. He remembered one fantasy that had long haunted him. As he lay half asleep in the forest on one hot afternoon of that memorable visit to the country, he had 'made believe' that a little companion had come to him out of the blue mists and the green light beneath the leaves—a white girl with long black hair, who had played with him and whispered her secrets in his ear, as his father lay sleeping under a tree; and from that summer afternoon, day by day, she had been beside him; she had visited him in the wilderness of London, and even in recent years there had come to him now and again the sense of her presence, in the midst of the heat and turmoil of the City. The last visit he remembered well; it was a few weeks before he married, and from the depths of some futile task he had looked up with puzzled eyes, wondering why the close air suddenly grew scented with green leaves, why the murmur of the trees and the wash of the river on the reeds came to his ears; and then that sudden rapture to which he had given a name and an individuality possessed him utterly. He knew then how the dull flesh of man can be like fire; and now, looking back from a new standpoint on this and other experiences, he realized how all that was real in his life had been unwelcomed, uncherished by him, had come to him, perhaps, in virtue of merely negative qualities on his part. And yet, as he reflected, he saw that there had been a chain of witnesses all through his life: again and again voices had whispered in his ear words in a strange language that he now recognized as his native tongue; the common street had not been lacking in visions of the true land of his birth; and in all the passing and repassing of the world he saw that there had been emissaries ready to guide his feet on the way of the great journey.

A week or two after the visit of Mr. Nixon, Darnell took his annual holiday.

There was no question of Walton-on-the-Naze, or of anything of the kind, as he quite agreed with his wife's longing for some substantial sum put by against the evil day. But the weather was still fine, and he lounged away the time in his garden beneath the tree, or he sauntered out on long aimless walks in the western purlieus of London, not unvisited by that old sense of some great ineffable beauty, concealed by the dim and dingy veils of grey interminable streets. Once, on a day of heavy rain he went to the 'box-room,' and began to turn over the papers in the old hair trunk—scraps and odds and ends of family history, some of them in his father's handwriting, others in faded ink, and there were a few ancient pocket-books, filled with manuscript of a still earlier time, and in these the ink was glossier and blacker than any writing fluids supplied by stationers of later days. Darnell had hung up the portrait of the ancestor in this room, and had bought a solid kitchen table and a chair; so that Mrs. Darnell, seeing him looking over his old documents, half thought of naming the room 'Mr. Darnell's study.' He had not glanced at these relics of his family for many years, but from the hour when the rainy morning sent him to them, he remained constant to research till the end of the holidays. It was a new interest, and he began to fashion in his mind a faint picture of his forefathers, and of their life in that grey old house in the river valley, in the western land of wells and streams and dark and ancient woods. And there were stranger things than mere notes on family history amongst that odd litter of old disregarded papers, and when he went back to his work in the City some of the men fancied that he was in some vague manner changed in appearance; but he only laughed when they asked him where he had been and what he had been doing with himself. But Mary noticed that every evening he spent at least an hour in the box-room; she was rather sorry at the waste of time involved in reading old papers about dead people. And one afternoon, as they were out together on a somewhat dreary walk towards Acton, Darnell stopped at a hopeless second-hand bookshop, and after scanning the rows of shabby books in the window, went in and purchased two volumes. They proved to be a Latin dictionary and grammar, and she was surprised to hear her husband declare his intention of acquiring the Latin language.

But, indeed, all his conduct impressed her as indefinably altered; and she began to be a little alarmed, though she could scarcely have formed her fears in words. But she knew that in some way that was all indefined and beyond the grasp of her thought their lives had altered since the summer, and no single thing wore quite the same aspect as before. If she looked out into the dull street with its rare loiterers, it was the same and yet it had altered, and if she opened the window in the early morning the wind that entered came with a changed breath that spoke some message that she could not understand. And day by day passed by in the old course, and not even the four walls were altogether familiar, and the voices of men and women sounded with strange notes, with the echo, rather, of a music that came over unknown hills. And day by day as she went about her household work, passing from shop to shop in those dull streets that were a network, a fatal labyrinth of grey desolation on every side, there came to her sense half-seen images of some other world, as if she walked in a dream, and every moment must bring her to light and to awakening, when the grey should fade, and regions long desired should appear in glory. Again and again it seemed as if that which was hidden would be shown even to the sluggish testimony of sense; and as she went to and fro from street to street of that dim and weary suburb, and looked on those grey material walls, they seemed as if a light glowed behind them, and again and again the mystic fragrance of incense was blown to her nostrils from across the verge of that world which is not so much impenetrable as ineffable, and to her ears came the dream of a chant that spoke of hidden choirs about all her ways. She struggled against these impressions, refusing her assent to the testimony of them, since all the pressure of credited opinion for three hundred years has been directed towards stamping out real knowledge, and so effectually has this been accomplished that we can only recover the truth through much anguish. And so Mary passed the days in a strange perturbation, clinging to common things and common thoughts, as if she feared that one morning she would wake up in an unknown world to a changed life. And Edward

Darnell went day by day to his labour and returned in the evening, always with that shining of light within his eyes and upon his face, with the gaze of wonder that was greater day by day, as if for him the veil grew thin and soon would disappear.

From these great matters both in herself and in her husband Mary shrank back, afraid, perhaps, that if she began the question the answer might be too wonderful. She rather taught herself to be troubled over little things; she asked herself what attraction there could be in the old records over which she supposed Edward to be poring night after night in the cold room upstairs. She had glanced over the papers at Darnell's invitation, and could see but little interest in them; there were one or two sketches, roughly done in pen and ink, of the old house in the west: it looked a shapeless and fantastic place, furnished with strange pillars and stranger ornaments on the projecting porch; and on one side a roof dipped down almost to the earth, and in the centre there was something that might almost be a tower rising above the rest of the building. Then there were documents that seemed all names and dates, with here and there a coat of arms done in the margin, and she came upon a string of uncouth Welsh names linked together by the word 'ap' in a chain that looked endless. There was a paper covered with signs and figures that meant nothing to her, and then there were the pocket-books, full of old-fashioned writing, and much of it in Latin, as her husband told her—it was a collection as void of significance as a treatise on conic sections, so far as Mary was concerned. But night after night Darnell shut himself up with the musty rolls, and more than ever when he rejoined her he bore upon his face the blazonry of some great adventure. And one night she asked him what interested him so much in the papers he had shown her.

He was delighted with the question. Somehow they had not talked much together for the last few weeks, and he began to tell her of the records of the old race from which he came, of the old strange house of grey stone between the forest and the river. The family went back and back, he said, far into the dim past, beyond the Normans, beyond the Saxons, far into the Roman days, and for many hundred years they had been petty kings, with a strong fortress high up on the hill, in the heart of the forest; and even now the great mounds remained, whence one could look through the trees towards the mountain on one side and across the yellow sea on the other. The real name of the family was not Darnell; that was assumed by one Iolo ap Taliesin ap Iorwerth in the sixteenth century—why, Darnell did not seem to understand. And then he told her how the race had dwindled in prosperity, century by century, till at last there was nothing left but the grey house and a few acres of land bordering the river.

'And do you know, Mary,' he said, 'I suppose we shall go and live there some day or other.

'My great-uncle, who has the place now, made money in business when he was a young man, and I believe he will leave it all to me. I know I am the only relation he has. How strange it would be.

'What a change from the life here.'

'You never told me that. Don't you think your great-uncle might leave his house and his money to somebody he knows really well? You haven't seen him since you were a little boy, have you?'

'No; but we write once a year. And from what I have heard my father say, I am sure the old man would never leave the house out of the family. Do you think you would like it?'

'I don't know. Isn't it very lonely?'

'I suppose it is. I forget whether there are any other houses in sight, but I don't think there are any at all near. But what a change! No City, no streets, no people passing to and fro; only the sound of the wind and the sight of the green leaves and the green hills, and the song of the voices of the earth.' . . . . He checked himself suddenly, as if he feared that he was about to tell some secret that must not yet be uttered; and indeed, as he spoke of the change from the little street in Shepherd's Bush to that ancient house in the woods of the far west, a change seemed already to possess himself, and his voice put on the modulation of an antique chant. Mary looked at him steadily and touched his arm, and he drew a long breath before he spoke again.

'It is the old blood calling to the old land,' he said. 'I was forgetting that I am a clerk in the City.'

It was, doubtless, the old blood that had suddenly stirred in him; the resurrection of the old spirit that for many centuries had been faithful to secrets that are now disregarded by most of us, that now day by day was quickened more and more in his heart, and grew so strong that it was hard to conceal. He was indeed almost in the position of the man in the tale, who, by a sudden electric shock, lost the vision of the things about him in the London streets, and gazed instead upon the sea and shore of an island in the Antipodes; for Darnell only clung with an effort to the interests and the atmosphere which, till lately, had seemed all the world to him; and the grey house and the wood and the river, symbols of the other sphere, intruded as it were into the landscape of the London suburb.

But he went on, with more restraint, telling his stories of far-off ancestors, how one of them, the most remote of all, was called a saint, and was supposed to possess certain mysterious secrets often alluded to in the papers as the 'Hidden Songs of Iolo Sant.' And then with an abrupt transition he recalled memories of his father and of the strange, shiftless life in dingy lodgings in the backwaters of London, of the dim stucco streets that were his first recollections, of forgotten squares in North London, and of the figure of his father, a grave bearded man who seemed always in a dream, as if he too sought for the vision of a land beyond the strong walls, a land where there were deep orchards and many shining hills, and fountains and water-pools gleaming under the leaves of the wood.

'I believe my father earned his living,' he went on, 'such a living as he did earn, at the Record Office and the British Museum. He used to hunt up things for lawyers and country parsons who wanted old deeds inspected. He never made much, and we were always moving from one lodging to another—always to out-of-the-way places where everything seemed to have run to seed. We never knew our neighbours—we moved too often for that—but my father had about half a dozen friends, elderly men like himself, who used to come to see us pretty often; and then, if there was any money, the lodging-house servant would go out for beer, and they would sit and smoke far into the night.

'I never knew much about these friends of his, but they all had the same look, the look of longing for something hidden. They talked of mysteries that I never understood, very little of their own lives, and when they did speak of ordinary affairs one could tell that they thought such matters as money and the want of it were unimportant trifles. When I grew up and went into the City, and met other young fellows and heard their way of talking, I wondered whether my father and his friends were not a little queer in their heads; but I know better now.'

So night after night Darnell talked to his wife, seeming to wander aimlessly from the dingy lodging-houses, where he had spent his boyhood in the company of his father and the other seekers, to the old house hidden in that far western valley, and the old race that had so long looked at the setting of the sun over the mountain. But in truth there was one end in all that he spoke, and Mary felt that beneath his words, however indifferent they might seem, there was hidden a purpose, that they were to embank on a great and marvellous adventure.

So day by day the world became more magical; day by day the work of separation was being performed, the gross accidents were being refined away. Darnell neglected no instruments that might be useful in the work; and now he neither lounged at home on Sunday mornings, nor did he accompany his wife to the Gothic blasphemy which pretended to be a church. They had discovered a little church of another fashion in a back street, and Darnell, who had found in one of the old notebooks the maxim Incredibilia sola Credenda, soon perceived how high and glorious a thing was that service at which he assisted. Our stupid ancestors taught us that we could become wise by studying books on 'science,' by meddling with test-tubes, geological specimens, microscopic preparations, and the like; but they who have cast off these follies know that they must read not 'science' books, but mass-books, and that the soul is made wise by the contemplation of mystic ceremonies and elaborate and curious rites. In such things Darnell found a wonderful mystery language, which spoke at once more secretly and more directly than the formal creeds; and he saw that, in a sense, the whole world is but a great ceremony or sacrament, which teaches under visible forms a hidden and transcendent doctrine. It was thus that he found in the ritual of the church a perfect image of the world; an image purged, exalted, and illuminate, a holy house built up of shining and translucent stones, in which the burning torches were more significant than the wheeling stars, and the fuming incense was a more certain token than the rising of the mist. His soul went forth with the albed procession in its white and solemn order, the mystic dance that signifies rapture and a joy above all joys, and when he beheld Love slain and rise again victorious he knew that he witnessed, in a figure, the consummation of all things, the Bridal of all Bridals, the mystery that is beyond all mysteries, accomplished from the foundation of the world. So day by day the house of his life became more magical.

And at the same time he began to guess that if in the New Life there are new and unheard-of joys, there are also new and unheard-of dangers. In his manuscript books which professed to deliver the outer sense of those mysterious 'Hidden Songs of Iolo Sant' there was a little chapter that bore the heading: Fons Sacer non in communem Vsum convertendus est, and by diligence, with much use of the grammar and dictionary, Darnell was able to construe the by no means complex Latin of his ancestor. The special book which contained the chapter in question was one of the most singular in the collection, since it bore the title Terra de Iolo, and on the surface, with an ingenious concealment of its real symbolism, it affected to give an account of the orchards, fields, woods, roads, tenements, and waterways in the possession of Darnell's ancestors. Here, then, he read of the Holy Well, hidden in the Wistman's Wood—

Sylva Sapientum—'a fountain of abundant water, which no heats of summer can ever dry, which no flood can ever defile, which is as a water of life, to them that thirst for life, a stream of cleansing to them that would be pure, and a medicine of such healing virtue that by it, through the might of God and the intercession of His saints, the most grievous wounds are made whole.'

But the water of this well was to be kept sacred perpetually, it was not to be used for any common purpose, nor to satisfy any bodily thirst; but ever to be esteemed as holy, 'even as the water which the priest hath hallowed.' And in the margin a comment in a later hand taught Darnell something of the meaning of these prohibitions. He was warned not to use the Well of Life as a mere luxury of mortal life, as a new sensation, as a means of making the insipid cup of everyday existence more palatable. 'For,' said the commentator, 'we are not called to sit as the spectators in a theatre, there to watch the play performed before us, but we are rather summoned to stand in the very scene itself, and there fervently to enact our parts in a great and wonderful mystery.'

Darnell could quite understand the temptation that was thus indicated. Though he had gone but a little way on the path, and had barely tested the over-runnings of that mystic well, he was already aware of the enchantment that was transmuting all the world about him, informing his life with a strange significance and romance. London seemed a city of the Arabian Nights, and its labyrinths of streets an enchanted maze; its long avenues of lighted lamps were as starry systems, and its immensity became for him an image of the endless universe. He could well imagine how pleasant it might be to linger in such a world as this, to sit apart and dream, beholding the strange pageant played before him; but the Sacred Well was not for common use, it was for the cleansing of the soul, and the healing of the grievous wounds of the spirit. There must be yet another transformation: London had become Bagdad; it must at last be transmuted to Syon, or in the phrase of one of his old documents, the City of the Cup.

And there were yet darker perils which the Iolo MSS. (as his father had named the collection) hinted at more or less obscurely. There were suggestions of an awful region which the soul might enter, of a transmutation that was unto death, of evocations which could summon the utmost forces of evil from their dark places—in a word, of that sphere which is represented to most of us under the crude and somewhat childish symbolism of Black Magic. And here again he was not altogether without a dim comprehension of what was meant. He found himself recalling an odd incident that had happened long ago, which had remained all the years in his mind unheeded, amongst the many insignificant recollections of his childhood, and now rose before him, clear and distinct and full of meaning. It was on that memorable visit to the old house in the west, and the whole scene returned, with its smallest events, and the voices seemed to sound in his ears. It was a grey, still day of heavy heat that he remembered: he had stood on the lawn after breakfast, and wondered at the great peace and silence of the world. Not a leaf stirred in the trees on the lawn, not a whisper came from the myriad leaves of the wood; the flowers gave out sweet and heavy odours as if they breathed the dreams of the summer night; and far down the valley, the winding river was like dim silver under that dim and silvery sky, and the far hills and woods and fields vanished in the mist. The stillness of the air held him as with a charm; he leant all the morning against the rails that parted the lawn from the meadow, breathing the mystic breath of summer, and watching the fields brighten as with a sudden blossoming of shining flowers as the high mist grew thin for a moment before the hidden sun. As he watched thus, a man weary with heat, with some glance of horror in his eyes, passed him on his way to the house; but he stayed at his post till the old bell in the turret rang, and they dined all together, masters and servants, in the dark cool room that looked towards the still leaves of the wood. He could see that his uncle was upset about something, and when they had finished dinner he heard him tell his father that there was trouble at a farm; and it was settled that they should all drive over in the afternoon to some place with a strange name. But when the time came Mr. Darnell was too deep in old books and tobacco smoke to be stirred from his corner, and Edward and his uncle went alone in the dog-cart.

They drove swiftly down the narrow lane, into the road that followed the winding river, and crossed the bridge at Caermaen by the mouldering Roman walls, and then, skirting the deserted, echoing village, they came out on a broad white turnpike road, and the limestone dust followed them like a cloud. Then, suddenly, they turned to the north by such a road as Edward had never seen before. It was so narrow that there was barely room for the cart to pass, and the footway was of rock, and the banks rose high above them as they slowly climbed the long, steep way, and the untrimmed hedges on either side shut out the light. And the ferns grew thick and green upon the banks, and hidden wells dripped down upon them; and the old man told him how the lane in winter was a torrent of swirling water, so that no one could pass by it. On they went, ascending and then again descending, always in that deep hollow under the wild woven boughs, and the boy wondered vainly what the country was like on either side. And now the air grew darker, and the hedge on one bank was but the verge of a dark and rustling wood, and the grey limestone rocks had changed to dark-red earth flecked with green patches and veins of marl, and suddenly in the stillness from the depths of the wood a bird began to sing a melody that charmed the heart into another world, that sang to the child's soul of the blessed faery realm beyond the woods of the earth, where the wounds of man are healed. And so at last, after many turnings and windings, they came to a high bare land where the lane broadened out into a kind of common, and along the edge of this place there were scattered three or four old cottages, and one of them was a little tavern. Here they stopped, and a man came out and tethered the tired horse to a post and gave him water; and old Mr. Darnell took the child's hand and led him by a path across the fields. The boy could see the country now, but it was all a strange, undiscovered land; they were in the heart of a wilderness of hills and valleys that he had never looked upon, and they were going down a wild, steep hillside, where the narrow path wound in and out amidst gorse and towering bracken, and the sun gleaming out for a moment, there was a gleam of white water far below in a narrow valley, where a little brook poured and rippled from stone to stone. They went down the hill, and through a brake, and then, hidden in dark-green orchards, they came upon a long, low whitewashed house, with a stone roof strangely coloured by the growth of moss and lichens. Mr. Darnell knocked at a heavy oaken door, and they came into a dim room where but little light entered through the thick glass in the deep-set window. There were heavy beams in the ceiling, and a great fire-place sent out an odour of burning wood that Darnell never forgot, and the room seemed to him full of women who talked all together in frightened tones. Mr. Darnell beckoned to a tall, grey old man, who wore corduroy knee-breeches, and the boy, sitting on a high straight-backed chair, could see the old man and his uncle passing to and fro across the window-panes, as they walked together on the garden path. The women stopped their talk for a moment, and one of them brought him a glass of milk and an apple from some cold inner chamber; and then, suddenly, from a room above there rang out a shrill and terrible shriek, and then, in a young girl's voice, a more terrible song. It was not like anything the child had ever heard, but as the man recalled it to his memory, he knew to what song it might be compared—to a certain chant indeed that summons the angels and archangels to assist in the great Sacrifice. But as this song chants of the heavenly army, so did that seem to summon all the hierarchy of evil, the hosts of Lilith and Samael; and the words that rang out with such awful modulations—neumata inferorum—were in some unknown tongue that few men have even heard on earth.

The women glared at one another with horror in their eyes, and he saw one or two of the oldest of them clumsily making an old sign upon their breasts. Then they began to speak again, and he remembered fragments of their talk.

'She has been up there,' said one, pointing vaguely oven her shoulder.

'She'd never know the way,' answered another. 'They be all gone that went there.'

'There be nought there in these days.'

'How can you tell that, Gwenllian? 'Tis not for us to say that.'

'My great-grandmother did know some that had been there,' said a very old woman. 'She told me how they was taken afterwards.'

And then his uncle appeared at the door, and they went their way as they had come. Edward Darnell never heard any more of it, nor whether the girl died or recovered from her strange attack; but the scene had haunted his mind in boyhood, and now the recollection of it came to him with a certain note of warning, as a symbol of dangers that might be in the way.

It would be impossible to carry on the history of Edward Darnell and of Mary his wife to a greater length, since from this point their legend is full of impossible events, and seems to put on the semblance of the stories of the Graal. It is certain, indeed, that in this world they changed their lives, like King Arthur, but this is a work which no chronicler has cared to describe with any amplitude of detail. Darnell, it is true, made a little book, partly consisting of queer verse which might have been written by an inspired infant, and partly made up of 'notes and exclamations' in an odd dog-Latin which he had picked up from the 'Iolo MSS.', but it is to be feared that this work, even if published in its entirety, would cast but little light on a perplexing story. He called this piece of literature 'In Exitu Israel,' and wrote on the title page the motto, doubtless of his own composition, 'Nunc certe scio quod omnia legenda; omnes historiæ, omnes fabulæ, omnis Scriptura sint de ME narrata.' It is only too evident that his Latin was not learnt at the feet of Cicero; but in this dialect he relates the great history of the 'New Life' as it was manifested to him. The 'poems' are even stranger. One, headed (with an odd reminiscence of old-fashioned books) 'Lines written on looking down from a Height in London on a Board School suddenly lit up by the Sun' begins thus:—

One day when I was all alone
I found a wondrous little stone,
It lay forgotten on the road
Far from the ways of man's abode.
When on this stone mine eyes I cast
I saw my Treasure found at last.
I pressed it hard against my face,
I covered it with my embrace,
I hid it in a secret place.
And every day I went to see
This stone that was my ecstasy;
And worshipped it with flowers rare,
And secret words and sayings fair.
O stone, so rare and red and wise
O fragment of far Paradise,
O Star, whose light is life! O Sea,
Whose ocean is infinity!
Thou art a fire that ever burns,
And all the world to wonder turns;
And all the dust of the dull day
By thee is changed and purged away,
So that, where'er I look, I see
A world of a Great Majesty.
The sullen river rolls all gold,
The desert park's a faery wold,
When on the trees the wind is borne
I hear the sound of Arthur's horn
I see no town of grim grey ways,
But a great city all ablaze
With burning torches, to light up
The pinnacles that shrine the Cup.
Ever the magic wine is poured,
Ever the Feast shines on the board,
Ever the song is borne on high
That chants the holy Magistry—

Etc. etc. etc.

From such documents as these it is clearly impossible to gather
any very definite information.

But on the last page Darnell has written— 'So I awoke from a dream of a London suburb, of daily labour, of weary, useless little things; and as my eyes were opened I saw that I was in an ancient wood, where a clear well rose into grey film and vapour beneath a misty, glimmering heat. And a form came towards me from the hidden places of the wood, and my love and I were united by the well.'

THE SHINING PYRAMID

Part 1. The Arrow-head Character

"Haunted, you said?"

"Yes, haunted. Don't you remember, when I saw you three years ago, you told me about your place in the west with the ancient woods hanging all about it, and the wild, domed hills, and the ragged land? It has always remained a sort of enchanted picture in my mind as I sit at my desk and hear the traffic rattling in the Street in the midst of whirling London. But when did you come up?"

"The fact is, Dyson, I have only just got out of the train. I drove to the station early this morning and caught the 10.45."

"Well, I am very glad you looked in on me. How have you been getting on since we last met? There is no Mrs. Vaughan, I suppose?"

"No," said Vaughan, "I am still a hermit, like yourself. I have done nothing but loaf about."

Vaughn had lit his pipe and sat in the elbow chair, fidgeting and glancing about him in a somewhat dazed and restless manner. Dyson had wheeled round his chair when his visitor entered and sat with one arm fondly reclining on the desk of his bureau, and touching the litter of manuscript.

"And you are still engaged in the old task?" said Vaughan, pointing to the pile of papers and the teeming pigeon-holes.

"Yes, the vain pursuit of literature, as idle as alchemy, and as entrancing. But you have come to town for some time I suppose; what shall we do to-night?"

"Well, I rather wanted you to try a few days with me down in the west. It would do you a lot of good. I'm sure."

"You are very kind, Vaughan, but London in September is hard to leave. Doré could not have designed anything more wonderful and mystic than Oxford Street as I saw it the other evening; the sunset flaming, the blue haze transmuting the plain street into a road 'far in the spiritual city.'"

"I should like you to come down though. You would enjoy roaming over our hills. Does this racket go on all day and night? It quite bewilders me; I wonder how you can work through it. I am sure you would revel in the great peace of my old home among the woods."

Vaughan lit his pipe again, and looked anxiously at Dyson to see if his inducements had had any effect, but the man of letters shook his head, smiling, and vowed in his heart a firm allegiance to the streets.

"You cannot tempt me," he said.

'Well, you may be right. Perhaps, after all, I was wrong to speak of the peace of the country. There, when a tragedy does occur, it is like a stone thrown into a pond; the circles of disturbance keep on widening, and it seems as if the water would never be still again."

"Have you ever any tragedies where you are?"

"I can hardly say that. But I was a good deal disturbed about a month ago by something that happened; it may or may not have been a tragedy in the usual sense of the word."

"What was the occurrence?"

"Well, the fact is a girl disappeared in a way which seems highly mysterious. Her parents, people of the name of Trevor, are well-to-do farmers, and their eldest daughter Annie was a sort of village beauty; she was really remarkably handsome. One afternoon she thought she would go and see her aunt, a widow who farms her own land, and as the two houses are only about five or six miles apart, she started off, telling her parents she would take the short cut over the hills. She never got to her aunt's, and she never was seen again. That's putting it in a few words."

"What an extraordinary thing! I suppose there are no disused mines, are there, on the hills? I don't think you quite run to anything so formidable as a precipice?"

"No; the path the girl must have taken had no pitfalls of any description; it is just a track over wild, bare hillside, far, even from a byroad. One may walk for miles without meeting a soul, but it is perfectly safe."

"And what do people say about it?"

"Oh, they talk nonsense—among themselves. You have no notion as to how superstitious English cottagers are in out-of-the-way parts like mine. They are as bad as the Irish, every whit, and even more secretive."

"But what do they say?"

"Oh, the poor girl is supposed to have 'gone with the fairies,' or to have been 'taken by the fairies.' Such stuff!" he went on, "one would laugh if it were not for the real tragedy of the case."

Dyson looked somewhat interested.

"Yes," he said, "'fairies' certainly strike a little curiously on the ear in these days. But what do the police say? I presume they do not accept the fairy-tale hypothesis?"

"No; but they seem quite at fault. What I am afraid of is that Annie Trevor must have fallen in with some scoundrels on her way. Castletown is a large seaport, you know, and some of the worst of the foreign sailors

106

occasionally desert their ships and go on the tramp up and down the country. Not many years ago a Spanish sailor named Garcia murdered a whole family for the sake of plunder that was not worth sixpence. They are hardly human, some of these fellows, and I am dreadfully afraid the poor girl must have come to an awful end."

"But no foreign sailor was seen by anyone about the country?"

"No; there is certainly that; and of course country people are quick to notice anyone whose appearance and dress are a little out of the common. Still it seems as if my theory were the only possible explanation."

"There are no data to go upon," said Dyson, thoughtfully. "There was no question of a love affair, or anything of the kind, I suppose?"

"Oh, no, not a hint of such a thing. I am sure if Annie were alive she would have contrived to let her mother know of her safety."

"No doubt, no doubt. Still it is barely possible that she is alive and yet unable to communicate with her friends. But all this must have disturbed you a good deal."

"Yes, it did; I hate a mystery, and especially a mystery which is probably the veil of horror. But frankly, Dyson, I want to make a clean breast of it; I did not come here to tell you all this."

"Of course not," said Dyson, a little surprised at Vaughan's uneasy manner. "You came to have a chat on more cheerful topics."

"No, I did not. What I have been telling you about happened a month ago, but something which seems likely to affect me more personally has taken place within the last few days, and to be quite plain, I came up to town with the idea that you might be able to help me. You recollect that curious case you spoke to me about on our last meeting; something about a spectacle-maker."

"Oh, yes, I remember that. I know I was quite proud of my acumen at the time; even to this day the police have no idea why those peculiar yellow spectacles were wanted. But, Vaughan, you really look quite put out; I hope there is nothing serious?"

"No, I think I have been exaggerating, and I want you to reassure me. But what has happened is very odd."

"And what has happened?"

"I am sure that you will laugh at me, but this is the story. You must know there is a path, a right of way, that goes through my land, and to be precise, close to the wall of the kitchen garden. It is not used by many people; a woodman now and again finds it useful, and five or six children who go to school in the village pass twice a day. Well, a few days ago I was taking a walk about the place before breakfast, and I happened to stop to fill my pipe just by the large doors in the garden wall. The wood, I must tell you, comes to within a few feet of the wall, and the track I spoke of runs right in the shadow of the trees. I thought the shelter from a brisk wind that was blowing rather pleasant, and I stood there smoking with my eyes on the ground. Then something caught my attention. Just under the wall, on the short grass; a number of small flints were arranged in a pattern; something like this": and Mr. Vaughan caught at a pencil and piece of paper, and dotted down a few strokes.

"You see," he went on, "there were, I should think, twelve little stones neatly arranged in lines, and spaced at equal distances, as I have shown it on the paper. They were pointed stones, and the points were very carefully directed one way."

"Yes," said Dyson, without much interest, "no doubt the children you have mentioned had been playing there on their way from school. Children, as you know, are very fond of making such devices with oyster shells or flints or flowers, or with whatever comes in their way."

"So I thought; I just noticed these flints were arranged in a sort of pattern and then went on. But the next morning I was taking the same round, which, as a matter of fact, is habitual with me, and again I saw at the same spot a device in flints. This time it was really a curious pattern; something like the spokes of a wheel, all meeting at a common centre, and this centre formed by a device which looked like a bowl; all, you understand done in flints."

"You are right," said Dyson, "that seems odd enough. Still it is reasonable that your half-a-dozen school children are responsible for these fantasies in stone."

"Well, I thought I would set the matter at rest. The children pass the gate every evening at half-past five, and I walked by at six, and found the device just as I had left it in the morning. The next day I was up and about at a quarter to seven, and I found the whole thing had been changed. There was a pyramid outlined in flints upon the grass. The children I saw going by an hour and a half later, and they ran past the spot without glancing to right or left. In the evening I watched them going home, and this morning when I got to the gate at six o'clock there was a thing like a half moon waiting for me."

"So then the series runs thus: firstly ordered lines, then, the device of the spokes and the bowl, then the pyramid, and finally, this morning, the half moon. That is the order, isn't it?"

"Yes; that is right. But do you know it has made me feel very uneasy? I suppose it seems absurd, but I can't help thinking that some kind of signalling is going on under my nose, and that sort of thing is disquieting."

"But what have you to dread? You have no enemies?"

"No; but I have some very valuable old plate."

"You are thinking of burglars then?" said Dyson, with an accent of considerable interest, "but you must know your neighbours. Are there any suspicious characters about?"

"Not that I am aware of. But you remember what I told you of the sailors."

"Can you trust your servants?"

"Oh, perfectly. The plate is preserved in a strong room; the butler, an old family servant, alone knows where the key is kept. There is nothing wrong there. Still, everybody is aware that I have a lot of old silver, and all country folks are given to gossip. In that way information may have got abroad in very undesirable quarters."

"Yes, but I confess there seems something a little unsatisfactory in the burglar theory. Who is signalling to whom? I cannot see my way to accepting such an explanation. What put the plate into your head in connection with these flints signs, or whatever one may call them?"

"It was the figure of the Bowl," said Vaughan. "I happen to possess a very large and very valuable Charles II punch-bowl. The chasing is really exquisite, and the thing is worth a lot of money. The sign I described to you was exactly the same shape as my punch-bowl."

"A queer coincidence certainly. But the other figures or devices: you have nothing shaped like a pyramid?"

"Ah, you will think that queerer. As it happens, this punch-bowl of mine, together with a set of rare old ladles, is kept in a mahogany chest of a pyramidal shape. The four sides slope upwards, the narrow towards the top."

"I confess all this interests me a good deal," said Dyson. "let us go on then. What about the other figures; how about the Army, as we may call the first sign, and the Crescent or Half moon?"

"Ah, there is no reference that I can make out of these two. Still, you see I have some excuse for curiosity at all events. I should be very vexed to lose any of the old plate; nearly all the pieces have been in the family for generations. And I cannot get it out of my head that some scoundrels mean to rob me, and are communicating with one another every night."

"Frankly," said Dyson, "I can make nothing of it; I am as much in the dark as yourself. Your theory seems certainly the only possible explanation, and yet the difficulties are immense."

He leaned back in his chair, and the two men faced each other, frowning, and perplexed by so bizarre a problem.

"By the way," said Dyson, after a long pause, "what is your geological formation down there?"

Mr. Vaughan looked up, a good deal surprised by the question.

"Old red sandstone and limestone, I believe," he said. "We are just beyond the coal measures, you know."

"But surely there are no flints either in the sandstone or the limestone?"

"No, I never see any flints in the fields. I confess that did strike me as a little curious."

"I should think so! It is very important. By the way, what size were the flints used in making these devices?"

"I happen to have brought one with me; I took it this morning."

"From the Half moon?"

"Exactly. Here it is."

He handed over a small flint, tapering to a point, and about three inches in length.

Dyson's face blazed up with excitement as he took the thing from Vaughan.

"Certainly," he said, after a moment's pause, "you have some curious neighbours in your country. I hardly think they can harbour any designs on your punch-bowl. Do you know this is a flint arrowhead of vast antiquity, and not only that, but an arrow-head of a unique kind? I have seen specimens from all parts of the world, but there are features about this thing that are quite peculiar." He laid down his pipe, and took out a book from a drawer.

"We shall just have time to catch the 5.45 to Castletown," he said.

Part 2. The Eyes on the Wall

Mr. Dyson drew in a long breath of the air of the hills and felt all the enchantment of the scene about him. It was very early morning, and he stood on the terrace in the front of the house.

Vaughan's ancestor had built on the lower slope of a great hill, in the shelter of a deep and ancient wood that gathered on three sides about the house, and on the fourth side, the southwest, the land fell gently away and sank to the valley, where a brook wound in and out in mystic esses, and the dark and gleaming alders tracked the stream's course to the eye. On the terrace in the sheltered place no wind blew, and far beyond, the trees were still. Only one sound broke in upon the silence, and Dyson heard the noise of the brook singing far below, the song of clear and shining water rippling over the stones, whispering and murmuring as it sank to dark deep pools.

Across the stream, just below the house, rose a grey stone bridge, vaulted and buttressed, a fragment of the Middle Ages, and then beyond the bridge the hills rose again, vast and rounded like bastions, covered here and there with dark woods and thickets of undergrowth, but the heights were all bare of trees, showing only grey turf and patches of bracken, touched here and there with the gold of fading fronds; Dyson looked to the north and south, and still he saw the wall of the hills, and the ancient woods, and the stream drawn in and out between them; all grey and dim with morning mist beneath a grey sky in a hushed and haunted air.

Mr. Vaughan's voice broke in upon the silence.

"I thought you would be too tired to be about so early," he said. "I see you are admiring the view. It is very pretty, isn't it, though I suppose old Meyrick Vaughan didn't think much about the scenery when he built the house. A queer grey, old place, isn't it?"

"Yes, and how it fits into the surroundings; it seems of a piece with the grey hills and the grey bridge below."

"I am afraid I have brought you down on false pretences, Dyson," said Vaughan, as they began to walk up and down the terrace. "I have been to the place, and there is not a sign of anything this morning."

"Ah, indeed. Well, suppose we go round together."

They walked across the lawn and went by a path through the ilex shrubbery to the back of the house. There Vaughan pointed out the track leading down to the valley and up to the heights above the wood, and presently they stood beneath the garden wall, by the door.

"Here, you see, it was," said Vaughan, pointing to a spot on the turf. "I was standing just where you are now that morning I first saw the flints."

"Yes, quite so. That morning it was the Army, as I call it; then the Bowl, then the Pyramid, and, yesterday, the Half moon. What a queer old stone that is," he went on, pointing to a block of limestone rising out of the turf just beneath the wall. 'It looks like a sort of dwarf pillar, but I suppose it is natural."

"Oh, yes, I think so. I imagine it was brought here, though, as we stand on the red sandstone. No doubt it was used as a foundation stone for some older building."

"Very likely," Dyson was peering about him attentively, looking from the ground to the wall, and from the wall to the deep wood that hung almost over the garden and made the place dark even in the morning.

"Look here," said Dyson at length, "it is certainly a case of children this time. Look at that." He was bending down and staring at the dull red surface of the mellowed bricks of the wall.

Vaughan came up and looked hard where Dyson's finger was pointing, and could scarcely distinguish a faint mark in deeper red.

"What is it?" he said. "I can make nothing of it."

"Look a little more closely. Don't you see it is an attempt to draw the human eye?"

"Ah, now I see what you mean. My sight is not very sharp. Yes, so it is, it is meant for an eye, no doubt, as you say. I thought the children learnt drawing at school."

"Well, it is an odd eye enough. Do you notice the peculiar almond shape; almost like the eye of a Chinaman?"

Dyson looked meditatively at the work of the undeveloped artist, and scanned the wall again, going down on his knees in the minuteness of his inquisition.

"I should like very much," he said at length, "to know how a child in this out of the way place could have any idea of the shape of the Mongolian eye. You see the average child has a very distinct impression of the subject; he draws a circle, or something like a circle, and put a dot in the centre. I don't think any child imagines that the eye is really made like that; it's just a convention of infantile art. But this almond-shaped thing puzzles me extremely. Perhaps it may be derived from a gilt Chinaman on a tea-canister in the grocer's shop. Still that's hardly likely."

"But why are you so sure it was done by a child?"

"Why! Look at the height. These old-fashioned bricks are little more than two inches thick; there are twenty courses from the ground to the sketch if we call it so; that gives a height of three and a half feet. Now, just imagine you are going to draw something on this wall. Exactly; your pencil, if you had one, would touch the wall somewhere on the level with your eyes, that is, more than five feet from the ground. It seems, therefore, a very simple deduction to conclude that this eye on the wall was drawn by a child about ten years old."

"Yes, I had not thought of that. Of course one of the children must have done it."

"I suppose so; and yet as I said, there is something singularly unchildlike about those two lines, and the eyeball itself, you see, is almost an oval. To my mind, the thing has an odd, ancient air; and a touch that is not altogether pleasant. I cannot help fancying that if we could see a whole face from the same hand it would not be altogether agreeable. However, that is nonsense, after all, and we are not getting farther in our investigations. It is odd that the flint series has come to such an abrupt end."

The two men walked away towards the house, and as they went in at the porch there was a break in the grey sky, and a gleam of sunshine on the grey hill before them.

All the day Dyson prowled meditatively about the fields and woods surrounding the house. He was thoroughly and completely puzzled by the trivial circumstances he proposed to elucidate, and now he again took the flint arrow-head from his pocket, turning it over and examining it with deep attention. There was something about the thing that was altogether different from the specimens he had seen at the museums and private collections; the shape was of a distinct type, and around the edge there was a line of little punctured dots, apparently a suggestion of ornament. Who, thought Dyson, could possess such things in so remote a place; and who, possessing the flints, could have put them to the fantastic use of designing meaningless figures under Vaughan's garden wall? The rank absurdity of the whole affair offended him unutterably; and as one theory after another rose in his mind only to be rejected, he felt strongly tempted to take the next train back to town. He had seen the silver plate which Vaughan treasured, and had inspected the punch-bowl, the gem of the collection, with close attention; and what he saw and his interview with the butler convinced him that a plot to rob the strong box was out of the limits of enquiry. The chest in which the bowl was kept, a heavy piece of mahogany, evidently dating from the beginning of the century, was certainly strongly suggestive of a pyramid, and Dyson was at first inclined to the inept manoeuvres of the detective, but a little sober thought convinced him of the impossibility of the burglary hypothesis, and he cast wildly about for something more satisfying. He asked Vaughan if there were any gipsies in the neighbourhood, and heard that the Romany had not been seen for years. This dashed him a good deal, as he knew the gipsy habit of leaving queer hieroglyphics on the line of march, and had been much elated when the thought occurred to him. He was facing Vaughan by the old-fashioned hearth when he put the question, and leaned back in his chair in disgust at the destruction of his theory.

"It is odd," said Vaughan, "but the gipsies never trouble us here. Now and then the farmers find traces of fires in the wildest part of the hills, but nobody seems to know who the fire-lighters are."

"Surely that looks like gipsies?"

"No, not in such places as those. Tinkers and gipsies and wanderers of all sorts stick to the roads and don't go very far from the farmhouses."

"Well, I can make nothing of it. I saw the children going by this afternoon, and, as you say, they ran straight on. So we shall have no more eyes on the wall at all events."

"No, I must waylay them one of these days and find out who is the artist."

The next morning when Vaughan strolled in his usual course from the lawn to the back of the house he found Dyson already awaiting him by the garden door, and evidently in a state of high excitement, for he beckoned furiously with his hand, and gesticulated violently.

"What is it?" asked Vaughan. "The flints again?"

"No; but look here, look at the wall. There; don't you see it?"

"There's another of those eyes!"

"Exactly. Drawn, you see, at a little distance from the first, almost on the same level, but slightly lower."

"What on earth is one to make of it? It couldn't have been done by the children; it wasn't there last night, and they won't pass for another hour. What can it mean?"

"I think the very devil is at the bottom of all this," said Dyson. "Of course, one cannot resist the conclusion that these infernal almond eyes are to be set down to the same agency as the devices in the arrow-heads; and where that conclusion is to lead us is more than I can tell. For my part, I have to put a strong check on my imagination, or it would run wild."

"Vaughan," he said, as they turned away from the wall, "has it struck you that there is one point—a very curious point—in common between the figures done in flints and the eyes drawn on the wall?"

"What is that?" asked Vaughan, on whose face there had fallen a certain shadow of indefinite dread.

"It is this. We know that the signs of the Army, the Bowl, the Pyramid, and the Half moon must have been done at night. Presumably they were meant to be seen at night. Well, precisely the same reasoning applies to those eyes on the wall."

"I do not quite see your point."

"Oh, surely. The nights are dark just now, and have been very cloudy, I know, since I came down. Moreover, those overhanging trees would throw that wall into deep shadow even on a clear night."

"Well?"

"What struck me was this. What very peculiarly sharp eyesight, they, whoever 'they' are, must have to be able to arrange arrow-heads in intricate order in the blackest shadow of the wood, and then draw the eyes on the wall without a trace of bungling, or a false line."

"I have read of persons confined in dungeons for many years who have been able to see quite well in the dark," said Vaughan.

"Yes," said Dyson, "there was the abbé in Monte Cristo. But it is a singular point."

Part 3. The Search for the Bowl

"Who was that old man that touched his hat to you just now?" said Dyson, as they came to the bend of the lane near the house.

"Oh, that was old Trevor. He looks very broken, poor old fellow."

"Who is Trevor?"

"Don't you remember? I told you the story that afternoon I came to your rooms—about a girl named Annie Trevor, who disappeared in the most inexplicable manner about five weeks ago. That was her father."

"Yes, yes, I recollect now. To tell the truth I had forgotten all about it. And nothing has been heard of the girl?"

"Nothing whatever. The police are quite at fault."

"I am afraid I did not pay very much attention to the details you gave me. Which way did the girl go?"

"Her path would take her right across those wild hills above the house: the nearest point in the track must be about two miles from here."

"Is it near that little hamlet I saw yesterday?"

"You mean Croesyceiliog, where the children came from? No; it goes more to the north."

"Ah, I have never been that way."

They went into the house, and Dyson shut himself up in his room, sunk deep in doubtful thought, but yet with the shadow of a suspicion growing within him that for a while haunted his brain, all vague and fantastic, refusing to take definite form. He was sitting by the open window and looking out on the valley and saw, as if in a picture, the intricate winding of the brook, the grey bridge, and the vast hills rising beyond; all still and without a breath of wind to stir the mystic hanging woods, and the evening sunshine glowed warm on the bracken, and down below a faint mist, pure white, began to rise from the stream. Dyson sat by the window as the day darkened and the huge bastioned hills loomed vast and vague, and the woods became dim and more shadowy: and the fancy that had seized him no longer appeared altogether impossible. He passed the rest of the evening in a reverie, hardly hearing what Vaughan said; and when he took his candle in the hall, he paused a moment before bidding his friend good-night.

"I want a good rest," he said. "I have got some work to do to-morrow."

"Some writing, you mean?"

"No. I am going to look for the Bowl."

"The Bowl! If you mean my punch-bowl, that is safe in the chest."

"I don't mean the punch-bowl. You may take my word for it that your plate has never been threatened. No; I will not bother you with any suppositions. We shall in all probability have something much stronger than suppositions before long. Good-night, Vaughan."

The next morning Dyson set off after breakfast. He took the path by the garden wall, and noted that there were now eight of the weird almond eyes dimly outlined on the brick.

"Six days more," he said to himself, but as he thought over the theory he had formed, he shrank, in spite of strong conviction, from such a wildly incredible fancy. He struck up through the dense shadows of the wood, and at length came out on the bare hillside, and climbed higher and higher over the slippery turf, keeping well to the north, and following the indications given him by Vaughan. As he went on, he seemed to mount ever higher above the world of human life and customary things; to his right he looked at a fringe of orchard and saw a faint blue smoke rising like a pillar; there was the hamlet from which the children came to school, and there the only sign of life, for the woods embowered and concealed Vaughan's old grey house. As he reached what seemed the summit of the hill, he realized for the first time the desolate loneliness and strangeness of the land; there was nothing but grey sky and grey hill, a high, vast plain that seemed to stretch on for ever and ever, and a faint glimpse of a blue-peaked mountain far away and to the north. At length he came to the path, a slight track scarcely noticeable, and from its position and by what Vaughan had told him he knew that it was the way the lost girl, Annie Trevor, must have taken. He followed the path on the bare hill-top, noticing the great limestone rocks that cropped out of the turf, grim and hideous, and of an aspect as forbidding as an idol of the South Seas; and suddenly he halted, astonished, although he had found what he searched for.

Almost without warning the ground shelved suddenly away on all sides, and Dyson looked down into a circular depression, which might well have been a Roman amphitheatre, and the ugly crags of limestone rimmed it round as if with a broken wall. Dyson walked round the hollow, and noted the position of the stones, and then turned on his way home.

"This," he thought to himself, "is more than curious. The Bowl is discovered, but where is the Pyramid?"

"My dear Vaughan," he said, when he got back, "I may tell you that I have found the Bowl, and that is all I shall tell you for the present. We have six days of absolute inaction before us; there is really nothing to be done."

Part 4. The Secret of the Pyramid

"I have just been round the garden," said Vaughan one morning. "I have been counting those infernal eyes, and I find there are fourteen of them. For heaven's sake, Dyson, tell me what the meaning of it all is."

"I should be very sorry to attempt to do so. I may have guessed this or that, but I always make it a principle to keep my guesses to myself. Besides, it is really not worth while anticipating events; you will remember my telling you that we had six days of inaction before us? Well, this is the sixth day, and the last of idleness. To-night, I propose we take a stroll."

"A stroll! Is that all the action you mean to take?"

"Well, it may show you some very curious things. To be plain, I want you to start with me at nine o'clock this evening for the hills. We may have to be out all night, so you had better wrap up well, and bring some of that brandy."

"Is it a joke?" asked Vaughan, who was bewildered with strange events and strange surmises.

"No, I don't think there is much joke in it. Unless I am much mistaken we shall find a very serious explanation of the puzzle. You will come with me, I am sure?"

"Very good. Which way do you want to go?"

"By the path you told me of; the path Annie Trevor is supposed to have taken."

Vaughan looked white at the mention of the girl's name.

"I did not think you were on that track," he said. "I thought it was the affair of those devices in flint and of the eyes on the wall that you were engaged on. It's no good saying any more, but I will go with you."

At a quarter to nine that evening the two men set out, taking the path through the wood, and up the hill-side. It was a dark and heavy night, the sky was thick with clouds, and the valley full of mist, and all the way they seemed to walk in a world of shadow and gloom, hardly speaking, and afraid to break the haunted silence. They came out at last on the steep hill-side, and instead of the oppression of the wood there was the long, dim sweep of the turf, and higher, the fantastic limestone rocks hinted horror through the darkness, and the wind sighed as it passed across the mountain to the sea, and in its passage beat chill about their hearts. They seemed to walk on and on for hours, and the dim outline of the hill still stretched before them, and the haggard rocks still loomed through the darkness, when suddenly Dyson whispered, drawing his breath quickly, and coming close to his companion:

"Here," he said, "we will lie down. I do not think there is anything yet."

"I know the place," said Vaughan, after a moment. "I have often been by in the daytime. The country people are afraid to come here, I believe; it is supposed to be a fairies' castle, or something of the kind. But why on earth have we come here?"

"Speak a little lower," said Dyson. "It might not do us any good if we are overheard."

"Overheard here! There is not a soul within three miles of us."

"Possibly not; indeed, I should say certainly not. But there might be a body somewhat nearer."

"I don't understand you in the least," said Vaughan, whispering to humour Dyson, "but why have we come here?"

"Well, you see this hollow before us is the Bowl. I think we had better not talk even in whispers."

They lay full length upon the turf; the rock between their faces and the Bowl, and now and again, Dyson, slouching his dark, soft hat over his forehead, put out the glint of an eye, and in a moment drew back, not daring to take a prolonged view. Again he laid an ear to the ground and listened, and the hours went by, and the darkness seemed to blacken, and the faint sigh of the wind was the only sound.

Vaughan grew impatient with this heaviness of silence, this watching for indefinite terror; for to him there was no shape or form of apprehension, and he began to think the whole vigil a dreary farce.

"How much longer is this to last?" he whispered to Dyson, and Dyson who had been holding his breath in the agony of attention put his mouth to Vaughan's ear and said:

"Will you listen?" with pauses between each syllable, and in the voice with which the priest pronounces the awful words.

Vaughan caught the ground with his hands, and stretched forward, wondering what he was to hear. At first there was nothing, and then a low and gentle noise came very softly from the Bowl, a faint sound, almost indescribable, but as if one held the tongue against the roof of the mouth and expelled the breath. He listened eagerly and presently the noise grew louder, and became a strident and horrible hissing as if the pit beneath boiled with fervent heat, and Vaughan, unable to remain in suspense any longer, drew his cap half over his face in imitation of Dyson, and looked down to the hollow below.

It did, in truth, stir and seethe like an infernal caldron. The whole of the sides and bottom tossed and writhed with vague and restless forms that passed to and fro without the sound of feet, and gathered thick here and there and seemed to speak to one another in those tones of horrible sibilance, like the hissing of snakes, that he had heard. It was as if the sweet turf and the cleanly earth had suddenly become quickened with some foul writhing growth. Vaughan could not draw back his face, though he felt Dyson's finger touch him, but he peered into the quaking mass and saw faintly that there were things like faces and human limbs, and yet he felt his inmost soul chill with the sure belief that no fellow soul or human thing stirred in all that tossing and hissing host. He looked aghast, choking back sobs of horror, and at length the loathsome forms gathered thickest about some vague object in the middle of the hollow, and the hissing of their speech grew more venomous, and he saw in the uncertain light the abominable limbs, vague and yet too plainly seen, writhe and intertwine, and he thought he heard, very faint, a low human moan striking through the noise of speech that was not of man. At his heart something seemed to whisper ever "the worm of corruption, the worm that dieth not," and grotesquely the image was pictured to his imagination of a piece of putrid offal stirring through and through with bloated and horrible creeping things. The writhing of the dusky limbs continued, they seemed clustered round the dark form in the middle of the hollow, and the sweat dripped and poured off Vaughan's forehead, and fell cold on his hand beneath his face.

Then, it seemed done in an instant, the loathsome mass melted and fell away to the sides of the Bowl, and for a moment Vaughan saw in the middle of the hollow the tossing of human arms.

But a spark gleamed beneath, a fire kindled, and as the voice of a woman cried out loud in a shrill scream of utter anguish and terror, a great pyramid of flame spired up like a bursting of a pent fountain, and threw a blaze of light upon the whole mountain. In that instant Vaughan saw the myriads beneath; the things made in the form of men but stunted like children hideously deformed, the faces with the almond eyes burning with evil and unspeakable lusts; the ghastly yellow of the mass of naked flesh and then as if by magic the place was empty, while the fire roared and crackled, and the flames shone abroad.

"You have seen the Pyramid," said Dyson in his ear, "the Pyramid of fire."

Part 5. The Little People

"Then you recognize the thing?"

"Certainly. It is a brooch that Annie Trevor used to wear on Sundays; I remember the pattern. But where did you find it? You don't mean to say that you have discovered the girl?"

"My dear Vaughan, I wonder you have not guessed where I found the brooch. You have not forgotten last night already?"

"Dyson," said the other, speaking very seriously, "I have been turning it over in my mind this morning while you have been out. I have thought about what I saw, or perhaps I should say about what I thought I saw, and the only conclusion I can come to is this, that the thing won't bear recollection. As men live, I have lived soberly and honestly, in the fear of God, all my days, and all I can do is believe that I suffered from some monstrous delusion, from some phantasmagoria of the bewildered senses. You know we went home together in silence, not a word passed between us as to what I fancied I saw; had we not better agree to keep silence on the subject? When I took my walk in the peaceful morning sunshine, I thought all the earth seemed full of praise, and passing by that wall I noticed there were no more signs recorded, and I blotted out those that remained. The mystery is over, and we can live quietly again. I think some poison has been working for the last few weeks; I have trod on the verge of madness, but I am sane now."

Mr. Vaughan had spoken earnestly, and bent forward in his chair and glanced at Dyson with something of entreaty.

"My dear Vaughan," said the other, after a pause, "what's the use of this? It is much too late to take that tone; we have gone too deep. Besides you know as well as I that there is no delusion in the case; I wish there were with all my heart. No, in justice to myself I must tell you the whole story, so far as I know it."

"Very good," said Vaughan with a sigh, "if you must, you must."

"Then," said Dyson, "we will begin with the end if you please. I found this brooch you have just identified in the place we have called the Bowl. There was a heap of grey ashes, as if a fire had been burning, indeed, the embers were still hot, and this brooch was lying on the ground, just outside the range of the flame. It must have dropped accidentally from the dress of the person who was wearing it. No, don't interrupt me; we can pass now to the beginning, as we have had the end. Let us go back to that day you came to see me in my rooms in London. So far as I can remember, soon after you came in you mentioned, in a somewhat casual manner, that an unfortunate and mysterious incident had occurred in your part of the country; a girl named Annie Trevor had gone to see a relative, and had disappeared. I confess freely that what you said did not greatly interest me; there are so many reasons which may make it extremely convenient for a man and more especially a woman to vanish from the circle of their relations and friends. I suppose, if we were to consult the police, one would find that in London somebody disappears mysteriously every other week, and the officers would, no doubt, shrug their shoulders, and tell you that by the law of averages it could not be otherwise. So I was very culpably careless to your story, and besides, here is another reason for my lack of interest; your tale was inexplicable. You could only suggest a blackguard sailor on the tramp, but I discarded the explanation immediately.

"For many reasons, but chiefly because the occasional criminal, the amateur in brutal crime, is always found out, especially if he selects the country as the scene of his operations. You will remember the case of that Garcia you mentioned; he strolled into a railway station the day after the murder, his trousers covered with blood, and the works of the Dutch clock, his loot, tied in a neat parcel. So rejecting this, your only suggestion, the whole tale became, as I say, inexplicable, and, therefore, profoundly uninteresting. Yes, therefore, it is a perfectly valid conclusion. Do you ever trouble your head about problems which you know to be insoluble? Did you ever bestow much thought on the old puzzle of Achilles and the tortoise? Of course not, because you knew it was a hopeless quest, and so when you told me the story of a country girl who had disappeared I simply placed the whole thing down in the category of the insoluble, and thought no more about the matter. I was mistaken, so it has turned out; but if you remember, you immediately passed on to an affair which interested you more intensely, because personally, I need not go over the very singular narrative of the flint signs, at first I thought it all trivial, probably some children's game, and if not that a hoax of some sort; but your showing me the arrow-head awoke my acute interest. Here, I saw, there was something widely removed from the commonplace, and matter of real curiosity; and as soon as I came here I set to work to find the solution, repeating to myself again and again the signs you had described. First came the sign we have agreed to call the Army; a number of serried lines of flints, all pointing in the same way. Then the lines, like the spokes of a wheel, all converging towards the figure of a Bowl, then the triangle or Pyramid, and last of all the Half moon. I confess that I exhausted conjecture in my efforts to unveil this mystery, and as you will understand it was a duplex or rather triplex problem. For I had not merely to ask myself: what do these figures mean? but also, who can possibly be responsible for the designing of them? And again, who can possibly possess such valuable things, and knowing their value thus throw them down by the wayside? This line of thought led me to suppose that the person or persons in question did not know the value of unique flint arrow-heads, and yet this did not lead me far, for a well-educated man might easily be ignorant on such a subject. Then came the complication of the eye on the wall, and you remember that we could not avoid the conclusion that in the two cases the same agency was at work. The peculiar position of these eyes on the wall made me inquire if there was such a thing as a dwarf anywhere in the neighbourhood, but I found that there was not, and I knew that the children who pass by every day had nothing to do with the matter. Yet I felt convinced that whoever drew the eyes must be from three and a half to four feet high, since, as I pointed out at the time, anyone who draws on a perpendicular surface chooses by instinct a spot about level with his face. Then again, there was the question of the peculiar shape of the eyes; that marked Mongolian character of which the English countryman could have no conception, and for a final cause of confusion the obvious fact that the designer or designers must be able practically to see in the dark. As you remarked, a man who has been confined for many years in an extremely dark cell or dungeon might acquire that power; but since the days of Edmond Dantès, where would such a prison be found in Europe? A sailor, who had been immured for a considerable period in some horrible Chinese oubliette, seemed the individual I was in search of, and though it looked improbable, it was not absolutely impossible that a sailor or, let us say, a man employed on shipboard, should be a dwarf. But how to account for my imaginary sailor being in possesion of prehistoric arrow-heads? And the possession granted, what was the meaning and object of these mysterious signs of flint, and the almond-shaped eyes? Your theory of a contemplated burglary I saw, nearly from the first, to be quite untenable, and I confess I was utterly at a loss for a working hypothesis. It was a mere accident which put me on the track; we passed poor old Trevor, and your mention of his name and of the disappearance of his daughter, recalled the story which I had forgotten, or which remained unheeded. Here, then, I said to myself, is another problem, uninteresting, it is true, by itself; but what if it prove to be in relation with all these enigmas which torture me? I shut myself in my room, and endeavoured to dismiss all prejudice from my mind, and I went over everything de novo, assuming for theory's sake that the disappearance of

Annie Trevor had some connection with the flint signs and the eyes on the wall. This assumption did not lead me very far, and I was on the point of giving the whole problem up in despair, when a possible significance of the Bowl struck me. As you know there is a 'Devil's Punch-bowl' in Surrey, and I saw that the symbol might refer to some feature in the country. Putting the two extremes together, I determined to look for the Bowl near the path which the lost girl had taken, and you know how I found it. I interpreted the sign by what I knew, and read the first, the Army, thus:

"'there is to be a gathering or assembly at the Bowl in a fortnight (that is the Half moon) to see the Pyramid, or to build the Pyramid.'

"The eyes, drawn one by one, day by day, evidently checked off the days, and I knew that there would be fourteen and no more. Thus far the way seemed pretty plain; I would not trouble myself to inquire as to the nature of the assembly, or as to who was to assemble in the loneliest and most dreaded place among these lonely hills. In Ireland or China or the West of America the question would have been easily answered; a muster of the disaffected, the meeting of a secret society; vigilantes summoned to report: the thing would be simplicity itself; but in this quiet corner of England, inhabited by quiet folk, no such suppositions were possible for a moment. But I knew that I should have an opportunity of seeing and watching the assembly, and I did not care to perplex myself with hopeless research; and in place of reasoning a wild fancy entered into judgment: I remembered what people had said about Annie Trevor's disappearance, that she had been 'taken by the fairies.' I tell you, Vaughan, I am a sane man as you are, my brain is not, I trust, mere vacant space to let to any wild improbability, and I tried my best to thrust the fantasy away. And the hint came of the old name of fairies, 'the little people,' and the very probable belief that they represent a tradition of the prehistoric Turanian inhabitants of the country, who were cave dwellers: and then I realized with a shock that I was looking for a being under four feet in height, accustomed to live in darkness, possessing stone instruments, and familiar with the Mongolian cast of features! I say this, Vaughan, that I should be ashamed to hint at such visionary stuff to you, if it were not for that which you saw with your very eyes last night, and I say that I might doubt the evidence of my senses, if they were not confirmed by yours. But you and I cannot look each other in the face and pretend delusion; as you lay on the turf beside me I felt your flesh shrink and quiver, and I saw your eyes in the light of the flame. And so I tell you without any shame what was in my mind last night as we went through the wood and climbed the hill, and lay hidden beneath the rock.

"There was one thing that should have been most evident that puzzled me to the very last. I told you how I read the sign of the Pyramid; the assembly was to see a pyramid, and the true meaning of the symbol escaped me to the last moment. The old derivation from 'up, fire,' though false, should have set me on the track, but it never occurred to me.

"I think I need say very little more. You know we were quite helpless, even if we had foreseen what was to come. Ah, the particular place where these signs were displayed? Yes, that is a curious question. But this house is, so far as I can judge, in a pretty central situation amongst the hills; and possibly, who can say yes or no, that queer, old limestone pillar by your garden wall was a place of meeting before the Celt set foot in Britain. But there is one thing I must add: I don't regret our inability to rescue the wretched girl. You saw the appearance of those things that gathered thick and writhed in the Bowl; you may be sure that what lay bound in the midst of them was no longer fit for earth."

"So?" said Vaughan.

"So she passed in the Pyramid of Fire," said Dyson, "and they passed again to the underworld, to the places beneath the hills."

THE TERROR: A MYSTERY

CHAPTER I
The Coming of the Terror

After two years we are turning once more to the morning's news with a sense of appetite and glad expectation. There were thrills at the beginning of the war; the thrill of horror and of a doom that seemed at once incredible and certain; this was when Namur fell and the German host swelled like a flood over the French fields, and drew very near to the walls of Paris. Then we felt the thrill of exultation when the good news came that the awful tide had been turned back, that Paris and the world were safe; for awhile at all events.

Then for days we hoped for more news as good as this or better. Has Von Kluck been surrounded? Not to-day, but perhaps he will be surrounded to-morrow. But the days became weeks, the weeks drew out to months; the battle in the West seemed frozen. Now and again things were done that seemed hopeful, with promise of events still better. But Neuve Chapelle and Loos dwindled into disappointments as their tale was told fully; the lines in the West remained, for all practical purposes of victory, immobile. Nothing seemed to happen; there was nothing to read save the record of operations that were clearly trifling and insignificant. People speculated as to the reason of this inaction; the hopeful said that Joffre had a plan, that he was "nibbling," others declared that we were short of munitions, others again that the new levies were not yet ripe for battle. So the months went by, and almost two years of war had been completed before the motionless English line began to stir and quiver as if it awoke from a long sleep, and began to roll onward, overwhelming the enemy.

The secret of the long inaction of the British Armies has been well kept. On the one hand it was rigorously protected by the censorship, which severe, and sometimes severe to the point of absurdity—"the captains and the ... depart," for instance—became in this particular matter ferocious. As soon as the real significance of that which was happening, or beginning to happen, was perceived by the authorities, an underlined circular was issued to the newspaper proprietors of Great Britain and Ireland. It warned each proprietor that he might impart the contents of this circular to one other person only, such person being the responsible editor of his paper, who was to keep the communication secret under the severest penalties. The circular forbade any mention of certain events that

126

had taken place, that might take place; it forbade any kind of allusion to these events or any hint of their existence, or of the possibility of their existence, not only in the Press, but in any form whatever. The subject was not to be alluded to in conversation, it was not to be hinted at, however obscurely, in letters; the very existence of the circular, its subject apart, was to be a dead secret.

These measures were successful. A wealthy newspaper proprietor of the North, warmed a little at the end of the Throwsters' Feast (which was held as usual, it will be remembered), ventured to say to the man next to him: "How awful it would be, wouldn't it, if...." His words were repeated, as proof, one regrets to say, that it was time for "old Arnold" to "pull himself together"; and he was fined a thousand pounds. Then, there was the case of an obscure weekly paper published in the county town of an agricultural district in Wales. The Meiros Observer (we will call it) was issued from a stationer's back premises, and filled its four pages with accounts of local flower shows, fancy fairs at vicarages, reports of parish councils, and rare bathing fatalities. It also issued a visitors' list, which has been known to contain six names.

This enlightened organ printed a paragraph, which nobody noticed, which was very like paragraphs that small country newspapers have long been in the habit of printing, which could hardly give so much as a hint to any one—to any one, that is, who was not fully instructed in the secret. As a matter of fact, this piece of intelligence got into the paper because the proprietor, who was also the editor, incautiously left the last processes of this particular issue to the staff, who was the Lord-High-Every-thing-Else of the establishment; and the staff put in a bit of gossip he had heard in the market to fill up two inches on the back page. But the result was that the Meiros Observer ceased to appear, owing to "untoward circumstances" as the proprietor said; and he would say no more. No more, that is, by way of explanation, but a great deal more by way of execration of "damned, prying busybodies."

-oOo-

Now a censorship that is sufficiently minute and utterly remorseless can do amazing things in the way of hiding ... what it wants to hide. Before the war, one would have thought otherwise; one would have said that, censor or no censor, the fact of the murder at X or the fact of the bank robbery at Y would certainly become known; if not through the Press, at all events through rumor and the passage of the news from mouth to mouth. And this would be true—of England three hundred years ago, and of savage tribelands of to-day. But we have grown of late to such a reverence for the printed word and such a reliance on it, that the old faculty of disseminating news by word of mouth has become atrophied. Forbid the Press to mention the fact that Jones has been murdered, and it is marvelous how few people will hear of it, and of those who hear how few will credit the story that they have heard. You meet a man in the train who remarks that he has been told something about a murder in Southwark; there is all the difference in the world between the impression you receive from such a chance communication and that given by half a dozen lines of print with name, and street and date and all the facts of the case. People in trains repeat all sorts of tales, many of them false; newspapers do not print accounts of murders that have not been committed.

Then another consideration that has made for secrecy. I may have seemed to say that the old office of rumor no longer exists; I shall be reminded of the strange legend of "the Russians" and the mythology of the "Angels of Mons." But let me point out, in the first place, that both these absurdities depended on the papers for their wide dissemination. If there had been no newspapers or magazines Russians and Angels would have made but a brief, vague appearance of the most shadowy kind—a few would have heard of them, fewer still would have believed in them, they would have been gossiped about for a bare week or two, and so they would have vanished away.

And, then, again, the very fact of these vain rumors and fantastic tales having been so widely believed for a time was fatal to the credit of any stray mutterings that may have got abroad. People had been taken in twice; they had seen how grave persons, men of credit, had preached and lectured about the shining forms that had saved the British Army at Mons, or had testified to the trains, packed with gray-coated Muscovites, rushing through the land at dead of night: and now there was a hint of something more amazing than either of the discredited legends. But this time there was no word of confirmation to be found in daily paper, or weekly review, or parish magazine, and so the few that heard either laughed, or, being serious, went home and jotted down notes for essays on "War-time Psychology: Collective Delusions."

-oOo-

I followed neither of these courses. For before the secret circular had been issued my curiosity had somehow been aroused by certain paragraphs concerning a "Fatal Accident to Well-known Airman." The propeller of the airplane had been shattered, apparently by a collision with a flight of pigeons; the blades had been broken and the machine had fallen like lead to the earth. And soon after I had seen this account, I heard of some very odd circumstances relating to an explosion in a great munition factory in the Midlands. I thought I saw the possibility of a connection between two very different events.

-oOo-

It has been pointed out to me by friends who have been good enough to read this record, that certain phrases I have used may give the impression that I ascribe all the delays of the war on the Western front to the extraordinary circumstances which occasioned the issue of the Secret Circular. Of course this is not the case, there were many reasons for the immobility of our lines from October 1914 to July 1916. These causes have been evident enough and have been openly discussed and deplored. But behind them was something of infinitely greater moment. We lacked men, but men were pouring into the new army; we were short of shells, but when the shortage was proclaimed the nation set itself to mend this matter with all its energy. We could undertake to supply the defects of our army both in men and munitions—if the new and incredible danger could be overcome. It has been overcome; rather, perhaps, it has ceased to exist; and the secret may now be told.

I have said my attention was attracted by an account of the death of a well-known airman. I have not the habit of preserving cuttings, I am sorry to say, so that I cannot be precise as to the date of this event. To the best of my belief it was either towards the end of May or the beginning of June 1915. The newspaper paragraph announcing the death of Flight-Lieutenant Western-Reynolds was brief enough; accidents, and fatal accidents, to the men who are storming the air for us are, unfortunately, by no means so rare as to demand an elaborated notice. But the manner in which Western-Reynolds met his death struck me as extraordinary, inasmuch as it revealed a new danger in the element that we have lately conquered. He was brought down, as I said, by a flight of birds; of pigeons, as appeared by what was found on the bloodstained and shattered blades of the propeller. An eye-witness of the accident, a fellow-officer, described how Western-Reynolds set out from the aerodrome on a fine afternoon, there being hardly any wind. He was going to France; he had made the journey to and fro half a dozen times or more, and felt perfectly secure and at ease.

"'Wester' rose to a great height at once, and we could scarcely see the machine. I was turning to go when one of the fellows called out, 'I say! What's this?' He pointed up, and we saw what looked like a black cloud coming from the south at a tremendous rate. I saw at once it wasn't a cloud; it came with a swirl and a rush quite different from any cloud I've ever seen. But for a second I couldn't make out exactly what it was. It altered its shape and turned into a great crescent, and wheeled and veered about as if it was looking for something. The man who had called out had got his glasses, and was staring for all he was worth. Then he shouted that it was a tremendous flight of birds, 'thousands of them.' They went on wheeling and beating about high up in the air, and we were watching them, thinking it was interesting, but not supposing that they would make any difference to 'Wester,' who was just about out of sight. His machine was just a speck. Then the two arms of the crescent drew in as quick as lightning, and these thousands of birds shot in a solid mass right up there across the sky, and flew away somewhere about nor'-nor'-by-west. Then Henley, the man with the glasses, called out, 'He's down!' and started running, and I went after him. We got a car and as we were going along Henley told me that he'd seen the machine drop dead, as if it came out of that cloud of birds. He thought then that they must have mucked up the propeller somehow. That turned out to be the case. We found the propeller blades all broken and covered with blood and pigeon feathers, and carcasses of the birds had got wedged in between the blades, and were sticking to them."

This was the story that the young airman told one evening in a small company. He did not speak "in confidence," so I have no hesitation in reproducing what he said. Naturally, I did not take a verbatim note of his conversation, but I have something of a knack of remembering talk that interests me, and I think my reproduction is very near to the tale that I heard. And let it be noted that the flying man told his story without any sense or indication of a sense that the incredible, or all but the incredible, had happened. So far as he knew, he said, it was the first accident of the kind. Airmen in France had been bothered once or twice by birds—he thought they were eagles—flying viciously at them, but poor old "Wester" had been the first man to come up against a flight of some thousands of pigeons.

"And perhaps I shall be the next," he added, "but why look for trouble? Anyhow, I'm going to see Toodle-oo to-morrow afternoon."

-oOo-

Well, I heard the story, as one hears all the varied marvels and terrors of the air; as one heard some years ago of "air pockets," strange gulfs or voids in the atmosphere into which airmen fell with great peril; or as one heard of the experience of the airman who flew over the Cumberland mountains in the burning summer of 1911, and as he swam far above the heights was suddenly and vehemently blown upwards, the hot air from the rocks striking his plane as if it had been a blast from a furnace chimney. We have just begun to navigate a strange region; we must expect to encounter strange adventures, strange perils. And here a new chapter in the chronicles of these perils and adventures had been opened by the death of Western-Reynolds; and no doubt invention and contrivance would presently hit on some way of countering the new danger.

It was, I think, about a week or ten days after the airman's death that my business called me to a northern town, the name of which, perhaps, had better remain unknown. My mission was to inquire into certain charges of extravagance which had been laid against the working people, that is, the munition workers of this especial town. It was said that the men who used to earn £2 10s. a week were now getting from seven to eight pounds, that "bits of girls" were being paid two pounds instead of seven or eight shillings, and that, in consequence, there was an orgy of foolish extravagance. The girls, I was told, were eating chocolates at four, five, and six shillings a pound, the women were ordering thirty-pound pianos which they couldn't play, and the men bought gold chains at ten and twenty guineas apiece.

I dived into the town in question and found, as usual, that there was a mixture of truth and exaggeration in the stories that I had heard. Gramophones, for example: they cannot be called in strictness necessaries, but they were undoubtedly finding a ready sale, even in the more expensive brands. And I thought that there were a great many very spick and span perambulators to be seen on the pavement; smart perambulators, painted in tender shades of color and expensively fitted.

"And how can you be surprised if people will have a bit of a fling?" a worker said to me. "We're seeing money for the first time in our lives, and it's bright. And we work hard for it, and we risk our lives to get it. You've heard of explosion yonder?"

He mentioned certain works on the outskirts of the town. Of course, neither the name of the works nor of the town had been printed; there had been a brief notice of "Explosion at Munition Works in the Northern District: Many Fatalities." The working man told me about it, and added some dreadful details.

"They wouldn't let their folks see bodies; screwed them up in coffins as they found them in shop. The gas had done it."

"Turned their faces black, you mean?"

"Nay. They were all as if they had been bitten to pieces."

This was a strange gas.

I asked the man in the northern town all sorts of questions about the extraordinary explosion of which he had spoken to me. But he had very little more to say. As I have noted already, secrets that may not be printed are often deeply kept; last summer there were very few people outside high official circles who knew anything about the "Tanks," of which we have all been talking lately, though these strange instruments of war were being exercised and tested in a park not far from London. So the man who told me of the explosion in the munition factory was most likely genuine in his profession that he knew nothing more of the disaster. I found out that he was a smelter employed at a furnace on the other side of the town to the ruined factory; he didn't know even what they had been making there; some very dangerous high explosive, he supposed. His information was really nothing more than a bit of gruesome gossip, which he had heard probably at third or fourth or fifth hand. The horrible detail of faces "as if they had been bitten to pieces" had made its violent impression on him, that was all.

I gave him up and took a tram to the district of the disaster; a sort of industrial suburb, five miles from the center of the town. When I asked for the factory, I was told that it was no good my going to it as there was nobody there. But I found it; a raw and hideous shed with a walled yard about it, and a shut gate. I looked for signs of destruction, but there was nothing. The roof was quite undamaged; and again it struck me that this had been a strange accident. There had been an explosion of sufficient violence to kill workpeople in the building, but the building itself showed no wounds or scars.

A man came out of the gate and locked it behind him. I began to ask him some sort of question, or rather, I began to "open" for a question with "A terrible business here, they tell me," or some such phrase of convention. I got no farther. The man asked me if I saw a policeman walking down the street. I said I did, and I was given the choice of getting about my business forthwith or of being instantly given in charge as a spy. "Th'ast better be gone and quick about it," was, I think, his final advice, and I took it.

Well, I had come literally up against a brick wall. Thinking the problem over, I could only suppose that the smelter or his informant had twisted the phrases of the story. The smelter had said the dead men's faces were "bitten to pieces"; this might be an unconscious perversion of "eaten away." That phrase might describe well enough the effect of strong acids, and, for all I knew of the processes of munition-making, such acids might be used and might explode with horrible results in some perilous stage of their admixture.

It was a day or two later that the accident to the airman, Western-Reynolds, came into my mind. For one of those instants which are far shorter than any measure of time there flashed out the possibility of a link between the two disasters. But here was a wild impossibility, and I drove it away. And yet I think that the thought, mad as it seemed, never left me; it was the secret light that at last guided me through a somber grove of enigmas.

-oOo-

It was about this time, so far as the date can be fixed, that a whole district, one might say a whole county, was visited by a series of extraordinary and terrible calamities, which were the more terrible inasmuch as they continued for some time to be inscrutable mysteries. It is, indeed, doubtful whether these awful events do not still remain mysteries to many of those concerned; for before the inhabitants of this part of the country had time to join one link of evidence to another the circular was issued, and thenceforth no one knew how to distinguish undoubted fact from wild and extravagant surmise.

The district in question is in the far west of Wales; I shall call it, for convenience, Meirion. In it there is one seaside town of some repute with holiday-makers for five or six weeks in the summer, and dotted about the county there are three or four small old towns that seem drooping in a slow decay, sleepy and gray with age and forgetfulness. They remind me of what I have read of towns in the west of Ireland. Grass grows between the uneven stones of the pavements, the signs above the shop windows decline, half the letters of these signs are missing, here and there a house has been pulled down, or has been allowed to slide into ruin, and wild greenery springs up through the fallen stones, and there is silence in all the streets. And, it is to be noted, these are not places that were once magnificent. The Celts have never had the art of building, and so far as I can see, such towns as Towy and Merthyr Tegveth and Meiros must have been always much as they are now, clusters of poorish, meanly-built houses, ill-kept and down at heel.

And these few towns are thinly scattered over a wild country where north is divided from south by a wilder mountain range. One of these places is sixteen miles from any station; the others are doubtfully and deviously connected by single-line railways served by rare trains that pause and stagger and hesitate on their slow journey up mountain passes, or stop for half an hour or more at lonely sheds called stations, situated in the midst of desolate marshes. A few years ago I traveled with an Irishman on one of these queer lines, and he looked to right and saw the bog with its yellow and blue grasses and stagnant pools, and he looked to left and saw a ragged hillside, set with gray stone walls. "I can hardly believe," he said, "that I'm not still in the wilds of Ireland."

Here, then, one sees a wild and divided and scattered region a land of outland hills and secret and hidden valleys. I know white farms on this coast which must be separate by two hours of hard, rough walking from any other habitation, which are invisible from any other house. And inland, again, the farms are often ringed about by thick groves of ash, planted by men of old days to shelter their roof-trees from rude winds of the mountain and stormy winds of the sea; so that these places, too, are hidden away, to be surmised only by the wood smoke that rises from the green surrounding leaves. A Londoner must see them to believe in them; and even then he can scarcely credit their utter isolation.

Such, then in the main is Meirion, and on this land in the early summer of last year terror descended—a terror without shape, such as no man there had ever known.

It began with the tale of a little child who wandered out into the lanes to pick flowers one sunny afternoon, and never came back to the cottage on the hill.

CHAPTER II
Death in the Village

The child who was lost came from a lonely cottage that stands on the slope of a steep hillside called the Allt, or the height. The land about it is wild and ragged; here the growth of gorse and bracken, here a marshy hollow of reeds and rushes, marking the course of the stream from some hidden well, here thickets of dense and tangled undergrowth, the outposts of the wood. Down through this broken and uneven ground a path leads to the lane at the bottom of the valley; then the land rises again and swells up to the cliffs over the sea, about a quarter of a mile away. The little girl, Gertrude Morgan, asked her mother if she might go down to the lane and pick the purple flowers—these were orchids—that grew there, and her mother gave her leave, telling her she must be sure to be back by tea-time, as there was apple-tart for tea.

She never came back. It was supposed that she must have crossed the road and gone to the cliff's edge, possibly in order to pick the sea-pinks that were then in full blossom. She must have slipped, they said, and fallen into the sea, two hundred feet below. And, it may be said at once, that there was no doubt some truth in this conjecture, though it stopped very far short of the whole truth. The child's body must have been carried out by the tide, for it was never found.

The conjecture of a false step or of a fatal slide on the slippery turf that slopes down to the rocks was accepted as being the only explanation possible. People thought the accident a strange one because, as a rule, country children living by the cliffs and the sea become wary at an early age, and Gertrude Morgan was almost ten years old. Still, as the neighbors said, "that's how it must have happened, and it's a great pity, to be sure." But this would not do when in a week's time a strong young laborer failed to come to his cottage after the day's work. His body was found on the rocks six or seven miles from the cliffs where the child was supposed to have fallen; he was going home by a path that he had used every night of his life for eight or nine years, that he used of dark nights in perfect security, knowing every inch of it. The police asked if he drank, but he was a teetotaler; if he were subject to fits, but he wasn't. And he was not murdered for his wealth, since agricultural laborers are not wealthy. It was only possible again to talk of slippery turf and a false step; but people began to be frightened. Then a woman was found with her neck broken at the bottom of a disused quarry near Llanfihangel, in the middle of the county. The "false step" theory was eliminated here, for the quarry was guarded with a natural hedge of gorse bushes. One would have to struggle and fight through sharp thorns to destruction in such a place as this; and indeed the gorse bushes were broken as if some one had rushed furiously through them, just above the place where the woman's body was found. And this was strange: there was a dead sheep lying beside her in the pit, as if the woman and the sheep together had been chased over the brim of the quarry. But chased by whom, or by what? And then there was a new form of terror.

This was in the region of the marshes under the mountain. A man and his son, a lad of fourteen or fifteen, set out early one morning to work and never reached the farm where they were bound. Their way skirted the marsh, but it was broad, firm and well metalled, and it had been raised about two feet above the bog. But when search was made in the evening of the same day Phillips and his son were found dead in the marsh, covered with black slime and pondweed. And they lay some ten yards from the path, which, it would seem, they must have left deliberately. It was useless of course, to look for tracks in the black ooze, for if one threw a big stone into it a few seconds removed all marks of the disturbance. The men who found the two bodies beat about the verges and purlieus of the marsh in hope of finding some trace of the murderers; they went to and fro over the rising ground where the black cattle were grazing, they searched the alder thickets by the brook; but they discovered nothing.

-oOo-

Most horrible of all these horrors, perhaps, was the affair of the Highway, a lonely and unfrequented by-road that winds for many miles on high and lonely land. Here, a mile from any other dwelling, stands a cottage on the edge of a dark wood. It was inhabited by a laborer named Williams, his wife, and their three children. One hot summer's evening, a man who had been doing a day's gardening at a rectory three or four miles away, passed the cottage, and stopped for a few minutes to chat with Williams, the laborer, who was pottering about his garden, while the children were playing on the path by the door. The two talked of their neighbors and of the potatoes till Mrs. Williams appeared at the doorway and said supper was ready, and Williams turned to go into the house. This was about eight o'clock, and in the ordinary course the family would have their supper and be in bed by nine, or by half-past nine at latest. At ten o'clock that night the local doctor was driving home along the Highway. His horse shied violently and then stopped dead just opposite the gate to the cottage. The doctor got down, frightened at what he saw; and there on the roadway lay Williams, his wife, and the three children, stone dead, all of them. Their skulls were battered in as if by some heavy iron instrument; their faces were beaten into a pulp.

CHAPTER III
The Doctors Theory

It is not easy to make any picture of the horror that lay dark on the hearts of the people of Meirion. It was no longer possible to believe or to pretend to believe that these men and women and children had met their deaths through strange accidents. The little girl and the young laborer might have slipped and fallen over the cliffs, but the woman who lay dead with the dead sheep at the bottom of the quarry, the two men who had been lured into the ooze of the marsh, the family who were found murdered on the Highway before their own cottage door; in these cases there could be no room for the supposition of accident. It seemed as if it were impossible to frame any conjecture or outline of a conjecture that would account for these hideous and, as it seemed, utterly purposeless crimes. For a time people said that there must be a madman at large, a sort of country variant of Jack the Ripper, some horrible pervert who was possessed by the passion of death, who prowled darkling about that lonely land, hiding in woods and in wild places, always watching and seeking for the victims of his desire.

Indeed, Dr. Lewis, who found poor Williams, his wife and children miserably slaughtered on the Highway, was convinced at first that the presence of a concealed madman in the countryside offered the only possible solution to the difficulty.

"I felt sure," he said to me afterwards, "that the Williams's had been killed by a homicidal maniac. It was the nature of the poor creatures' injuries that convinced me that this was the case. Some years ago thirty-seven or thirty-eight years ago as a matter of fact—I had something to do with a case which on the face of it had a strong likeness to the Highway murder. At that time I had a practice at Usk, in Monmouthshire. A whole family living in a cottage by the roadside were murdered one evening; it was called, I think, the Llangibby murder; the cottage was near the village of that name. The murderer was caught in Newport; he was a Spanish sailor, named Garcia, and it appeared that he had killed father, mother, and the three children for the sake of the brass works of an old Dutch clock, which were found on him when he was arrested.

"Garcia had been serving a month's imprisonment in Usk Jail for some small theft, and on his release he set out to walk to Newport, nine or ten miles away; no doubt to get another ship. He passed the cottage and saw the man working in his garden. Garcia stabbed him with his sailor's knife. The wife rushed out; he stabbed her. Then he went into the cottage and stabbed the three children, tried to set the place on fire, and made off with the clockworks. That looked like the deed of a madman, but Garcia wasn't mad—they hanged him, I may say—he was merely a man of a very low type, a degenerate who hadn't the slightest value for human life. I am not sure, but I think he came from one of the Spanish islands, where the people are said to be degenerates, very likely from too much inter-breeding.

"But my point is that Garcia stabbed to kill and did kill, with one blow in each case. There was no senseless hacking and slashing. Now those poor people on the Highway had their heads smashed to pieces by what must have been a storm of blows. Any one of them would have been fatal, but the murderer must have gone on raining blows with his iron hammer on people who were already stone dead. And that sort of thing is the work of a madman, and nothing but a madman. That's how I argued the matter out to myself just after the event.

"I was utterly wrong, monstrously wrong. But who could have suspected the truth?"

Thus Dr. Lewis, and I quote him, or the substance of him, as representative of most of the educated opinion of the district at the beginnings of the terror. People seized on this theory largely because it offered at least the comfort of an explanation, and any explanation, even the poorest, is better than an intolerable and terrible mystery. Besides, Dr. Lewis's theory was plausible; it explained the lack of purpose that seemed to characterize the murders. And yet—there were difficulties even from the first. It was hardly possible that a strange madman should be able to keep hidden in a countryside where any stranger is instantly noted and noticed; sooner or later he would be seen as he prowled along the lanes or across the wild places. Indeed, a drunken, cheerful, and altogether harmless tramp was arrested by a farmer and his man in the fact and act of sleeping off beer under a hedge; but the vagrant was able to prove complete and undoubted alibis, and was soon allowed to go on his wandering way.

Then another theory, or rather a variant of Dr. Lewis's theory, was started. This was to the effect that the person responsible for the outrages was, indeed, a madman; but a madman only at intervals. It was one of the members of the Porth Club, a certain Mr. Remnant, who was supposed to have originated this more subtle explanation. Mr. Remnant was a middle-aged man, who, having nothing particular to do, read a great many books by way of conquering the hours. He talked to the club—doctors, retired colonels, parsons, lawyers—about "personality," quoted various psychological textbooks in support of his contention that personality was sometimes fluid and unstable, went back to "Dr. Jekyll and Mr. Hyde" as good evidence of this proposition, and laid stress on Dr. Jekyll's speculation that the human soul, so far from being one and indivisible, might, possibly turn out to be a mere polity, a state in which dwelt many strange and incongruous citizens, whose characters were not merely unknown but altogether unsurmised by that form of consciousness which so rashly assumed that it was not only the president of the republic but also its sole citizen.

"The long and the short of it is," Mr. Remnant concluded, "that any one of us may be the murderer, though he hasn't the faintest notion of the fact. Take Llewelyn there."

Mr. Payne Llewelyn was an elderly lawyer, a rural Tulkinghorn. He was the hereditary solicitor to the Morgans of Pentwyn. This does not sound anything tremendous to the Saxons of London; but the style is far more than noble to the Celts of West Wales; it is immemorial; Teilo Sant was of the collaterals of the first known chief of the race. And Mr. Payne Llewelyn did his best to look like the legal adviser of this ancient house. He was weighty, he was cautious, he was sound, he was secure. I have compared him to Mr. Tulkinghorn of Lincoln's Inn Fields; but Mr. Llewelyn would most certainly never have dreamed of employing his leisure in peering into the cupboards where the family skeletons were hidden. Supposing such cupboards to have existed, Mr. Payne Llewelyn would have risked large out-of-pocket expenses to furnish them with double, triple, impregnable locks. He was a new man, an advena, certainly; for he was partly of the Conquest, being descended on one side from Sir Payne Turberville; but he meant to stand by the old stock.

"Take Llewelyn now," said Mr. Remnant. "Look here, Llewelyn, can you produce evidence to show where you were on the night those people were murdered on the Highway? I thought not."

Mr. Llewelyn, an elderly man, as I have said, hesitated before speaking.

"I thought not," Remnant went on. "Now I say that it is perfectly possible that Llewelyn may be dealing death throughout Meirion, although in his present personality he may not have the faintest suspicion that there is another Llewelyn within him, a Llewelyn who follows murder as a fine art."

-oOo-

Mr. Payne Llewelyn did not at all relish Mr. Remnant's suggestion that he might well be a secret murderer, ravening for blood, remorseless as a wild beast. He thought the phrase about his following murder as a fine art was both nonsensical and in the worst taste, and his opinion was not changed when Remnant pointed out that it was used by De Quincey in the title of one of his most famous essays.

"If you had allowed me to speak," he said with some coldness of manner, "I would have told you that on Tuesday last, the night on which those unfortunate people were murdered on the Highway I was staying at the Angel Hotel, Cardiff. I had business in Cardiff, and I was detained till Wednesday afternoon."

Having given this satisfactory alibi, Mr. Payne Llewelyn left the club, and did not go near it for the rest of the week.

Remnant explained to those who stayed in the smoking room that, of course, he had merely used Mr. Llewelyn as a concrete example of his theory, which, he persisted, had the support of a considerable body of evidence.

"There are several cases of double personality on record," he declared. "And I say again that it is quite possible that these murders may have been committed by one of us in his secondary personality. Why, I may be the murderer in my Remnant B. state, though Remnant A. knows nothing whatever about it, and is perfectly convinced that he could not kill a fowl, much less a whole family. Isn't it so, Lewis?"

Dr. Lewis said it was so, in theory, but he thought not in fact.

"Most of the cases of double or multiple personality that have been investigated," he said, "have been in connection with the very dubious experiments of hypnotism, or the still more dubious experiments of spiritualism. All that sort of thing, in my opinion, is like tinkering with the works of a clock—amateur tinkering, I mean. You fumble about with the wheels and cogs and bits of mechanism that you don't really know anything about; and then you find your clock going backwards or striking 240 at tea-time. And I believe it's just the same thing with these psychical research experiments; the secondary personality is very likely the result of the tinkering and fumbling with a very delicate apparatus that we know nothing about. Mind, I can't say that it's impossible for one of us to be the Highway murderer in his B. state, as Remnant puts it. But I think it's extremely improbable. Probability is the guide of life, you know, Remnant," said Dr. Lewis, smiling at that gentleman, as if to say that he also had done a little reading in his day. "And it follows" therefore, that improbability is also the guide of life. When you get a very high degree of probability, that is, you are justified in taking it as a certainty; and on the other hand, if a supposition is highly improbable, you are justified in treating it as an impossible one. That is, in nine hundred and ninety-nine cases out of a thousand."

"How about the thousandth case?" said Remnant. "Supposing these extraordinary crimes constitute the thousandth case?"

The doctor smiled and shrugged his shoulders, being tired of the subject. But for some little time highly respectable members of Porth society would look suspiciously at one another wondering whether, after all, there mightn't be "something in it." However, both Mr. Remnant's somewhat crazy theory and Dr. Lewis's plausible theory became untenable when two more victims of an awful and mysterious death were offered up in, sacrifice, for a man was found dead in the Llanfihangel quarry, where the woman had been discovered. And on the same day a girl of fifteen was found broken on the jagged rocks under the cliffs near Porth. Now, it appeared that these two deaths must have occurred at about the same time, within an hour of one another, certainly; and the distance between the quarry and the cliffs by Black Rock is certainly twenty miles.

"A motor could do it," one man said.

But it was pointed out that there was no high road between the two places; indeed, it might be said that there was no road at all between them. There was a network of deep, narrow, and tortuous lands that wandered into one another at all manner of queer angles for, say, seventeen miles; this in the middle, as it were, between Black Rock and the quarry at Llanfihangel. But to get to the high land of the cliffs one had to take a path that went through two miles of fields; and the quarry lay a mile away from the nearest by-road in the midst of gorse and bracken and broken land. And, finally, there was no track of motor-car or motor-bicycle in the lanes which must have been followed to pass from one place to the other.

"What about an airplane, then?" said the man of the motor-car theory. Well, there was certainly an aerodrome not far from one of the two places of death; but somehow, nobody believed that the Flying Corps harbored a homicidal maniac. It seemed clear, therefore, that there must be more than one person concerned in the terror of Meirion. And Dr. Lewis himself abandoned his own theory.

"As I said to Remnant at the Club," he remarked, "improbability is the guide of life. I can't believe that there are a pack of madmen or even two madmen at large in the country. I give it up."

And now a fresh circumstance or set of circumstances became manifest to confound judgment and to awaken new and wild surmises. For at about this time people realized that none of the dreadful events that were happening all about them was so much as mentioned in the Press. I have already spoken of the fate of the Meiros Observer. This paper was suppressed by the authorities because it had inserted a brief paragraph about some person who had been "found dead under mysterious circumstances"; I think that paragraph referred to the first death of Llanfihangel quarry. Thenceforth, horror followed on horror, but no word was printed in any of the local journals. The curious went to the newspaper offices—there were two left in the county—but found nothing save a firm refusal to discuss the matter. And the Cardiff papers were drawn and found blank; and the London Press was apparently ignorant of the fact that crimes that had no parallel were terrorizing a whole countryside. Everybody wondered what could have happened, what was happening; and then it was whispered that the coroner would allow no inquiry to be made as to these deaths of darkness.

"In consequence of instructions received from the Home Office," one coroner was understood to have said, "I have to tell the jury that their business will be to hear the medical evidence and to bring in a verdict immediately in accordance with that evidence. I shall disallow all questions."

One jury protested. The foreman refused to bring in any verdict at all.

"Very good," said the coroner. "Then I beg to inform you, Mr. Foreman and gentlemen of the jury, that under the Defense of the Realm Act, I have power to supersede your functions, and to enter a verdict according to the evidence which has been laid before the Court as if it had been the verdict of you all."

The foreman and jury collapsed and accepted what they could not avoid. But the rumors that got abroad of all this, added to the known fact that the terror was ignored in the Press, no doubt by official command, increased the panic that was now; arising, and gave it a new direction. Clearly, people reasoned, these Government restrictions and prohibitions could only refer to the war, to some great danger in connection with the war. And that being so, it followed that the outrages which must be kept so secret were the work of the enemy, that is of concealed German agents.

CHAPTER IV
The Spread of the Terror

It is time, I think, for me to make one point clear. I began this history with certain references to an extraordinary accident to an airman whose machine fell to the ground after collision with a huge flock of pigeons; and then to an explosion in a northern munition factory, an explosion, as I noted, of a very singular kind. Then I deserted the neighborhood of London, and the northern district, and dwelt on a mysterious and terrible series of events which occurred in the summer of 1915 in a Welsh county, which I have named, for convenience, Meirion.

Well, let it be understood at once that all this detail that I have given about the occurrences in Meirion does not imply that the county in the far west was alone or especially afflicted by the terror that was over the land. They tell me that in the villages about Dartmoor the stout Devonshire hearts sank as men's hearts used to sink in the time of plague and pestilence. There was horror, too, about the Norfolk Broads, and far up by Perth no one would venture on the path that leads by Scone to the wooded heights above the Tay. And in the industrial districts: I met a man by chance one day in an odd London corner who spoke with horror of what a friend had told him.

"'Ask no questions, Ned,' he says to me, 'but I tell yow a' was in Bairnigan t'other day, and a' met a pal who'd seen three hundred coffins going out of a works not far from there.'"

And then the ship that hovered outside the mouth of the Thames with all sails set and beat to and fro in the wind, and never answered any hail, and showed no light! The forts shot at her and brought down one of the masts, but she went suddenly about with a change of wind under what sail still stood, and then veered down Channel, and drove ashore at last on the sandbanks and pinewoods of Arcachon, and not a man alive on her, but only rattling heaps of bones! That last voyage of the Semiramis would be something horribly worth telling; but I only heard it at a distance as a yarn, and only believed it because it squared with other things that I knew for certain.

This, then, is my point; I have written of the terror as it fell on Meirion, simply because I have had opportunities of getting close there to what really happened. Third or fourth or fifth hand in the other places; but round about Porth and Merthyr Tegveth I have spoken with people who have seen the tracks of the terror with their own eyes.

Well, I have said that the people of that far western county realized, not only that death was abroad in their quiet lanes and on their peaceful hills, but that for some reason it was to be kept all secret. Newspapers might not print any news of it, the very juries summoned to investigate it were allowed to investigate nothing. And so they concluded that this veil of secrecy must somehow be connected with the war; and from this position it was not a long way to a further inference: that the murderers of innocent men and women and children were either Germans or agents of Germany. It would be just like the Huns, everybody agreed, to think out such a devilish scheme as this; and they always thought out their schemes beforehand. They hoped to seize Paris in a few weeks, but when they were beaten on the Marne they had their trenches on the Aisne ready to fall back on: it had all been prepared years before the war. And so, no doubt, they had devised this terrible plan against England in case they could not beat us in open fight: there were people ready, very likely, all over the country, who were prepared to murder and destroy everywhere as soon as they got the word. In this way the Germans intended to sow terror throughout England and fill our hearts with panic and dismay, hoping so to weaken their enemy at home that he would lose all heart over the war abroad. It was the Zeppelin notion, in another form; they were committing these horrible and mysterious outrages thinking that we should be frightened out of our wits.

It all seemed plausible enough; Germany had by this time perpetrated so many horrors and had so excelled in devilish ingenuities that no abomination seemed too abominable to be probable, or too ingeniously wicked to be beyond the tortuous malice of the Hun. But then came the questions as to who the agents of this terrible design were, as to where they lived, as to how they contrived to move unseen from field to field, from lane to lane. All sorts of fantastic attempts were made to answer these questions; but it was felt that they remained unanswered. Some suggested that the murderers landed from submarines, or flew from hiding places on the West Coast of Ireland, coming and going by night; but there were seen to be flagrant impossibilities in both these suggestions. Everybody agreed that the evil work was no doubt the work of Germany; but nobody could begin to guess how it was done. Somebody at the Club asked Remnant for his theory.

"My theory," said that ingenious person, "is that human progress is simply a long march from one inconceivable to another. Look at that airship of ours that came over Porth yesterday: ten years ago that would have been an inconceivable sight. Take the steam engine, stake printing, take the theory of gravitation: they were all inconceivable till somebody thought of them. So it is, no doubt, with this infernal dodgery that we're talking about: the Huns have found it out, and we haven't; and there you are. We can't conceive how these poor people have been murdered, because the method's inconceivable to us."

The club listened with some awe to this high argument. After Remnant had gone, one member said:

"Wonderful man, that." "Yes," said Dr. Lewis. "He was asked whether he knew something. And his reply really amounted to 'No, I don't,' But I have never heard it better put."

-oOo-

It was, I suppose, at about this time when the people were puzzling their heads as to the secret methods used by the Germans or their agents to accomplish their crimes that a very singular circumstance became known to a few of the Porth people. It related to the murder of the Williams family on the Highway in front of their cottage door. I do not know that I have made it plain that the old Roman road called the Highway follows the course of a long, steep hill that goes steadily westward till it slants down and droops towards the sea. On either side of the road the ground falls away, here into deep shadowy woods, here to high pastures, now and again into a field of corn, but for the most part into the wild and broken land that is characteristic of Arfon. The fields are long and narrow, stretching up the steep hillside; they fall into sudden dips and hollows, a well springs up in the midst of one and a grove of ash and thorn bends over it, shading it; and beneath it the ground is thick with reeds and rushes. And then may come on either side of such a field territories glistening with the deep growth of bracken, and rough with gorse and rugged with thickets of blackthorn, green lichen hanging strangely from the branches; such are the lands on either side of the Highway.

Now on the lower slopes of it, beneath the Williams's cottage, some three or four fields down the hill, there is a military camp. The place has been used as a camp for many years, and lately the site has been extended and huts have been erected. But a considerable number of the men were under canvas here in the summer of 1915.

On the night of the Highway murder this camp, as it appeared afterwards, was the scene of the extraordinary panic of the horses.

-oOo-

A good many men in the camp were asleep in their tents soon after 9:30, when the Last Post was sounded. They woke up in panic. There was a thundering sound on the steep hillside above them, and down upon the tents came half a dozen horses, mad with fright, trampling the canvas, trampling the men, bruising dozens of them and killing two.

Everything was in wild confusion, men groaning and screaming in the darkness, struggling with the canvas and the twisted ropes, shouting out, some of them, raw lads enough, that the Germans had landed, others wiping the blood from their eyes, a few, roused suddenly from heavy sleep, hitting out at one another, officers coming up at the double roaring out orders to the sergeants, a party of soldiers who were just returning to camp from the village seized with fright at what they could scarcely see or distinguish, at the wildness of the shouting and cursing and groaning that they could not understand, bolting out of the camp again and racing for their lives back to the village: everything in the maddest confusion of wild disorder.

Some of the men had seen the horses galloping down the hill as if terror itself was driving them. They scattered off into the darkness, and somehow or another found their way back in the night to their pasture above the camp. They were grazing there peacefully in the morning, and the only sign of the panic of the night before was the mud they had scattered all over themselves as they pelted through a patch of wet ground. The farmer said they were as quiet a lot as any in Meirion; he could make nothing of it.

"Indeed," he said, "I believe they must have seen the devil himself to be in such a fright as that: save the people!"

Now all this was kept as quiet as might be at the time when it happened; it became known to the men of the Porth Club in the days when they were discussing the difficult question of the German outrages, as the murders were commonly called. And this wild stampede of the farm horses was held by some to be evidence of the extraordinary and unheard of character of the dreadful agency that was at work. One of the members of the club had been told by an officer who was in the camp at the time of the panic that the horses that came charging down were in a perfect fury of fright, that he had never seen horses in such a state, and so there was endless speculation as to the nature of the sight or the sound that had driven half a dozen quiet beasts into raging madness.

Then, in the middle of this talk, two or three other incidents, quite as odd and incomprehensible, came to be known, borne on chance trickles of gossip that came into the towns from outland farms, or were carried by cottagers tramping into Porth on market day with a fowl or two and eggs and garden stuff; scraps and fragments of talk gathered by servants from the country folk and repeated—to their mistresses. And in such ways it came out that up at Plas Newydd there had been a terrible business over swarming the bees; they had turned as wild as wasps and much more savage. They had come about the people who were taking the swarms like a cloud. They settled on one man's face so that you could not see the flesh for the bees crawling all over it, and they had stung him so badly that the doctor did not know whether he would get over it, and they had chased a girl who had come out to see the swarming, and settled on her and stung her to death. Then they had gone off to a brake below the farm and got into a hollow tree there, and it was not safe to go near it, for they would come out at you by day or by night.

And much the same thing had happened, it seemed, at three or four farms and cottages where bees were kept. And there were stories, hardly so clear or so credible, of sheep dogs, mild and trusted beasts, turning as savage as wolves and injuring the farm boys in a horrible manner—in one case it was said with fatal results. It was certainly true that old Mrs. Owen's favorite Brahma-Dorking cock had gone mad; she came into Porth one Saturday morning with her face and her neck all bound up and plastered. She had gone out to her bit of a field to feed the poultry the night before, and the bird had flown at her and attacked her most savagely, inflicting some very nasty wounds before she could beat it off.

"There was a stake handy, lucky for me," she said, "and I did beat him and beat him till the life was out of him. But what is come to the world, whatever?"

-oOo-

Now Remnant, the man of theories, was also a man of extreme leisure. It was understood that he had succeeded to ample means when he was quite a young man, and after tasting the savors of the law, as it were, for half a dozen terms at the board of the Middle Temple, he had decided that it would be senseless to bother himself with passing examinations for a profession which he had not the faintest intention of practising. So he turned a deaf ear to the call of "Manger" ringing through the Temple Courts, and set himself out to potter amiably through the world. He had pottered all over Europe, he had looked at Africa, and had even put his head in at the door of the East, on a trip which included the Greek isles and Constantinople. Now getting into the middle fifties, he had settled at Porth for the sake, as he said, of the Gulf Stream and the fuchsia hedges, and pottered over his books and his theories and the local gossip. He was no more brutal than the general public, which revels in the details of mysterious crime; but it must be said that the terror, black though it was, was a boon to him. He peered and investigated and poked about with the relish of a man to whose life a new zest has been added. He listened attentively to the strange tales of bees and dogs and poultry that came into Porth with the country baskets of butter, rabbits, and green peas; and he evolved at last a most extraordinary theory.

Full of this discovery, as he thought it, he went one night to see Dr. Lewis and take his view of the matter.

"I want to talk to you," said Remnant to the doctor, "about what I have called provisionally, the Z Ray."

CHAPTER V
The Incident of the Unknown Tree

Dr. Lewis, smiling indulgently, and quite prepared for some monstrous piece of theorizing, led Remnant into the room that overlooked the terraced garden and the sea.

The doctor's house, though it was only a ten minutes' walk from the center of the town, seemed remote from all other habitations. The drive to it from the road came through a deep grove of trees and a dense shrubbery, trees were about the house on either side, mingling with neighboring groves, and below, the garden fell down, terrace by green terrace, to wild growth, a twisted path amongst red rocks, and at last to the yellow sand of a little cove. The room to which the doctor took Remnant looked over these terraces and across the water to the dim boundaries of the bay. It had French windows that were thrown wide open, and the two men sat in the soft light of the lamp—this was before the days of severe lighting regulations in the Far West—and enjoyed the sweet odors and the sweet vision of the summer evening. Then Remnant began:

"I suppose, Lewis, you've heard these extraordinary stories of bees and dogs and things that have been going about lately?"

"Certainly I have heard them. I was called in at Plas Newydd, and treated Thomas Trevor, who's only just out of danger, by the way. I certified for the poor child, Mary Trevor. She was dying when I got to the place. There was no doubt she was stung to death by bees, and I believe there were other very similar cases at Llantarnam and Morwen; none fatal, I think. What about them?"

"Well: then there are the stories of good-tempered old sheepdogs turning wicked and 'savaging' children?"

"Quite so. I haven't seen any of these cases professionally; but I believe the stories are accurate enough."

"And the old woman assaulted by her own poultry?"

"That's perfectly true. Her daughter put some stuff of their own concoction on her face and neck, and then she came to me. The wounds seemed going all right, so I told her to continue the treatment, whatever it might be."

"Very good," said Mr. Remnant. He spoke now with an italic impressiveness. "Don't you see the link between all this and the horrible things that have been happening about here for the last month?"

Lewis stared at Remnant in amazement. He lifted his red eyebrows and lowered them in a kind of scowl. His speech showed traces of his native accent.

"Great burning!" he exclaimed. "What on earth are you getting at now? It is madness. Do you mean to tell me that you think there is some connection between a swarm or two of bees that have turned nasty, a cross dog, and a wicked old barn-door cock and these poor people that have been pitched over the cliffs and hammered to death on the road? There's no sense in it, you know."

"I am strongly inclined to believe that there is a great deal of sense in it," replied Remnant, with extreme calmness. "Look here, Lewis, I saw you grinning the other day at the club when I was telling the fellows that in my opinion all these outrages had been committed, certainly by the Germans, but by some method of which we have no conception. But what I meant to say when I talked about inconceivables was just this: that the Williams's and the rest of them have been killed in some way that's not in theory at all, not in our theory, at all events, some way we've not contemplated, not thought of for an instant. Do you see my point?"

"Well, in a sort of way. You mean there's an absolute originality in the method? I suppose that is so. But what next?"

Remnant seemed to hesitate, partly from a sense of the portentous nature of what he was about to say, partly from a sort of half-unwillingness to part with so profound a secret.

"Well," he said, "you will allow that we have two sets of phenomena of a very extraordinary kind occurring at the same time. Don't you think that it's only reasonable to connect the two sets with one another."

"So the philosopher of Tenterden steeple and the Goodwin Sands thought, certainly," said Lewis. "But what is the connection? Those poor folks on the Highway weren't stung by bees or worried by a dog. And horses don't throw people over cliffs or stifle them in marshes."

"No; I never meant to suggest anything so absurd. It is evident to me that in all these cases of animals turning suddenly savage the cause has been terror, panic, fear. The horses that went charging into the camp were mad with fright, we know. And I say that in the other instances we have been discussing the cause was the same. The creatures were exposed to an infection of fear, and a frightened beast or bird or insect uses its weapons, whatever they may be. If, for example, there had been anybody with those horses when they took their panic they would have lashed out at him with their heels."

"Yes, I dare say that that is so. Well."

"Well; my belief is that the Germans have made an extraordinary discovery. I have called it the Z Ray. You know that the ether is merely an hypothesis; we have to suppose that it's there to account for the passage of the Marconi current from one place to another. Now, suppose that there is a psychic ether as well as a material ether, suppose that it is possible to direct irresistible impulses across this medium, suppose that these impulses are towards murder or suicide; then I think that you have an explanation of the terrible series of events that have been happening in Meirion for the last few weeks. And it is quite clear to my mind that the horses and the other creatures have been exposed to this Z Ray, and that it has produced on them the effect of terror, with ferocity as the result of terror. Now what do you say to that? Telepathy, you know, is well established; so is hypnotic suggestion. You have only to look in the Encyclopædia Britannica' to see that, and suggestion is so strong in some cases as to be an irresistible imperative. Now don't you feel that putting telepathy and suggestion together, as it were, you have more than the elements of what I call the Z Ray? I feel myself that I have more to go on in making my hypothesis than the inventor of the steam engine had in making his hypothesis when he saw the lid of the kettle bobbing up and down. What do you say?"

Dr. Lewis made no answer. He was watching the growth of a new, unknown tree in his garden.

-oOo-

The doctor made no answer to Remnant's question. For one thing, Remnant was profuse in his eloquence—he has been rigidly condensed in this history—and Lewis was tired of the sound of his voice. For another thing, he found the Z Ray theory almost too extravagant to be bearable, wild enough to tear patience to tatters. And then as the tedious argument continued Lewis became conscious that there was something strange about the night.

It was a dark summer night. The moon was old and faint, above the Dragon's Head across the bay, and the air was very still. It was so still that Lewis had noted that not a leaf stirred on the very tip of a high tree that stood out against the sky; and yet he knew that he was listening to some sound that he could not determine or define. It was not the wind in the leaves, it was not the gentle wash of the water of the sea against the rocks; that latter sound he could distinguish quite easily. But there was something else. It was scarcely a sound; it was as if the air itself trembled and fluttered, as the air trembles in a church when they open the great pedal pipes of the organ.

The doctor listened intently. It was not an illusion, the sound was not in his own head, as he had suspected for a moment; but for the life of him he could not make out whence it came or what it was. He gazed down into the night over the terraces of his garden, now sweet with the scent of the flowers of the night; tried to peer over the tree-tops across the sea towards the Dragon's Head. It struck him suddenly that this strange fluttering vibration of the air might be the noise of a distant aeroplane or airship; there was not the usual droning hum, but this sound might be caused by a new type of engine. A new type of engine? Possibly it was an enemy airship; their range, it had been said, was getting longer; and Lewis was just going to call Remnant's attention to the sound, to its possible cause, and to the possible danger that might be hovering over them, when he saw something that caught his breath and his heart with wild amazement and a touch of terror.

He had been staring upward into the sky, and, about to speak to Remnant, he had let his eyes drop for an instant. He looked down towards the trees in the garden, and saw with utter astonishment that one had changed its shape in the few hours that had passed since the setting of the sun. There was a thick grove of ilexes bordering the lowest terrace, and above them rose one tall pine, spreading its head of sparse, dark branches dark against the sky.

As Lewis glanced down over the terraces he saw that the tall pine tree was no longer there. In its place there rose above the ilexes what might have been a greater ilex; there was the blackness of a dense growth of foliage rising like a broad and far-spreading and rounded cloud over the lesser trees.

Here, then was a sight wholly incredible, impossible. It is doubtful whether the process of the human mind in such a case has ever been analyzed and registered; it is doubtful whether it ever can be registered. It is hardly fair to bring in the mathematician, since he deals with absolute truth (so far as mortality can conceive absolute truth); but how would a mathematician feel if he were suddenly confronted with a two-sided triangle? I suppose he would instantly become a raging madman; and Lewis, staring wide-eyed and wild-eyed at a dark and spreading tree which his own experience informed him was not there, felt for an instant that shock which should affront us all when we first realize the intolerable antinomy of Achilles and the Tortoise. Common sense tells us that Achilles will flash past the tortoise almost with the speed of the lightning;

the inflexible truth of mathematics assures us that till the earth boils and the heavens cease to endure the Tortoise must still be in advance; and thereupon we should, in common decency, go mad. We do not go mad, because, by special grace, we are certified that, in the final: court of appeal, all science is a lie, even the highest science of all; and so we simply grin at Achilles and the Tortoise, as we grin at Darwin, deride Huxley, and laugh at Herbert Spencer.

Dr. Lewis did not grin. He glared into the dimness of the night, at the great spreading tree that he knew could not be there. And as he gazed he saw that what at first appeared the dense blackness of foliage was fretted and starred with wonderful appearances of lights and colors.

Afterwards he said to me: "I remember thinking to myself: 'Look here, I am not delirious; my temperature is perfectly normal. I am not drunk; I only had a pint of Graves with my dinner, over three hours ago. I have not eaten any poisonous fungus; I have not taken Anhelonium Lewinii experimentally. So, now then! What is happening?'"

The night had gloomed over; clouds obscured the faint moon and the misty stars. Lewis rose, with some kind of warning and inhibiting gesture to Remnant, who, he was conscious was gaping at him in astonishment. He walked to the open French window, and took a pace forward on to the path outside, and looked, very intently, at the dark shape of the tree, down below the sloping garden, above the washing of the waves. He shaded the light of the lamp behind him by holding his hands on each side of his eyes.

The mass of the tree—the tree that couldn't be there—stood out against the sky, but not so clearly, now that the clouds had rolled up. Its edges, the limits of its leafage, were not so distinct. Lewis thought that he could detect some sort of quivering movement in it; though the air was at a dead calm. It was a night on which one might hold up a lighted match and watch it burn without any wavering or inclination of the flame.

"You know," said Lewis, "how a bit of burnt paper will sometimes hang over the coals before it goes up the chimney, and little worms of fire will shoot through it. It was like that, if you should be standing some distance away. Just threads and hairs of yellow light I saw, and specks and sparks of fire, and then a twinkling of a ruby no bigger than a pin point, and a green wandering in the black, as if an emerald were crawling, and then little veins of deep blue. 'Woe is me!' I said to myself in Welsh, 'What is all this color and burning?'

"And, then, at that very moment there came a thundering rap at the door of the room inside, and there was my man telling me that I was wanted directly up at the Garth, as old Mr. Trevor Williams had been taken very bad. I knew his heart was not worth much, so I had to go off directly, and leave Remnant to make what he could of it all."

CHAPTER VI
Mr. Remnant's Z Ray

Dr. Lewis was kept some time at the Garth. It was past twelve when he got back to his house.

He went quickly to the room that overlooked the garden and the sea and threw open the French window and peered into the darkness. There, dim indeed against the dim sky but unmistakable, was the tall pine with its sparse branches, high above the dense growth of the ilex trees. The strange boughs which had amazed him had vanished; there was no appearance now of colors or of fires.

He drew his chair up to the open window and sat there gazing and wondering far into the night, till brightness came upon the sea and sky, and the forms of the trees in the garden grew clear and evident. He went up to his bed at last filled with a great perplexity, still asking questions to which there was no answer.

The doctor did not say anything about the strange tree to Remnant. When they next met, Lewis said that he had thought there was a man hiding amongst the bushes—this in explanation of that warning gesture he had used, and of his going out into the garden and staring into the night. He concealed the truth because he dreaded the Remnant doctrine that would undoubtedly be produced; indeed, he hoped that he had heard the last of the theory of the Z Ray. But Remnant firmly reopened this subject.

"We were interrupted just as I was putting my case to you," he said. "And to sum it all up, it amounts to this: that the Huns have made one of the great leaps of science. They are sending 'suggestions' (which amount to irresistible commands) over here, and the persons affected are seized with suicidal or homicidal mania. The people who were killed by falling over the cliffs or into the quarry probably committed suicide; and so with the man and boy who were found in the bog. As to the Highway case, you remember that Thomas Evans said that he stopped and talked to Williams on the night of the murder. In my opinion Evans was the murderer. He came under the influence of the Ray, became a homicidal maniac in an instant, snatched Williams's spade from his hand and killed him and the others."

"The bodies were found by me on the road."

"It is possible that the first impact of the Ray produces violent nervous excitement, which would manifest itself externally. Williams might have called to his wife to come and see what was the matter with

Evans. The children would naturally follow their mother. It seems to me simple. And as for the animals—the horses, dogs, and so forth, they as I say, were no doubt panic stricken by the Ray, and hence driven to frenzy."

"Why should Evans have murdered Williams instead of Williams murdering Evans? Why should the impact of the Ray affect one and not the other?"

"Why does one man react violently to a certain drug, while it makes no impression on another man? Why is A able to drink a bottle of whisky and remain sober, while B is turned into something very like a lunatic after he has drunk three glasses?"

"It is a question of idiosyncrasy," said the doctor.

"Is idiosyncrasy Greek for 'I don't know'?" asked Remnant.

"Not at all," said Lewis, smiling blandly. "I mean that in some diatheses whisky—as you have mentioned whisky—appears not to be pathogenic, or at all events not immediately pathogenic. In other cases, as you very justly observed, there seems to be a very marked cachexia associated with the exhibition of the spirit in question, even in comparatively small doses."

Under this cloud of professional verbiage Lewis escaped from the Club and from Remnant. He did not want to hear any more about that Dreadful Ray, because he felt sure that the Ray was all nonsense. But asking himself why he felt this certitude in the matter he had to confess that he didn't know. An aeroplane, he reflected, was all nonsense before it was made; and he remembered talking in the early nineties to a friend of his about the newly discovered X Rays. The friend laughed incredulously, evidently didn't believe a word of it, till Lewis told him that there was an article on the subject in the current number of the Saturday Review; whereupon the unbeliever said, "Oh, is that so? Oh, really. I see," and was converted on the X Ray faith on the spot. Lewis, remembering this talk, marveled at the strange processes of the human mind, its illogical and yet all-compelling ergos, and wondered whether he himself was only waiting for an article on the Z Ray in the Saturday Review to become a devout believer in the doctrine of Remnant.

But he wondered with far more fervor as to the extraordinary thing he had seen in his own garden with his own eyes. The tree that changed all its shape for an hour or two of the night, the growth of strange boughs, the apparition of secret fires among them, the sparkling of emerald and ruby lights: how could one fail to be afraid with great amazement at the thought of such a mystery?

-oOo-

Dr. Lewis's thoughts were distracted from the incredible adventure of the tree by the visit of his sister and her husband. Mr. and Mrs. Merritt lived in a well-known manufacturing town of the Midlands, which was now, of course, a center of munition work. On the day of their arrival at Porth, Mrs. Merritt, who was tired after the long, hot journey, went to bed early, and Merritt and Lewis went into the room by the garden for their talk and tobacco. They spoke of the year that had passed since their last meeting, of the weary dragging of the war, of friends that had perished in it, of the hopelessness of an early ending of all this misery. Lewis said nothing of the terror that was on the land. One does not greet a tired man who is come to a quiet, sunny place for relief from black smoke and work and worry with a tale of horror. Indeed, the doctor saw that his brother-in-law looked far from well. And he seemed "jumpy"; there was an occasional twitch of his mouth that Lewis did not like at all.

"Well," said the doctor, after an interval of silence and port wine, "I am glad to see you here again. Porth always suits you. I don't think you're looking quite up to your usual form. But three weeks of Meirion air will do wonders."

"Well, I hope it will," said the other. "I am not up to the mark. Things are not going well at Midlingham."

"Business is all right, isn't it?"

"Yes. Business is all right. But there are other things that are all wrong. We are living under a reign of terror. It comes to that."

"What on earth do you mean?"

"Well, I suppose I may tell you what I know. It's not much. I didn't dare write it. But do you know that at every one of the munition works in Midlingham and all about it there's a guard of soldiers with drawn bayonets and loaded rifles day and night? Men with bombs, too. And machine-guns at the big factories."

"German spies?"

"You don't want Lewis guns to fight spies with. Nor bombs. Nor a platoon of men. I woke up last night. It was the machine-gun at Benington's Army Motor Works. Firing like fury. And then bang! bang! bang! That was the hand bombs."

"But what against?"

"Nobody knows."

"Nobody knows what is happening," Merritt repeated, and he went on to describe the bewilderment and terror that hung like a cloud over the

158

great industrial city in the Midlands, how the feeling of concealment, of some intolerable secret danger that must not be named, was worst of all.

"A young fellow I know," he said, "was on short leave the other day from the front, and he spent it with his people at Belmont—that's about four miles out of Midlingham, you know. 'Thank God,' he said to me, 'I am going back to-morrow. It's no good saying that the Wipers salient is nice, because it isn't. But it's a damned sight better than this. At the front you know what you're up against anyhow.' At Midlingham everybody has the feeling that we're up against something awful and we don't know what; it's that that makes people inclined to whisper. There's terror in the air."

Merritt made a sort of picture of the great town cowering in its fear of an unknown danger.

"People are afraid to go about alone at nights in the outskirts. They make up parties at the stations to go home together if it's anything like dark, or if there are any lonely bits on their way."

"But why? I don't understand. What are they afraid of?"

"Well, I told you about my being awakened up the other night with the machine-guns at the motor works rattling away, and the bombs exploding and making the most terrible noise. That sort of thing alarms one, you know. It's only natural."

"Indeed, it must be very terrifying. You mean, then, there is a general nervousness about, a vague sort of apprehension that makes people inclined to herd together?"

"There's that, and there's more. People have gone out that have never come back. There were a couple of men in the train to Holme, arguing about the quickest way to get to Northend, a sort of outlying part of Holme where they both lived. They argued all the way out of Midlingham, one saying that the high road was the quickest though it was the longest way. 'It's the quickest going because it's the cleanest going,' he said."

"The other chap fancied a short cut across the fields, by the canal. 'It's half the distance,' he kept on. 'Yes, if you don't lose your way,' said the other. Well, it appears they put an even half-crown on it, and each was to try his own way when they got out of the train. It was arranged that they were to meet at the 'Wagon' in Northend. 'I shall be at the "Wagon" first,' said the man who believed in the short cut, and with that he climbed over the stile and made off across the fields. It wasn't late enough to be really dark, and a lot of them thought he might win the stakes. But he never turned up at the Wagon—or anywhere else for the matter of that."

"What happened to him?"

"He was found lying on his back in the middle of a field—some way from the path. He was dead. The doctors said he'd-been suffocated. Nobody knows how. Then there have been other cases. We whisper about them at Midlingham, but we're afraid to speak out."

Lewis was ruminating all this profoundly. Terror in Meirion and terror far away in the heart of England; but at Midlingham, so far as he could gather from these stories of soldiers on guard, of crackling machine-guns, it was a case of an organized attack on the munitioning of the army. He felt that he did not know enough to warrant his deciding that the terror of Meirion and of Stratfordshire were one.

Then Merritt began again:

"There's a queer story going about, when the door's shut and the curtain's drawn, that is, as to a place right out in the country over the other side of Midlingham; on the opposite side to Dunwich. They've built one of the new factories out there, a great red brick town of sheds they tell me it is, with a tremendous chimney. It's not been finished more than a month or six weeks. They plumped it down right in the middle of the fields, by the line, and they're building huts for the workers as fast as they can but up to the present the men are billeted all about, up and down the line.

"About two hundred yards from this place there's an old footpath, leading from the station and the main road up to a small hamlet on the hillside. Part of the way this path goes by a pretty large wood, most of it thick undergrowth. I should think there must be twenty acres of wood, more or less. As it happens, I used this path once long ago; and I can tell you it's a black place of nights.

"A man had to go this way one night. He got along all right till he came to the wood. And then he said his heart dropped out of his body. It was awful to hear the noises in that wood. Thousands of men were in it, he swears that. It was full of rustling, and pattering of feet trying to go dainty, and the crack of dead boughs lying on the ground as some one trod on them, and swishing of the grass, and some sort of chattering speech going on, that sounded, so he said, as if the dead sat in their bones and talked! He ran for his life, anyhow; across fields, over hedges, through brooks. He must have run, by his tale, ten miles out of his way before he got home to his wife, and beat at the door, and broke in, and bolted it behind him.".

"There is something rather alarming about any wood at night," said Dr. Lewis.

Merritt shrugged his shoulders.

"People say that the Germans have landed, and that they are hiding in underground places all over the country."

CHAPTER VII
The Case of the Hidden Germans

Lewis gasped for a moment, silent in contemplation of the magnificence of rumor. The Germans already landed, hiding underground, striking by night, secretly, terribly, at the power of England! Here was a conception which made the myth of "The Russians" a paltry fable; before which the Legend of Mons was an ineffectual thing.

It was monstrous. And yet—

He looked steadily at Merritt; a square-headed, black-haired, solid sort of man. He had symptoms of nerves about him for the moment, certainly, but one could not wonder at that, whether the tales he told were true, or whether he merely believed them to be true. Lewis had known his brother-in-law for twenty years or more, and had always found him a sure man in his own small world. "But then," said the doctor to himself, "those men, if they once get out of the ring of that little world of theirs, they are lost. Those are the men that believed in Madame Blavatsky."

"Well," he said, "what do you think yourself? The Germans landed and hiding somewhere about the country: there's something extravagant in the notion, isn't there?"

"I don't know what to think. You can't get over the facts. There are the soldiers with their rifles and their guns at the works all over Stratfordshire, and those guns go off. I told you I'd heard them. Then who are the soldiers shooting at? That's what we ask ourselves at Midlingham."

"Quite so; I quite understand. It's an extraordinary state of things."

"It's more than extraordinary; it's an awful state of things. It's terror in the dark, and there's nothing worse than that. As that young fellow I was telling you about said, 'At the front you do know what you're up against.'"

"And people really believe that a number of Germans have somehow got over to England and have hid themselves underground?"

"People say they've got a new kind of poison-gas. Some think that they dig underground places and make the gas there, and lead it by secret pipes into the shops; others say that they throw gas bombs into the factories. It must be worse than anything they've used in France, from what the authorities say."

"The authorities? Do they admit that there are Germans in hiding about Midlingham?"

"No. They call it 'explosions.' But we know it isn't explosions. We know in the Midlands what an explosion sounds like and looks like. And we know that the people killed in these 'explosions' are put into their coffins in the works. Their own relations are not allowed to see them."

"And so you believe in the German theory?"

"If I do, it's because one must believe in something. Some say they've seen the gas. I heard that a man living in Dunwich saw it one night like a black cloud with sparks of fire in it floating over the tops of the trees by Dunwich Common."

The light of an ineffable amazement came into Lewis's eyes. The night of Remnant's visit, the trembling vibration of the air, the dark tree that had grown in his garden since the setting of the sun, the strange leafage that was starred with burning, with emerald and ruby fires, and all vanished away when he returned from his visit to the Garth; and such a leafage had appeared as a burning cloud far in the heart of England: what intolerable mystery, what tremendous doom was signified in this? But one thing was clear and certain: that the terror of Meirion was also the terror of the Midlands.

Lewis made up his mind most firmly that if possible all this should be kept from his brother-in-law. Merritt had come to Porth as to a city of refuge from the horrors of Midlingham; if it could be managed he should be spared the knowledge that the cloud of terror had gone before him and hung black over the western land. Lewis passed the port and said in an even voice:

"Very strange, indeed; a black cloud with sparks of fire?"

"I can't answer for it, you know; it's only a rumor."

"Just so; and you think or you're inclined to think that this and all the rest you've told me is to be put down to the hidden Germans?"

"As I say; because one must think something.

"I quite see your point. No doubt, if it's true, it's the most awful blow that has ever been dealt at any nation in the whole history of man. The enemy established in our vitals! But is it possible, after all? How could it have been worked?"

Merritt told Lewis how it had been worked, or rather, how people said it had been worked. The idea, he said, was that this was a part, and a most important part, of the great German plot to destroy England and the British Empire.

The scheme had been prepared years ago, some thought soon after the Franco-Prussian War. Moltke had seen that the invasion of England (in the ordinary sense of the term invasion) presented very great

163

difficulties. The matter was constantly in discussion in the inner military and high political circles, and the general trend of opinion in these quarters was that at the best, the invasion of England would involve Germany in the gravest difficulties, and leave France in the position of the *tertius gaudens*. This was the state of affairs when a very high Prussian personage was approached by the Swedish professor, Huvelius.

Thus Merritt, and here I would say in parenthesis that this Huvelius was by all accounts an extraordinary man. Considered personally and apart from his writings he would appear to have been a most amiable individual. He was richer than the generality of Swedes, certainly far richer than the average university professor in Sweden. But his shabby, green frock-coat, and his battered, furry hat were notorious in the university town where he lived. No one laughed, because it was well known that Professor Huvelius spent every penny of his private means and a large portion of his official stipend on works of kindness and charity. He hid his head in a garret, some one said, in order that others might be able to swell on the first floor. It was told of him that he restricted himself to a diet of dry bread and coffee for a month in order that a poor woman of the streets, dying of consumption, might enjoy luxuries in hospital.

And this was the man who wrote the treatise "De Facinore Humano"; to prove the infinite corruption of the human race.

Oddly enough, Professor Huvelius wrote the most cynical book in the world—Hobbes preaches rosy sentimentalism in comparison—with the very highest motives. He held that a very large part of human misery, misadventure, and sorrow was due to the false convention that the heart of man was naturally and in the main well disposed and kindly, if not exactly righteous. "Murderers, thieves, assassins, violators, and all the host of the abominable," he says in one passage, "are created by the false pretense and foolish credence of human virtue. A lion in a cage is a fierce beast, indeed; but what will he be if we declare him to be a lamb and open the doors of his den? Who will be guilty of the deaths of the men, women and children whom he will surely devour, save those who unlocked the cage?" And he goes on to show that kings and the rulers of the peoples could decrease the sum of human misery to a vast extent by acting on the doctrine of human wickedness. "War," he declares, "which is one of the worst of evils, will always continue to exist. But a wise king will desire a brief war rather than a lengthy one, a short evil rather than a long evil. And this not from the benignity of his heart towards his enemies, for we have seen that the human heart is naturally malignant, but because he desires to conquer, and to conquer easily, without a great expenditure of men or of treasure, knowing that if he can accomplish this feat his people will love him and his crown will be secure. So he will wage brief victorious wars, and not only spare his own nation, but the nation of the enemy, since in a short war the loss is less on both sides than in a long war. And so from evil will come good."

And how, asks Huvelius, are such wars to be waged? The wise prince, he replies, will begin by assuming the enemy to be infinitely corruptible and infinitely stupid, since stupidity and corruption are the chief characteristics of man. So the prince will make himself friends in the very councils of his enemy, and also amongst the populace, bribing the wealthy by proffering to them the opportunity of still greater wealth, and winning the poor by swelling words. "For, contrary to the common opinion, it is the wealthy who are greedy of wealth; while the populace are to be gained by talking to them about liberty, their unknown god. And so much are they enchanted by the words liberty, freedom, and such like, that the wise can go to the poor, rob them of what little they have, dismiss them with a hearty kick, and win their hearts and their votes for ever, if only they will assure them that the treatment which they have received is called liberty."

Guided by these principles, says Huvelius, the wise prince will entrench himself in the country that he desires to conquer; "nay, with but little trouble, he may actually and literally throw his garrisons into the heart of the enemy country before war has begun."

-oOo-

This is a long and tiresome parenthesis; but it is necessary as explaining the long tale which Merritt told his brother-in-law, he having received it from some magnate of the Midlands, who had traveled in Germany. It is probable that the story was suggested in the first place by the passage from Huvelius which I have just quoted.

Merritt knew nothing of the real Huvelius, who was all but a saint; he thought of the Swedish professor as a monster of iniquity, "worse," as he said, "than Neech"—meaning, no doubt, Nietzsche.

So he told the story of how Huvelius had sold his plan to the Germans; a plan for filling England with German soldiers. Land was to be bought in certain suitable and well-considered places, Englishmen were to be bought as the apparent owners of such land, and secret excavations were to be made, till the country was literally undermined. A subterranean Germany, in fact, was to be dug under selected districts of England; there were to be great caverns, underground cities, well drained, well ventilated, supplied with water, and in these places vast stores both of food and of munitions were to be accumulated, year after year, till "the Day" dawned. And then, warned in time, the secret garrison would leave shops, hotels, offices, villas, and vanish underground, ready to begin their work of bleeding England at the heart.

"That's what Henson told me," said Merritt at the end of his long story. "Henson, head of the Buckley Iron and Steel Syndicate. He has been a lot in Germany."

"Well," said Lewis, "of course, it may be so. If it is so, it is terrible beyond words."

Indeed, he found something horribly plausible in the story. It was an extraordinary plan, of course; an unheard of scheme; but it did not seem impossible. It was the Trojan Horse on a gigantic scale; indeed, he reflected, the story of the horse with the warriors concealed within it which was dragged into the heart of Troy by the deluded Trojans themselves might be taken as a prophetic parable of what had happened to England—if Henson's theory were well founded. And this theory certainly squared with what one had heard of German preparations in Belgium and in France: emplacements for guns ready for the invader, German manufactories which were really German forts on Belgian soil, the caverns by the Aisne made ready for the cannon; indeed, Lewis thought he remembered something about suspicious concrete tennis-courts on the heights commanding London. But a German army hidden under English ground! It was a thought to chill the stoutest heart.

And it seemed from that wonder of the burning tree, that the enemy mysteriously and terribly present at Midlingham, was present also in Meirion. Lewis, thinking of the country as he knew it, of its wild and desolate hillsides, its deep woods, its wastes and solitary places, could not but confess that no more fit region could be found for the deadly enterprise of secret men. Yet, he thought again, there was but little harm to be done in Meirion to the armies of England or to their munitionment. They were working for panic terror? Possibly that might be so; but the camp under the Highway? That should be their first object, and no harm had been done there.

Lewis did not know that since the panic of the horses men had died terribly in that camp; that it was now a fortified place, with a deep, broad trench, a thick tangle of savage barbed wire about it, and a machine-gun planted at each corner.

CHAPTER VIII
What Mr. Merritt Found

Mr. Merritt began to pick up his health and spirits a good deal. For the first morning or two of his stay at the doctor's he contented himself with a very comfortable deck chair close to the house, where he sat under the shade of an old mulberry tree beside his wife and watched the bright sunshine on the green lawns, on the creamy crests of the waves, on the headlands of that glorious coast, purple even from afar with the imperial glow of the heather, on the white farmhouses gleaming in the sunlight, high over the sea, far from any turmoil, from any troubling of men.

The sun was hot, but the wind breathed all the while gently, incessantly, from the east, and Merritt, who had come to this quiet place, not only from dismay, but from the stifling and oily airs of the smoky Midland town, said that that east wind, pure and clear and like well water from the rock, was new life to him. He ate a capital dinner, at the end of his first day at Porth and took rosy views. As to what they had been talking about the night before, he said to Lewis, no doubt there must be trouble of some sort, and perhaps bad trouble; still, Kitchener would soon put it all right.

So things went on very well. Merritt began to stroll about the garden, which was full of the comfortable spaces, groves, and surprises that only country gardens know. To the right of one of the terraces he found an arbor or summer-house covered with white roses, and he was as pleased as if he had discovered the Pole. He spent a whole day there, smoking and lounging and reading a rubbishy sensational story, and declared that the Devonshire roses had taken many years off his age. Then on the other side of the garden there was a filbert grove that he had never explored on any of his former visits; and again there was a find. Deep in the shadow of the filberts was a bubbling well, issuing from rocks, and all manner of green, dewy ferns growing about it and above it, and an angelica springing beside it. Merritt knelt on his knees, and hollowed his hand and drank the well water. He said (over his port) that night that if all water were like the water of the filbert well the world would turn to teetotalism. It takes a townsman to relish the manifold and exquisite joys of the country.

It was not till he began to venture abroad that Merritt found that something was lacking of the old rich peace that used to dwell in Meirion. He had a favorite walk which he never neglected, year after year. This walk led along the cliffs towards Meiros, and then one could turn inland and return to Porth by deep winding lanes that went over the Allt. So Merritt set out early one morning and got as far as a sentry-box at the foot of the path that led up to the cliff. There was a sentry pacing up and down in front of the box, and he called on Merritt to produce his pass, or to turn back to the main road. Merritt was a good deal put out, and asked the doctor about this strict guard. And the doctor was surprised.

"I didn't know they had put their bar up there," he said. "I suppose it's wise. We are certainly in the far West here; still, the Germans might slip round and raid us and do a lot of damage just because Meirion is the last place we should expect them to go for."

"But there are no fortifications, surely, on the cliff?"

"Oh, no; I never heard of anything of the kind there."

"Well, what's the point of forbidding the public to go on the cliff, then? I can quite understand putting a sentry on the top to keep a look-out for the enemy. What I don't understand is a sentry at the bottom who can't keep a look-out for anything, as he can't see the sea. And why warn the public off the cliffs? I couldn't facilitate a German landing by standing on Pengareg, even if I wanted to."

"It is curious," the doctor agreed. "Some military reasons, I suppose."

He let the matter drop, perhaps because the matter did not affect him. People who live in the country all the year round, country doctors certainly, are little given to desultory walking in search of the picturesque.

Lewis had no suspicion that sentries whose object was equally obscure were being dotted all over the country. There was a sentry, for example, by the quarry at Llanfihangel, where the dead woman and the dead sheep had been found some weeks before. The path by the quarry was used a good deal, and its closing would have inconvenienced the people of the neighborhood very considerably. But the sentry had his box by the side of the track and had his orders to keep everybody strictly to the path, as if the quarry were a secret fort.

It was not known till a month or two ago that one of these sentries was himself a victim of the terror. The men on duty at this place were given certain very strict orders, which from the nature of the case, must have seemed to them unreasonable. For old soldiers, orders are orders; but here was a young bank clerk, scarcely in training for a couple of months, who had not begun to appreciate the necessity of hard, literal obedience to an order which seemed to him meaningless. He found himself on a remote and lonely hillside, he had not the faintest notion that his every movement was watched; and he disobeyed a certain instruction that had been given him. The post was found deserted by the relief; the sentry's dead body was found at the bottom of the quarry.

This by the way; but Mr. Merritt discovered again and again that things happened to hamper his walks and his wanderings. Two or three miles from Porth there is a great marsh made by the Afon river before it falls into the sea, and here Merritt had been accustomed to botanize mildly. He had learned pretty accurately the causeways of solid ground that lead through the sea of swamp and ooze and soft yielding soil, and he set out one hot afternoon determined to make a thorough exploration of the marsh, and this time to find that rare Bog Bean, that he felt sure, must grow somewhere in its wide extent.

He got into the by-road that skirts the marsh, and to the gate which he had always used for entrance.

There was the scene as he had known it always, the rich growth of reeds and flags and rushes, the mild black cattle grazing on the "islands" of firm turf, the scented procession of the meadowsweet, the royal glory of the loosestrife, flaming pennons, crimson and golden, of the giant dock.

But they were bringing out a dead man's body through the gate.

A laboring man was holding open the gate on the marsh. Merritt, horrified, spoke to him and asked who it was, and how it had happened.

"They do say he was a visitor at Porth. Somehow he has been drowned in the marsh, whatever."

"But it's perfectly safe. I've been all over it a dozen times."

"Well, indeed, we did always think so. If you did slip by accident, like, and fall into the water, it was not so deep; it was easy enough to climb out again. And this gentleman was quite young, to look at him, poor man; and he has come to Meirion for his pleasure and holiday and found his death in it!"

"Did he do it on purpose? Is it suicide?"

"They say he had no reasons to do that."

Here the sergeant of police in charge of the party interposed, according to orders, which he himself did not understand.

"A terrible thing, sir, to be sure, and a sad pity; and I am sure this is not the sort of sight you have come to see down in Meirion this beautiful summer. So don't you think, sir, that it would be more pleasant like, if you would leave us to this sad business of ours? I have heard many gentlemen staying in Porth say that there is nothing to beat the view from the hill over there, not in the whole of Wales."

Every one is polite in Meirion, but somehow Merritt understood that, in English, this speech meant "move on."

Merritt moved back to Porth—he was not in the humor for any idle, pleasurable strolling after so dreadful a meeting with death. He made some inquiries in the town about the dead man, but nothing seemed known of him. It was said that he had been on his honeymoon, that he had been staying at the Porth Castle Hotel; but the people of the hotel declared that they had never heard of such a person. Merritt got the local paper at the end of the week; there was not a word in it of any fatal accident in the marsh. He met the sergeant of police in the street. That officer touched his helmet with the utmost politeness and a "hope you are enjoying yourself, sir; indeed you do look a lot better already"; but as to the poor man who was found drowned or stifled in the marsh, he knew nothing.

The next day Merritt made up his mind to go to the marsh to see whether he could find anything to account for so strange a death. What he found was a man with an armlet standing by the gate. The armlet had the letters "C.W." on it, which are understood to mean Coast Watcher. The Watcher "said he had strict instructions to keep everybody away from the marsh. Why? He didn't know, but some said that the river was changing its course since the new railway embankment was built, and the marsh had become dangerous to people who didn't know it thoroughly.

"Indeed, sir," he added, "it is part of my orders not to set foot on the other side of that gate myself, not for one scrag-end of a minute."

Merritt glanced over the gate incredulously. The marsh looked as it had always looked; there was plenty of sound, hard ground to walk on; he could see the track that he used to follow as firm as ever. He did not believe in the story of the changing course of the river, and Lewis said he had never heard of anything of the kind. But Merritt had put the question in the middle of general conversation; he had not led up to it from any discussion of the death in the marsh, and so the doctor was taken unawares. If he had known of the connection in Merritt's mind between the alleged changing of the Afon's course and the tragical event in the marsh, no doubt he would have confirmed the official explanation. He was, above all things, anxious to prevent his sister and her husband from finding out that the invisible hand of terror that ruled at Midlingham was ruling also in Meirion.

Lewis himself had little doubt that the man who was found dead in the marsh had been struck down by the secret agency, whatever it was, that had already accomplished so much of evil; but it was a chief part of the terror that no one knew for certain that this or that particular event was to be ascribed to it. People do occasionally fall over cliffs through their own carelessness, and as the case of Garcia, the Spanish sailor, showed, cottagers and their wives and children are now and then the victims of savage and purposeless violence. Lewis had never wandered about the marsh himself; but Remnant had pottered round it and about it, and declared that the man who met his death there—his name was never known, in Porth at all events—must either have committed suicide by deliberately lying prone in the ooze and stifling himself, or else must have been held down in it. There were no details available, so it was clear that the authorities had classified this death with the others; still, the man might have committed suicide, or he might have had a sudden seizure and fallen in the slimy water face-downwards. And so on: it was possible to believe that case A or B or C was in the category of ordinary accidents or ordinary crimes. But it was not possible to believe that A and B and C were all in that category. And thus it was to the end, and thus it is now. We know that the terror reigned, and how it reigned, but there were many dreadful events ascribed to its rule about which there must always be room for doubt.

For example, there was the case of the Mary Ann, the rowing-boat which came to grief in so strange a manner, almost under Merritt's eyes. In my opinion he was quite wrong in associating the sorry fate of the boat and her occupants with a system of signaling by flashlights which he detected or thought that he detected, on the afternoon in which the Mary Ann was capsized. I believe his signaling theory to be all nonsense, in spite of the naturalized German governess who was lodging with her employers in the suspected house. But, on the other hand, there is no doubt in my own mind that the boat was overturned and those in it drowned by the work of the terror.

CHAPTER IX
The Light on the Water

Let it be noted carefully that so far Merritt had not the slightest suspicion that the terror of Midlingham was quick over. Meirion. Lewis had watched and shepherded him carefully. He had let out no suspicion of what had happened in Meirion, and before taking his brother-in-law to the club he had passed round a hint among the members. He did not tell the truth about Midlingham—and here again is a point of interest, that as the terror deepened the general public cooperated voluntarily, and, one would say, almost subconsciously, with the authorities in concealing what they knew from one another—but he gave out a desirable portion of the truth: that his brother-in-law was "nervy," not by any means up to the mark, and that it was therefore desirable that he should be spared the knowledge of the intolerable and tragic mysteries which were being enacted all about them.

"He knows about that poor fellow who was found in the marsh," said Lewis, "and he has a kind of vague suspicion that there is something out of the common about the case; but no more than that."

"A clear case of suggested, or rather commanded suicide," said Remnant. "I regard it as a strong confirmation of my theory."

"Perhaps so," said the doctor, dreading lest he might have to hear about the Z Ray all over again. "But please don't let anything out to him; I want him to get built up thoroughly before he goes back to Midlingham."

Then, on the other hand, Merritt was as still as death about the doings of the Midlands; he hated to think of them, much more to speak of them; and thus, as I say, he and the men at the Porth Club kept their secrets from one another; and thus, from the beginning to the end of the terror, the links were not drawn together. In many cases, no doubt, A and B met every day and talked familiarly, it may be confidentially, on other matters of all sorts, each having in his possession half of the truth, which he concealed from the other. So the two halves were never put together to make a whole.

Merritt, as the doctor guessed, had a kind of uneasy feeling—it scarcely amounted to a suspicion—as to the business of the marsh; chiefly because he thought the official talk about the railway embankment and the course of the river rank nonsense. But finding that nothing more happened, he let the matter drop from his mind, and settled himself down to enjoy his holiday.

He found to his delight that there were no sentries or watchers to hinder him from the approach to Larnac Bay, a delicious cove, a place where the ashgrove and the green meadow and the glistening bracken sloped gently down to red rocks and firm yellow sands. Merritt remembered a rock that formed a comfortable seat, and here he established himself of a golden afternoon, and gazed at the blue of the sea and the crimson bastions and bays of the coast as it bent inward to Sarnau and swept out again southward to the odd-shaped promontory called the Dragon's Head. Merritt gazed on, amused by the antics of the porpoises who were tumbling and splashing and gamboling a little way out at sea, charmed by the pure and radiant air that was so different from the oily smoke that often stood for heaven at Midlingham, and charmed, too, by the white farmhouses dotted here and there on the heights of the curving coast.

Then he noticed a little row-boat at about two hundred yards from the shore. There were two or three people aboard, he could not quite make out how many, and they seemed to be doing something with a line; they were no doubt fishing, and Merritt (who disliked fish) wondered how people could spoil such an afternoon, such a sea, such pellucid and radiant air by trying to catch white, flabby, offensive, evil-smelling creatures that would be excessively nasty when cooked. He puzzled over this problem and turned away from it to the contemplation of the crimson headlands. And then he says that he noticed that signaling was going on. Flashing lights of intense brilliance, he declares, were coming from one of those farms on the heights of the coast; it was as if white fire was spouting from it. Merritt was certain, as the light appeared and disappeared, that some message was being sent, and he regretted that he knew nothing of heliography. Three short flashes, a long and very brilliant flash, then two short flashes. Merritt fumbled in his pocket for pencil and paper so that he might record these signals, and, bringing his eyes down to the sea level, he became aware, with amazement and horror, that the boat had disappeared. All that he could see was some vague, dark object far to westward, running out with the tide.

Now it is certain, unfortunately, that the Mary Ann was capsized and that two schoolboys and the sailor in charge were drowned. The bones of the boat were found amongst the rocks far along the coast, and the three bodies were also washed ashore. The sailor could not swim at all, the boys only a little, and it needs an exceptionally fine swimmer to fight against the outward suck of the tide as it rushes past Pengareg Point.

But I have no belief whatever in Merritt's theory. He held (and still holds, for all I know), that the flashes of light which he saw coming from Penyrhaul, the farmhouse oh the height, had some connection with the disaster to the Mary Ann. When it was ascertained that a family were spending their summer at the farm, and that the governess was a German, though a long naturalized German, Merritt could not see that there was anything left to argue about, though there might be many details to discover. But, in my opinion, all this was a mere mare's nest; the flashes of brilliant light were caused, no doubt, by the sun lighting up one window of the farmhouse after the other.

Still, Merritt was convinced from the very first, even before the damning circumstance of the German governess was brought to light; and on the evening of the disaster, as Lewis and he sat together after dinner, he was endeavoring to put what he called the common sense of the matter to the doctor.

"If you hear a shot," said Merritt, "and you see a man fall, you know pretty well what killed him."

There was a flutter of wild wings in the room. A great moth beat to and fro and dashed itself madly against the ceiling, the walls, the glass bookcase. Then a sputtering sound, a momentary dimming of the lamp. The moth had succeeded in its mysterious quest.

"Can you tell me," said Lewis as if he were answering Merritt, "why moths rush into the flame?"

-oOo-

Lewis had put his question as to the strange habits of the common moth to Merritt with the deliberate intent of closing the debate on death by heliograph. The query was suggested, of course, by the incident of the moth in the lamp, and Lewis thought that he had said, "Oh, shut up!" in a somewhat elegant manner. And, in fact Merritt looked dignified, remained silent, and helped himself to port.

That was the end that the doctor had desired. He had no doubt in his own mind that the affair of the Mary Ann was but one more item in the long account of horrors that grew larger almost with every day; and he was in no humor to listen to wild and futile theories as to the manner in which the disaster had been accomplished. Here was a proof that the terror that was upon them was mighty not only on the land but on the waters; for Lewis could not see that the boat could have been attacked by any ordinary means of destruction. From Merritt's story, it must have been in shallow water. The shore of Larnac Bay shelves very gradually, and the Admiralty charts showed the depth of water two hundred yards out to be only two fathoms; this would be too shallow for a submarine. And it could not have been shelled, and it could not have been torpedoed; there was no explosion. The disaster might have been due to carelessness; boys, he considered, will play the fool anywhere, even in a boat; but he did not think so; the sailor would have stopped them. And, it may be mentioned, that the two boys were as a matter of fact extremely steady, sensible young fellows, not in the least likely to play foolish tricks of any kind.

Lewis was immersed in these reflections, having successfully silenced his brother-in-law; he was trying in vain to find some clue to the horrible enigma. The Midlingham theory of a concealed German force, hiding in places under the earth, was extravagant enough, and yet it seemed the only solution that approached plausibility; but then again even a subterranean German host would hardly account for this wreckage of a boat, floating on a calm sea. And then what of the tree with the burning in it that had appeared in the garden there a few weeks ago, and the cloud with a burning in it that had shown over the trees of the Midland village?

I think I have, already written something of the probable emotions of the mathematician confronted suddenly with an undoubted two-sided triangle. I said, if I remember, that he would be forced, in decency, to go mad; and I believe that Lewis was very near to this point. He felt himself confronted with an intolerable problem that most instantly demanded solution, and yet, with the same breath, as it were, denied the possibility of there being any solution. People were being killed in an inscrutable manner by some inscrutable means, day after day, and one asked "why" and "how"; and there seemed no answer. In the Midlands, where every kind of munitionment was manufactured, the explanation of German agency was plausible; and even if the subterranean notion was to be rejected as savoring altogether too much of the fairytale, or rather of the sensational romance, yet it was possible that the backbone of the theory was true; the Germans might have planted their agents in some way or another in the midst of our factories. But here in Meirion, what serious effect could be produced by the casual and indiscriminate slaughter of a couple of schoolboys in a boat, of a harmless holiday-maker in a marsh? The creation of an atmosphere of terror and dismay? It was possible, of course, but it hardly seemed tolerable, in spite of the enormities of Louvain and of the Lusitania.

Into these meditations, and into the still dignified silence of Merritt broke the rap on the door of Lewis's man, and those words which harass the ease of the country doctor when he tries to take any ease: "You're wanted in the surgery, if you please, sir." Lewis bustled out, and appeared no more that night.

The doctor had been summoned to a little hamlet on the outskirts of Porth, separated from it by half a mile or three-quarters of road. One dignifies, indeed, this settlement without a name in calling it a hamlet; it was a mere row of four cottages, built about a hundred years ago for the accommodation of the workers in a quarry long since disused. In one of these cottages the doctor found a father and mother weeping and crying out to "doctor bach, doctor bach," and two frightened children, and one little body, still and dead. It was the youngest of the three, little Johnnie, and he was dead.

The doctor found that the child had been asphyxiated. He felt the clothes; they were dry; it was not a case of drowning. He looked at the neck; there was no mark of strangling. He asked the father how it had happened, and father and mother, weeping most lamentably, declared they had no knowledge of how their child had been killed: "unless it was the People that had done it." The Celtic fairies are still malignant. Lewis asked what had happened that evening; where had the child been?

"Was he with his brother and sister? Don't they know anything about it?"

Reduced into some sort of order from its original piteous confusion, this is the story that the doctor gathered.

All three children had been well and happy through the day. They had walked in with the mother, Mrs. Roberts, to Porth on a marketing expedition in the afternoon; they had returned to the cottage, had had their tea, and afterwards played about on the road in front of the house. John Roberts had come home somewhat late from his work, and it was after dusk when the family sat down to supper. Supper over, the three children went out again to play with other children from the cottage next door, Mrs. Roberts telling them that they might have half an hour before going to bed.

The two mothers came to the cottage gates at the same moment and called out to their children to come along and be quick about it. The two small families had been playing on the strip of turf across the road, just by the stile into the fields. The children ran across the road; all of them except Johnnie Roberts. His brother Willie said that just as their mother called them he heard Johnnie cry out:

"Oh, what is that beautiful shiny thing over the stile?"

CHAPTER X
The Child and the Moth

The little Roberts's ran across the road, up the path, and into the lighted room. Then they noticed that Johnnie had not followed them. Mrs. Roberts was doing something in the back kitchen, and Mr. Roberts had gone out to the shed to bring in some sticks for the next morning's fire. Mrs. Roberts heard the children run in and went on with her work. The children whispered to one another that Johnnie would "catch it" when their mother came out of the back room and found him missing; but they expected he would run in through the open door any minute. But six or seven, perhaps ten, minutes passed, and there was no Johnnie. Then the father and mother came into the kitchen together, and saw that their little boy was not there.

They thought it was some small piece of mischief—that the two other children had hidden the boy somewhere in the room: in the big cupboard perhaps.

"What have you done with him then?" said Mrs. Roberts. "Come out, you little rascal, directly in a minute."

There was no little rascal to come out, and Margaret Roberts, the girl, said that Johnnie had not come across the road with them: he must be still playing all by himself by the hedge.

"What did you let him stay like that for?" said Mrs. Roberts. "Can't I trust you for two minutes together? Indeed to goodness, you are all of you more trouble than you are worth." She went to the open door:

"Johnnie! Come you in directly, or you will be sorry for it. Johnnie!"

The poor woman called at the door. She went out to the gate and called there:

"Come you, little Johnnie. Come you, bachgen, there's a good boy. I do see you hiding there."

She thought he must be hiding in the shadow of the hedge, and that he would come running and laughing—"he was always such a happy little fellow"—to her across the road. But no little merry figure danced out of the gloom of the still, dark night; it was all silence.

It was then, as the mother's heart began to chill, though she still called cheerfully to the missing child, that the elder boy told how Johnnie had said there was something beautiful by the stile: "and perhaps he did climb over, and he is running now about the meadow, and has lost his way."

The father got his lantern then, and the whole family went crying and calling about the meadow, promising cakes and sweets and a fine toy to poor Johnnie if he would come to them.

They found the little body, under the ashgrove in the middle of the field. He was quite still and dead, so still that a great moth had settled on his forehead, fluttering away when they lifted him up.

Dr. Lewis heard this story. There was nothing to be done; little to be said to these most unhappy people.

"Take care of the two that you have left to you," said the doctor as he went away. "Don't let them out of your sight if you can help it. It is dreadful times that we are living in."

It is curious to record, that all through these dreadful times the simple little "season" went through its accustomed course at Porth. The war and its consequences had somewhat thinned the numbers of the summer visitors; still a very fair contingent of them occupied the hotels and boarding-houses and lodging-houses and bathed from the old-fashioned machines on one beach, or from the new-fashioned tents on the other, and sauntered in the sun, or lay stretched out in the shade under the trees that grow down almost to the water's edge. Porth never tolerated Ethiopians or shows of any kind on its sands, but "The Rockets" did very well during that summer in their garden entertainment, given in the castle grounds, and the fit-up companies that came to the Assembly Rooms are said to have paid their bills to a woman and to a man.

Porth depends very largely on its midland and northern custom, custom of a prosperous, well-established sort. People who think Llandudno overcrowded and Colwyn Bay too raw and red and new, come year after year to the placid old town in the southwest and delight in its peace; and as I say, they enjoyed themselves much as usual there in the summer of 1915. Now and then they became conscious, as Mr. Merritt became conscious, that they could not wander about quite in the old way; but they accepted sentries and coast-watchers and people who politely pointed out the advantages of seeing the view from this point rather than from that as very necessary consequences of the dreadful war that was being waged; nay, as a Manchester man said, after having been turned back from his favorite walk to Castell Coch, it was gratifying to think that they were so well looked after.

"So far as I can see," he added, "there's nothing to prevent a submarine from standing out there by Ynys Sant and landing half a dozen men in a collapsible boat in any of these little coves. And pretty fools we should look, shouldn't we, with our throats cut on the sands; or carried back to Germany in the submarine?" He tipped the coast-watcher half-a-crown.

"That's right, lad," he said, "you give us the tip."

Now here was a strange thing. The north-countryman had his thoughts on elusive submarines and German raiders; the watcher had simply received instructions to keep people off the Castell Coch fields, without reason assigned. And there can be no doubt that the authorities themselves, while they marked out the fields as in the "terror zone," gave their orders in the dark and were themselves profoundly in the dark as to the manner of the slaughter that had been done there; for if they had understood what had happened, they would have understood also that their restrictions were useless.

The Manchester man was warned off his walk about ten days after Johnnie Roberts's death. The Watcher had been placed at his post because, the night before, a young farmer had been found by his wife lying in the grass close to the Castle, with no scar on him, nor any mark of violence, but stone dead.

The wife of the dead man, Joseph Cradock, finding her husband lying motionless on the dewy turf, went white and stricken up the path to the village and got two men who bore the body to the farm. Lewis was sent for, and knew, at once when he saw the dead man that he had perished in the way that the little Roberts boy had perished—whatever that awful way might be. Cradock had been asphyxiated; and here again there was no mark of a grip on the throat. It might have been a piece of work by Burke and Hare, the doctor reflected; a pitch plaster might have been clapped over the man's mouth and nostrils and held there.

Then a thought struck him; his brother-in-law had talked of a new kind of poison gas that was said to be used against the munition workers in the Midlands: was it possible that the deaths of the man and the boy were due to some such instrument? He applied his tests but could find no trace of any gas having been employed. Carbonic acid gas? A man could not be killed with that in the open air; to be fatal that required a confined space, such a position as the bottom of a huge vat or of a well.

He did not know how Cradock had been killed; he confessed it to himself. He had been suffocated; that was all he could say.

It seemed that the man had gone out at about half-past nine to look after some beasts. The field in which they were was about five minutes' walk from the house. He told his wife he would be back in a quarter of an hour or twenty minutes. He did not return, and when he had been gone for three-quarters of an hour Mrs. Cradock went out to look for him. She went into the field where the beasts were, and everything seemed all right, but there was no trace of Cradock. She called out; there was no answer.

Now the meadow in which the cattle were pastured is high ground; a hedge divides it from the fields which fall gently down to the castle and the sea. Mrs. Cradock hardly seemed able to say why, having failed to find her husband among his beasts, she turned to the path which led to Castell Coch. She said at first that she had thought that one of the oxen might have broken through the hedge and strayed, and that Cradock had perhaps gone after it. And then, correcting herself, she said:

"There was that; and then there was something else that I could not make out at all. It seemed to me that the hedge did look different from usual. To be sure, things do look different at night, and there was a bit of sea mist about, but somehow it did look odd to me, and I said to myself, 'have I lost my way, then?'"

She declared that the shape of the trees in the hedge appeared to have changed, and besides, it had a look "as if it was lighted up, somehow," and so she went on towards the stile to see what all this could be, and when she came near everything was as usual. She looked over the stile and called and hoped to see her husband coming towards her or to hear his voice; but there was no answer, and glancing down the path she saw, or thought she saw, some sort of brightness on the ground, "a dim sort of light like a bunch of glow-worms in a hedge-bank.

"And so I climbed over the stile and went down the path, and the light seemed to melt away; and there was my poor husband lying on his back, saying not a word to me when I spoke to him and touched him."

-oOo-

So for Lewis the terror blackened and became altogether intolerable, and others, he perceived, felt as he did. He did not know, he never asked whether the men at the club had heard of these deaths of the child and the young farmer; but no one spoke of them. Indeed, the change was evident; at the beginning of the terror men spoke of nothing else; now it had become all too awful for ingenious chatter or labored and grotesque theories. And Lewis had received a letter from his brother-in-law at Midlingham; it contained the sentence, "I am afraid Fanny's health has not greatly benefited by her visit to Porth; there are still several symptoms I don't at all like." And this told him, in a phraseology that the doctor and Merritt had agreed upon, that the terror remained heavy in the Midland town.

180

-oOo-

It was soon after the death of Cradock that people began to tell strange tales of a sound that was to be heard of nights about the hills and valleys to the northward of Porth. A man who had missed the last train from Meiros and had been forced to tramp the ten miles between Meiros and Porth seems to have been the first to hear it. He said he had got to the top of the hill by Tredonoc, somewhere between half-past ten and eleven, when he first noticed an odd noise that he could not make out at all; it was like a shout, a long, drawn-out, dismal wail coming from a great way off, faint with distance. He stopped to listen, thinking at first that it might be owls hooting in the woods; but it was different, he said, from that: it was a long cry, and then there was silence and then it began over again. He could make nothing of it, and feeling frightened, he did not quite know of what, he walked on briskly and was glad to see the lights of Porth station.

He told his wife of this dismal sound that night, and she told the neighbors, and most of them thought that it was "all fancy"—or drink, or the owls after all. But the night after, two or three people, who had been to some small merrymaking in a cottage just off the Meiros road, heard the sound as they were going home, soon after ten. They, too, described it as a long, wailing cry, indescribably dismal in the stillness of the autumn night; "like the ghost of a voice," said one; "as if it came up from the bottom of the earth," said another.

CHAPTER XI
At Treff Loyne Farm

Let it be remembered, again and again, that, all the while that the terror lasted, there was no common stock of information as to the dreadful things that were being done. The press had not said one word upon it, there was no criterion by which the mass of the people could separate fact from mere vague rumor, no test by which ordinary misadventure or disaster could be distinguished from the achievements of the secret and awful force that was at work.

And so with every event of the passing day. A harmless commercial traveler might show himself in the course of his business in the tumbledown main street of Meiros and find himself regarded with looks of fear and suspicion as a possible worker of murder, while it is likely enough that the true agents of the terror went quite unnoticed. And since the real nature of all this mystery of death was unknown, it followed easily that the signs and warnings and omens of it were all the more unknown. Here was horror, there was horror; but there was no links to join one horror with another; no common basis of knowledge from which the connection between this horror and that horror might be inferred.

So there was no one who suspected at all that this dismal and hollow sound that was now heard of nights in the region to the north of Porth, had any relation at all to the case of the little girl who went out one afternoon to pick purple flowers and never returned, or to the case of the man whose body was taken out of the peaty slime of the marsh, or to the case of Cradock, dead in his fields, with a strange glimmering of light about his body, as his wife reported. And it is a question as to how far the rumor of this melancholy, nocturnal summons got abroad at all. Lewis heard of it, as a country doctor hears of most things, driving up and down the lanes, but he heard of it without much interest, with no sense that it was in any sort of relation to the terror. Remnant had been given the story of the hollow and echoing voice of the darkness in a colored and picturesque form; he employed a Tredonoc man to work in his garden once a week. The gardener had not heard the summons himself, but he knew a man who had done so.

"Thomas Jenkins, Pentoppin, he did put his head out late last night to see what the weather was like, as he was cutting a field of corn the next day, and he did tell me that when he was with the Methodists in Cardigan he did never hear no singing eloquence in the chapels that was like to it. He did declare it was like a wailing of Judgment Day."

Remnant considered the matter, and was inclined to think that the sound must be caused by a subterranean inlet of the sea; there might be, he supposed, an imperfect or half-opened or tortuous blow-hole in the Tredonoc woods, and the noise of the tide, surging up below, might very well produce that effect of a hollow wailing, far away. But neither he nor any one else paid much attention to the matter; save the few who heard the call at dead of night, as it echoed awfully over the black hills.

The sound had been heard for three or perhaps four nights, when the people coming out of Tredonoc church after morning service on Sunday noticed that there was a big yellow sheepdog in the churchyard. The dog, it appeared, had been waiting for the congregation; for it at once attached itself to them, at first to the whole body, and then to a group of half a dozen who took the turning to the right. Two of these presently went off over the fields to their respective houses, and four strolled on in the leisurely Sunday-morning manner of the country, and these the dog followed, keeping to heel all the time. The men were talking hay, corn and markets and paid no attention to the animal, and so they strolled along the autumn lane till they came to a gate in the hedge, whence a roughly made farm road went through the fields, and dipped down into the woods and to Treff Loyne farm.

Then the dog became like a possessed creature. He barked furiously. He ran up to one of the men and looked up at him, "as if he were begging for his life," as the man said, and then rushed to the gate and stood by it, wagging his tail and barking at intervals. The men stared and laughed.

"Whose dog will that be?" said one of them.

"It will be Thomas Griffith's, Treff Loyne," said another.

"Well, then, why doesn't he go home? Go home then!" He went through the gesture of picking up a stone from the road and throwing it at the dog. "Go home, then! Over the gate with you."

But the dog never stirred. He barked and whined and ran up to the men and then back to the gate. At last he came to one of them, and crawled and abased himself on the ground and then took hold of the man's coat and tried to pull him in the direction of the gate. The farmer shook the dog off, and the four went on their way; and the dog stood in the road and watched them and then put up its head and uttered a long and dismal howl that was despair.

The four farmers thought nothing of it; sheepdogs in the country are dogs to look after sheep, and their whims and fancies are not studied. But the yellow dog—he was a kind of degenerate collie—haunted the Tredonoc lanes from that day. He came to a cottage door one night and scratched at it, and when it was opened lay down, and then, barking, ran to the garden gate and waited, entreating, as it seemed, the cottager to follow him. They drove him away and again he gave that long howl of anguish. It was almost as bad, they said, as the noise that they had heard a few nights before. And then it occurred to somebody, so far as I can make out with no particular reference to the odd conduct of the Treff Loyne sheepdog, that Thomas Griffith had not been seen for some time past. He had missed market day at Porth, he had not been at Tredonoc church, where he was a pretty regular attendant on Sunday; and then, as heads were put together, it appeared that nobody had seen any of the Griffith family for days and days.

Now in a town, even in a small town, this process of putting heads together is a pretty quick business. In the country, especially in a countryside of wild lands and scattered and lonely farms and cottages, the affair takes time. Harvest was going on, everybody was busy in his own fields, and after the long day's hard work neither the farmer nor his men felt inclined to stroll about in search of news or gossip. A harvester at the day's end is ready for supper and sleep and for nothing else.

And so it was late in that week when it was discovered that Thomas Griffith and all his house had vanished from this world.

I have often been reproached for my curiosity over questions which are apparently of slight importance, or of no importance at all. I love to inquire, for instance, into the question of the visibility of a lighted candle at a distance. Suppose, that is, a candle lighted on a still, dark night in the country; what is the greatest distance at which you can see that there is a light at all? And then as to the human voice; what is its carrying distance, under good conditions, as a mere sound, apart from any matter of making out words that may be uttered?

They are trivial questions, no doubt, but they have always interested me, and the latter point has its application to the strange business of Treff Loyne. That melancholy and hollow sound, that wailing summons that appalled the hearts of those who heard it was, indeed, a human voice, produced in a very exceptional manner; and it seems to have been heard at points varying from a mile and a half to two miles from the farm. I do not know whether this is anything extraordinary; I do not know whether the peculiar method of production was calculated to increase or to diminish the carrying power of the sound.

Again and again I have laid emphasis in this story of the terror on the strange isolation of many of the farms and cottages in Meirion. I have done so in the effort to convince the townsman of something that he has never known. To the Londoner a house a quarter of a mile from the outlying suburban lamp, with no other dwelling within two hundred yards, is a lonely house, a place to fit with ghosts and mysteries and terrors. How can he understand then, the true loneliness of the white farmhouses of Meirion, dotted here and there, for the most part not even on the little lanes and deep winding byways, but set in the very heart of the fields, or alone on huge bastioned headlands facing the sea, and whether on the high verge of the sea or on the hills or in the hollows of the inner country, hidden from the sight of men, far from the sound of any common call. There is Penyrhaul, for example, the farm from which the foolish Merritt thought he saw signals of light being made: from seaward it is of course, widely visible; but from landward, owing partly to the curving and indented configuration of the bay, I doubt whether any other habitation views it from a nearer distance than three miles.

And of all these hidden and remote places, I doubt if any is so deeply buried as Treff Loyne. I have little or no Welsh, I am sorry to say, but I suppose that the name is corrupted from Trellwyn, or Tref-y-llwyn, "the place in the grove," and, indeed, it lies in the very heart of dark, overhanging woods. A deep, narrow valley runs down from the high lands of the Allt, through these woods, through steep hillsides of bracken and gorse, right down to the great marsh, whence Merritt saw the dead man being carried. The valley lies away from any road, even from that by-road, little better than a bridlepath, where the four farmers, returning from church were perplexed by the strange antics of the sheepdog. One cannot say that the valley is overlooked, even from a distance, for so narrow is it that the ashgroves that rim it on either side seem to meet and shut it in. I, at all events, have never found any high place from which Treff Loyne is visible; though, looking down from the Allt, I have seen blue wood-smoke rising from its hidden chimneys.

Such was the place, then, to which one September afternoon a party went up to discover what had happened to Griffith and his family. There were half a dozen farmers, a couple of policemen, and four soldiers, carrying their arms; those last had been lent by the officer commanding at the camp. Lewis, too, was of the party; he had heard by chance that no one knew what had become of Griffith and his family; and he was anxious about a young fellow, a painter, of his acquaintance, who had been lodging at Treff Loyne all the summer.

They all met by the gate of Tredonoc churchyard, and tramped solemnly along the narrow lane; all of them, I think, with some vague discomfort of mind, with a certain shadowy fear, as of men who do not quite know what they may encounter. Lewis heard the corporal and the three soldiers arguing over their orders.

"The Captain says to me," muttered the corporal, "'Don't hesitate to shoot if there's any trouble.' 'Shoot what, sir,' I says. 'The trouble,' says he, and that's all I could get out of him."

The men grumbled in reply; Lewis thought he heard some obscure reference to ratpoison, and wondered what they were talking about.

They came to the gate in the hedge, where the farm road led down to Treff Loyne. They followed this track, roughly made, with grass growing up between its loosely laid stones, down by the hedge from field to wood, till at last they came to the sudden walls of the valley, and the sheltering groves of the ash trees. Here the way curved down the steep hillside, and bent southward, and followed henceforward the hidden hollow of the valley, under the shadow of the trees.

Here was the farm enclosure; the outlying walls of the yard and the barns and sheds and outhouses. One of the farmers threw open the gate and walked into the yard, and forthwith began bellowing at the top of his voice:

"Thomas Griffith! Thomas Griffith! Where be you, Thomas Griffith?"

The rest followed him. The corporal snapped out an order over his shoulder, and there was a rattling metallic noise as the men fixed their bayonets and became in an instant dreadful dealers out of death, in place of harmless fellows with a feeling for beer.

"Thomas Griffith!" again bellowed the farmer.

There was no answer to this summons. But they found poor Griffith lying on his face at the edge of the pond in the middle of the yard. There was a ghastly wound in his side, as if a sharp stake had been driven into his body.

CHAPTER XII
The Letter of Wrath

It was a still September afternoon. No wind stirred in the hanging woods that were dark all about the ancient house of Treff Loyne; the only sound in the dim air was the lowing of the cattle; they had wandered, it seemed, from the fields and had come in by the gate of the farmyard and stood there melancholy, as if they mourned for their dead master. And the horses; four great, heavy, patient-looking beasts they were there too, and in the lower field the sheep were standing, as if they waited to be fed.

"You would think they all knew there was something wrong," one of the soldiers muttered to another. A pale sun showed for a moment and glittered on their bayonets. They were standing about the body of poor, dead Griffith, with a certain grimness growing on their faces and hardening there. Their corporal snapped something at them again; they were quite ready. Lewis knelt down by the dead man and looked closely at the great gaping wound in his side.

"He's been dead a long time," he said. "A week, two weeks, perhaps. He was killed by some sharp pointed weapon. How about the family? How many are there of them? I never attended them."

"There was Griffith, and his wife, and his son Thomas and Mary Griffith, his daughter. And I do think there was a gentleman lodging with them this summer."

That was from one of the farmers. They all looked at one another, this party of rescue, who knew nothing of the danger that had smitten this house of quiet people, nothing of the peril which had brought them to this pass of a farmyard with a dead man in it, and his beasts standing patiently about him, as if they waited for the farmer to rise up and give them their food. Then the party turned to the house. It was an old, sixteenth century building, with the singular round, "Flemish" chimney that is characteristic of Meirion. The walls were snowy with whitewash, the windows were deeply set and stone mullioned, and a solid, stone-tiled porch sheltered the doorway from any winds that might penetrate to the hollow of that hidden valley. The windows were shut tight. There was no sign of any life or movement about the place. The party of men looked at one another, and the churchwarden amongst the farmers, the sergeant of police, Lewis, and the corporal drew together.

"What is it to goodness, doctor?" said the churchwarden.

"I can tell you nothing at all—except that that poor man there has been pierced to the heart," said Lewis.

"Do you think they are inside and they will shoot us?" said another farmer. He had no notion of what he meant by "they," and no one of them knew better than he. They did not know what the danger was, or where it might strike them, or whether it was from without or from within. They stared at the murdered man, and gazed dismally at one another.

"Come!" said Lewis, "we must do something. We must get into the house and see what is wrong."

"Yes, but suppose they are at us while we are getting in," said the sergeant. "Where shall we be then, Doctor Lewis?"

The corporal put one of his men by the gate at the top of the farmyard, another at the gate by the bottom of the farmyard, and told them to challenge and shoot. The doctor and the rest opened the little gate of the front garden and went up to the porch and stood listening by the door. It was all dead silence. Lewis took an ash stick from one of the farmers and beat heavily three times on the old, black, oaken door studded with antique nails.

He struck three thundering blows, and then they all waited. There was no answer from within. He beat again, and still silence. He shouted to the people within, but there was no answer. They all turned and looked at one another, that party of quest and rescue who knew not what they sought, what enemy they were to encounter. There was an iron ring on the door. Lewis turned it but the door stood fast; it was evidently barred and bolted. The sergeant of police called out to open, but again there was no answer.

They consulted together. There was nothing for it but to blow the door open, and some one of them called in a loud voice to anybody that might be within to stand away from the door, or they would be killed. And at this very moment the yellow sheepdog came bounding up the yard from the woods and licked their hands and fawned on them and barked joyfully.

"Indeed now," said one of the farmers; "he did know that there was something amiss. A pity it was, Thomas Williams, that we did not follow him when he implored us last Sunday."

The corporal motioned the rest of the party back, and they stood looking fearfully about them at the entrance to the porch. The corporal disengaged his bayonet and shot into the keyhole, calling out once more before he fired. He shot and shot again; so heavy and firm was the ancient door, so stout its bolts and fastenings. At last he had to fire at the massive hinges, and then they all pushed together and the door lurched open and fell forward. The corporal raised his left hand and stepped back a few paces. He hailed his two men at the top and bottom of the farmyard. They were all right, they said. And so the party climbed and struggled over the fallen door into the passage, and into the kitchen of the farmhouse.

Young Griffith was lying dead before the hearth, before a dead fire of white wood ashes. They went on towards the "parlor," and in the doorway of the room was the body of the artist, Secretan, as if he had fallen in trying to get to the kitchen. Upstairs the two women, Mrs. Griffith and her daughter, a girl of eighteen, were lying together on the bed in the big bedroom, clasped in each others' arms.

They went about the house, searched the pantries, the back kitchen and the cellars; there was no life in it.

"Look!" said Dr. Lewis, when they came back to the big kitchen, "look! It is as if they had been besieged. Do you see that piece of bacon, half gnawed through?"

Then they found these pieces of bacon, cut from the sides on the kitchen wall, here and there about the house. There was no bread in the place, no milk, no water.

"And," said one of the farmers, "they had the best water here in all Meirion. The well is down there in the wood; it is most famous water. The old people did use to call it Ffynnon Teilo; it was Saint Teilo's Well, they did say."

"They must have died of thirst," said Lewis. "They have been dead for days and days."

The group of men stood in the big kitchen and stared at one another, a dreadful perplexity in their eyes. The dead were all about them, within the house and without it; and it was in vain to ask why they had died thus. The old man had been killed with the piercing thrust of some sharp weapon; the rest had perished, it seemed probable, of thirst; but what possible enemy was this that besieged the farm and shut in its inhabitants? There was no answer.

The sergeant of police spoke of getting a cart and taking the bodies into Porth, and Dr. Lewis went into the parlor that Secretan had used as a sitting-room, intending to gather any possessions or effects of the dead artist that he might find there. Half a dozen portfolios were piled up in one corner, there were some books on a side table, a fishing-rod and basket behind the door—that seemed all. No doubt there would be clothes and such matters upstairs, and Lewis was about to rejoin the rest of the party in the kitchen, when he looked down at some scattered papers lying with the books on the side table. On one of the sheets he read to his astonishment the words: "Dr. James Lewis, Porth." This was written in a staggering trembling scrawl, and examining the other leaves he saw that they were covered with writing.

The table stood in a dark corner of the room, and Lewis gathered up the sheets of paper and took them to the window-ledge and began to read, amazed at certain phrases that had caught his eye. But the manuscript was in disorder; as if the dead man who had written it had not been equal to the task of gathering the leaves into their proper sequence; it was some time before the doctor had each page in its place. This was the statement that he read, with ever-growing wonder, while a couple of the farmers were harnessing one of the horses in the yard to a cart, and the others were bringing down the dead women.

-oOo-

"I do not think that I can last much longer. We shared out the last drops of water a long time ago. I do not know how many days ago. We fall asleep and dream and walk about the house in our dreams, and I am often not sure whether I am awake or still dreaming, and so the days and nights are confused in my mind. I awoke not long ago, at least I suppose I awoke and found I was lying in the passage. I had a confused feeling that I had had an awful dream which seemed horribly real, and I thought for a moment what a relief it was to know that it wasn't true, whatever it might have been. I made up my mind to have a good long walk to freshen myself up, and then I looked round and found that I had been lying on the stones of the passage; and it all came back to me. There was no walk for me.

"I have not seen Mrs. Griffith or her daughter for a long while. They said they were going upstairs to have a rest. I heard them moving about the room at first, now I can hear nothing. Young Griffith is lying in the kitchen, before the hearth. He was talking to himself about the harvest and the weather when I last went into the kitchen. He didn't seem to know I was there, as he went gabbling on in a low voice very fast, and then he began to call the dog, Tiger.

"There seems no hope for any of us. We are in the dream of death...."

Here the manuscript became unintelligible for half a dozen lines. Secretan had written the words "dream of death" three or four times over. He had begun a fresh word and had scratched it out and then followed strange, unmeaning characters, the script, as Lewis thought, of a terrible language. And then the writing became clear, clearer than it was at the beginning of the manuscript, and the sentences flowed more easily, as if the cloud on Secretan's mind had lifted for a while. There was a fresh start, as it were, and the writer began again, in ordinary letter-form:

"DEAR LEWIS,

"I hope you will excuse all this confusion and wandering. I intended to begin a proper letter to you, and now I find all that stuff that you have been reading—if this ever gets into your hands. I have not the energy even to tear it up. If you read it you will know to what a sad pass I had come when it was written. It looks like delirium or a bad dream, and even now, though my mind seems to have cleared up a good deal, I have to hold myself in tightly to be sure that the experiences of the last days in this awful place are true, real things, not a long nightmare from which I shall wake up presently and find myself in my rooms at Chelsea.

"I have said of what I am writing, 'if it ever gets into your hands,' and I am not at all sure that it ever will. If what is happening here is happening everywhere else, then I suppose, the world is coming to an end. I cannot understand it, even now I can hardly believe it. I know that I dream such wild dreams and walk in such mad fancies that I have to look out and look about me to make sure that I am not still dreaming.

"Do you remember that talk we had about two months ago when I dined with you? We got on, somehow or other, to space and time, and I think we agreed that as soon as one tried to reason about space and time one was landed in a maze of contradictions. You said something to the effect that it was very curious but this was just like a dream. 'A man will sometimes wake himself from his crazy dream,' you said, 'by realizing that he is thinking nonsense.' And we both wondered whether these contradictions that one can't avoid if one begins to think of time and space may not really be proofs that the whole of life is a dream, and the moon and the stars bits of nightmare. I have often thought over that lately. I kick at the walls as Dr. Johnson kicked at the stone, to make sure that the things about me are there. And then that other question gets into my mind—is the world really coming to an end, the world as we have always known it; and what on earth will this new world be like? I can't imagine it; it's a story like Noah's Ark and the Flood. People used to talk about the end of the world and fire, but no one ever thought of anything like this.

"And then there's another thing that bothers me. Now and then I wonder whether we are not all mad together in this house. In spite of what I see and know, or, perhaps, I should say, because what I see and know is so impossible, I wonder whether we are not all suffering from a delusion. Perhaps we are our own gaolers, and we are really free to go out and live. Perhaps what we think we see is not there at all. I believe I have heard of whole families going mad together, and I may have come under the influence of the house, having lived in it for the last four months. I know there have been people who have been kept alive by their keepers forcing food down their throats, because they are quite sure that their throats are closed, so that they feel they are unable to swallow a morsel. I wonder now and then whether we are all like this in Treff Loyne; yet in my heart I feel sure that it is not so.

"Still, I do not want to leave a madman's letter behind me, and so I will not tell you the full story of what I have seen, or believe I have seen. If I am a sane man you will be able to fill in the blanks for yourself from your own knowledge. If I am mad, burn the letter and say nothing about it. Or perhaps—and indeed, I am not quite sure—I may wake up and hear Mary Griffith calling to me in her cheerful sing-song that breakfast will be ready 'directly, in a minute,' and I shall enjoy it and walk over to Porth and tell you the queerest, most horrible dream that a man ever had, and ask what I had better take.

"I think that it was on a Tuesday that we first noticed that there was something queer about, only at the time we didn't know that there was anything really queer in what we noticed. I had been out since nine o'clock in the morning trying to paint the marsh, and I found it a very tough job. I came home about five or six o'clock and found the family at Treff Loyne laughing at old Tiger, the sheepdog. He was making short runs from the farmyard to the door of the house, barking, with quick, short yelps. Mrs. Griffith and Miss Griffith were standing by the porch, and the dog would go to them, look in their faces, and then run up the farmyard to the gate, and then look back with that eager yelping bark, as if he were waiting for the women to follow him. Then, again and again, he ran up to them and tugged at their skirts as if he would pull them by main force away from the house.

"Then the men came home from the fields and he repeated this performance. The dog was running all up and down the farmyard, in and out of the barn and sheds yelping, barking; and always with that eager run to the person he addressed, and running away directly, and looking back as, if to see whether we were following him. When the house door was shut and they all sat down to supper, he would give them no peace, till at last they turned him out of doors. And then he sat in the porch and scratched at the door with his claws, barking all the while. When the daughter brought in my meal, she said: 'We can't think what is come to old Tiger, and indeed, he has always been a good dog, too.'

"The dog barked and yelped and whined and scratched at the door all through the evening. They let him in once, but he seemed to have become quite frantic. He ran up to one member of the family after another; his eyes were bloodshot and his mouth was foaming, and he tore at their clothes till they drove him out again into the darkness. Then he broke into a long, lamentable howl of anguish, and we heard no more of him."

CHAPTER XIII
The Last Words of Mr. Secretan

"I slept ill that night I awoke again and again from uneasy M dreams, and I seemed in my sleep to hear strange calls and noises and a sound of murmurs and beatings on the door. There were deep, hollow voices, too, that echoed in my sleep, and when I woke I could hear the autumn wind, mournful, on the hills above us. I started up once with a dreadful scream in my ears; but then the house was all still, and I fell again into uneasy sleep.

"It was soon after dawn when I finally roused myself. The people in the house were talking to each other in high voices, arguing about something that I did not understand.

"'It is those damned gipsies, I tell you,' said old Griffith.

"'What would they do a thing like that for?' asked Mrs. Griffith. 'If it was stealing now—'

"'It is more likely that John Jenkins has done it out of spite,' said the son. 'He said that he would remember you when we did catch him poaching.'"

"They seemed puzzled and angry, so far as I could make out, but not at all frightened. I got up and began to dress. I don't think I looked out of the window. The glass on my dressing-table is high and broad, and the window is small; one would have to poke one's head round the glass to see anything.

"The voices were still arguing downstairs. I heard the old man say, 'Well, here's for a beginning anyhow,' and then the door slammed.

"A minute later the old man shouted, I think, to his son. Then there was a great noise which I will not describe more particularly, and a dreadful screaming and crying inside the house and a sound of rushing feet. They all cried out at once to each other. I heard the daughter crying, 'it is no good, mother, he is dead, indeed they have killed him,' and Mrs. Griffith screaming to the girl to let her go. And then one of them rushed out of the kitchen and shot the great bolts of oak across the door, just as something beat against it with a thundering crash.

"I ran downstairs. I found them all in wild confusion, in an agony of grief and horror and amazement. They were like people who had seen something so awful that they had gone mad.

"I went to the window looking out on the farmyard. I won't tell you all that I saw. But I saw poor old Griffith lying by the pond, with the blood pouring out of his side.

194

"I wanted to go out to him and bring him in. But they told me that he must be stone dead, and such things also that it was quite plain that any one who went out of the house would not live more than a moment. We could not believe it, even as we gazed at the body of the dead man; but it was there. I used to wonder sometimes what one would feel like if one saw an apple drop from the tree and shoot up into the air and disappear. I think I know now how one would feel.

"Even then we couldn't believe that it would last. We were not seriously afraid for ourselves. We spoke of getting out in an hour or two, before dinner anyhow. It couldn't last, because it was impossible. Indeed, at twelve o'clock young Griffith said he would go down to the well by the back way and draw another pail of water. I went to the door and stood by it. He had not gone a dozen yards before they were on him. He ran for his life, and we had all we could do to bar the door in time. And then I began to get frightened.

"Still we could not believe in it. Somebody would come along shouting in an hour or two and it would all melt away and vanish. There could not be any real danger. There was plenty of bacon in the house, and half the weekly baking of loaves and some beer in the cellar and a pound or so of tea, and a whole pitcher of water that had been drawn from the well the night before. We could do all right for the day and in the morning it would have all gone away.

"But day followed day and it was still there. I knew Treff Loyne was a lonely place—that was why I had gone there, to have a long rest from all the jangle and rattle and turmoil of London, that makes a man alive and kills him too. I went to Treff Loyne because it was buried in the narrow valley under the ash trees, far away from any track. There was not so much as a footpath that was near it; no one ever came that way. Young Griffith had told me that it was a mile and a half to the nearest house, and the thought of the silent peace and retirement of the farm used to be a delight to me.

"And now this thought came back without delight, with terror. Griffith thought that a shout might be heard on a still night up away on the Allt, 'if a man was listening for it,' he added, doubtfully. My voice was clearer and stronger than his, and on the second night I said I would go up to my bedroom and call for help through the open window. I waited till it was all dark and still, and looked out through the window before opening it. And then I saw over the ridge of the long barn across the yard what looked like a tree, though I knew there was no tree there. It was a dark mass against the sky, with wide-spread boughs, a tree of thick, dense growth. I wondered what this could be, and I threw open the window, not only because I was going to call for help, but because I wanted to see more clearly what the dark growth over the barn really was.

"I saw in the depth of the dark of it points of fire, and colors in light, all glowing and moving, and the air trembled. I stared out into the night, and the dark tree lifted over the roof of the barn and rose up in the air and floated towards me. I did not move till at the last moment when it was close to the house; and then I saw what it was and banged the window down only just in time. I had to fight, and I saw the tree that was like a burning cloud rise up in the night and sink again and settle over the barn.

"I told them downstairs of this. They sat with white faces, and Mrs. Griffith said that ancient devils were let loose and had come out of the trees and out of the old hills because of the wickedness that was on the earth. She began to, murmur something to herself, something that sounded to me like broken-down Latin.

"I went up to my room again an hour later, but the dark tree swelled over the barn. Another day went by, and at dusk I looked out, but the eyes of fire were watching me. I dared not open the window.

"And then I thought of another plan. There was the great old fireplace, with the round Flemish chimney going high above the house. If I stood beneath it and shouted I thought perhaps the sound might be carried better than if I called out of the window; for all I knew the round chimney might act as a sort of megaphone. Night after night, then, I stood in the hearth and called for help from nine o'clock to eleven. I thought of the lonely place, deep in the valley of the ashtrees, of the lonely hills and lands about it. I thought of the little cottages far away and hoped that my voice might reach to those within them. I thought of the winding lane high on the Allt, and of the few men that came there of nights; but I hoped that my cry might come to one of them.

"But we had drunk up the beer, and we would only let ourselves have water by little drops, and on the fourth night my throat was dry, and I began to feel strange and weak; I knew that all the voice I had in my lungs would hardly reach the length of the field by the farm.

"It was then we began to dream of wells and fountains, and water coming very cold, in little drops, out of rocky places in the middle of a cool wood. We had given up all meals; now and then one would cut a lump from the sides of bacon on the kitchen wall and chew a bit of it, but the saltness was like fire.

"There was a great shower of rain one night. The girl said we might open a window and hold out bowls and basins and catch the rain. I spoke

196

of the cloud with burning eyes. She said 'we will go to the window in the dairy at the back, and one of us can get some water at all events,' She stood up with her basin on the stone slab in the dairy and looked out and heard the plashing of the rain, falling very fast. And she unfastened the catch of the window and had just opened it gently with one hand, for about an inch, and had her basin in the other hand. 'And then,' said she, 'there was something that began to tremble and shudder and shake as it did when we went to the Choral Festival at St. Teilo's, and the organ played, and there was the cloud and the burning close before me.'

"And then we began to dream, as I say. I woke up in my sitting-room one hot afternoon when the sun was shining, and I had been looking and searching in my dream all through the house, and I had gone down to the old cellar that wasn't used, the cellar with the pillars and the vaulted room, with an iron pike in my hand. Something said to me that there was water there, and in my dream I went to a heavy stone by the middle pillar and raised it up, and there beneath was a bubbling well of cold, clear water, and I had just hollowed my hand to drink it when I woke. I went into the kitchen and told young Griffith. I said I was sure there was water there. He shook his head, but he took up the great kitchen poker and we went down to the old cellar. I showed him the stone by the pillar, and he raised it up. But there was no well.

"Do you know, I reminded myself of many people whom I have met in life? I would not be convinced. I was sure that, after all, there was a well there. They had a butcher's cleaver in the kitchen and I took it down to the old cellar and hacked at the ground with it. The others didn't interfere with me. We were getting past that. We hardly ever spoke to one another. Each one would be wandering about the house, upstairs and downstairs, each one of us, I suppose, bent on his own foolish plan and mad design, but we hardly ever spoke. Years ago, I was an actor for a bit, and I remember how it was on first nights; the actors treading softly up and down the wings, by their entrance, their lips moving and muttering over the words of their parts, but without a word for one another. So it was with us. I came upon young Griffith one evening evidently trying to make a subterranean passage under one of the walls of the house. I knew he was mad, as he knew I was mad when he saw me digging for a well in the cellar; but neither said anything to the other.

"Now we are past all this. We are too weak. We dream when we are awake and when we dream we think we wake. Night and day come and go and we mistake one for another; I hear Griffith murmuring to himself about the stars when the sun is high at noonday, and at midnight I have found myself thinking that I walked in bright sunlit meadows beside cold, rushing streams that flowed from high rocks.

"Then at the dawn figures in black robes, carrying lighted tapers in their hands pass slowly about and about; and I hear great rolling organ music that sounds as if some tremendous rite were to begin, and voices crying in an ancient song shrill from the depths of the earth.

"Only a little while ago I heard a voice which sounded as if it were at my very ears, but rang and echoed and resounded as if it were rolling and reverberated from the vault of some cathedral, chanting in terrible modulations. I heard the words quite clearly.

-oOo-

"Incipit liber iræ Domini Dei nostri. (Here beginneth The Book of the Wrath of the Lord our God.)

"And then the voice sang the word Aleph, prolonging it, it seemed through ages, and a light was extinguished as it began the chapter:

"In that day, saith the Lord, there shall be a cloud over the land, and in the cloud a burning and a shape of fire, and out of the cloud shall issue forth my messengers; they shall run all together, they shall not turn aside; this shall be a day of exceeding bitterness, without salvation. And on every high hill, saith the Lord of Hosts, I will set my sentinels, and my armies shall encamp in the place of every valley; in the house that is amongst rushes I will execute judgment, and in vain shall they fly for refuge to the munitions of the rocks. In the groves of the woods, in the places where the leaves are as a tent above them, they shall find the sword of the slayer; and they that put their trust in walled cities shall be confounded. Woe unto the armed man, woe unto him that taketh pleasure in the strength of his artillery, for a little thing shall smite him, and by one that hath no might shall he be brought down into the dust. That which is low shall be set on high; I will make the lamb and the young sheep to be as the lion from the swellings of Jordan; they shall not spare, saith the Lord, and the doves shall be as eagles on the hill Engedi; none shall be found that may abide the onset of their battle.

"Even now I can hear the voice rolling far away, as if it came from the altar of a great church and I stood at the door. There are lights very far away in the hollow of a vast darkness, and one by one they are put out. I hear a voice chanting again with that endless modulation that climbs and aspires to the stars, and shines there, and rushes down to the dark depths of the earth, again to ascend; the word is Zain."

Here the manuscript lapsed again, and finally into utter, lamentable confusion. There were scrawled lines wavering across the page on which Secretan seemed to have been trying to note the unearthly music that swelled in his dying ears. As the scrapes and scratches of ink showed, he had tried hard to begin a new sentence. The pen had dropped at last out of his hand upon the paper, leaving a blot and a smear upon it.

Lewis heard the tramp of feet along the passage; they were carrying out the dead to the cart.

CHAPTER XIV
The End of the Terror

Dr. Lewis maintained that we should never begin to understand the real significance of life until we began to study just those aspects of it which we now dismiss and overlook as utterly inexplicable, and therefore, unimportant.

We were discussing a few months ago the awful shadow of the terror which at length had passed away from the land. I had formed my opinion, partly from observation, partly from certain facts which had been communicated to me, and the pass-words having been exchanged, I found that Lewis had come by very different ways to the same end.

"And yet," he said, "it is not a true end, or rather, it is like all the ends of human inquiry, it leads one to a great mystery. We must confess that what has happened might have happened at any time in the history of the world. It did not happen till a year ago as a matter of fact, and therefore we made up our minds that it never could happen; or, one would better say, it was outside the range even of imagination. But this is our way. Most people are quite sure that the Black Death—otherwise the Plague—will never invade Europe again. They have made up their complacent minds that it was due to dirt and bad drainage. As a matter of fact the Plague had nothing to do with dirt or with drains; and there is nothing to prevent its ravaging England to-morrow. But if you tell people so, they won't believe you. They won't believe in anything that isn't there at the particular moment when you are talking to them. As with the Plague, so with the Terror. We could not believe that such a thing could ever happen. Remnant said, truly enough, that whatever it was, it was outside theory, outside our theory. Flatland cannot believe in the cube or the sphere."

I agreed with all this. I added that sometimes the world was incapable of seeing, much less believing, that which was before its own eyes.

"Look," I said, "at any eighteenth century print of a Gothic cathedral. You will find that the trained artistic eye even could not behold in any true sense the building that was before it. I have seen an old print of Peterborough Cathedral that looks as if the artist had drawn it from a clumsy model, constructed of bent wire and children's bricks.

"Exactly; because Gothic was outside the aesthetic theory (and therefore vision) of the time. You can't believe what you don't see: rather, you can't see what you don't believe. It was so during the time of the Terror. All this bears out what Coleridge said as to the necessity of having the idea before the facts could be of any service to one. Of course, he was right; mere facts, without the correlating idea, are nothing and lead to no conclusion. We had plenty of facts, but we could make nothing of them. I went home at the tail of that dreadful procession from Treff Loyne in a state of mind very near to madness. I heard one of the soldiers saying to the other: 'There's no rat that'll spike a man to the heart, Bill.' I don't know why, but I felt that if I heard any more of such talk as that I should go crazy; it seemed to me that the anchors of reason were parting. I left the party and took the short cut across the fields into Porth. I looked up Davies in the High Street and arranged with him that he should take on any cases I might have that evening, and then I went home and gave my man his instructions to send people on. And then I shut myself up to think it all out—if I could.

"You must not suppose that my experiences of that afternoon had afforded me the slightest illumination. Indeed, if it had not been that I had seen poor old Griffith's body lying pierced in his own farmyard, I think I should have been inclined to accept one of Secretan's hints, and to believe that the whole family had fallen a victim to a collective delusion or hallucination, and had shut themselves up and died of thirst through sheer madness. I think there have been such cases. It's the insanity of inhibition, the belief that you can't do something which you are really perfectly capable of doing. But; I had seen the body of the murdered man and the wound that had killed him.

"Did the manuscript left by Secretan give me no hint? Well, it seemed to me to make confusion worse confounded. You have seen it; you know that in certain places it is evidently mere delirium, the wanderings of a dying mind. How was I to separate the facts from the phantasms—lacking the key to the whole enigma. Delirium is often a sort of cloud-castle, a sort of magnified and distorted shadow of actualities, but it is a very difficult thing, almost an impossible thing, to reconstruct the real house from the distortion of it, thrown on the clouds of the patient's brain. You see, Secretan in writing that extraordinary document almost insisted on the fact that he was not in his proper sense; that for days he had been part asleep, part awake, part delirious. How was one to judge his statement, to separate delirium from fact? In one thing he stood confirmed; you remember he speaks of calling for help up the old chimney of Treff Loyne; that did seem to fit in with the tales of a hollow, moaning cry that had been heard upon the Allt: so far one could take him as a recorder of actual experiences. And I looked in the old cellars of the farm and found a frantic sort of rabbit-hole dug by one of the pillars; again he was confirmed. But what was one to make of that story of the chanting voice, and the letters of the Hebrew alphabet, and the chapter out of some unknown Minor Prophet? When one has the key it is easy enough to sort out the facts, or the hints of facts from the delusions; but I hadn't the key on that September evening. I was forgetting the 'tree' with lights and fires in it; that, I think, impressed me more than anything with the feeling that Secretan's story was, in the main, a true story. I had seen a like appearance down there in my own garden; but what was it?

"Now, I was saying that, paradoxically, it is only by the inexplicable things that life can be explained. We are apt to say, you know, 'a very odd coincidence' and pass the matter by, as if there were no more to be said, or as if that were the end of it. Well, I believe that the only real path lies through the blind alleys."

"How do you mean?"

"Well, this is an instance of what I mean. I told you about Merritt, my brother-in-law, and the capsizing of that boat, the Mary Ann. He had seen, he said, signal lights flashing from one of the farms on the coast, and he was quite certain that the two things were intimately connected as cause and effect. I thought it all nonsense, and I was wondering how I was going to shut him up when a big moth flew into the room through that window, fluttered about, and succeeded in burning itself alive in the lamp. That gave me my cue; I asked Merritt if he knew why moths made for lamps or something of the kind; I thought it would be a hint to him that I was sick of his flashlights and his half-baked theories. So it was—he looked sulky and held his tongue.

"But a few minutes later I was called out by a man who had found his little boy dead in a field near his cottage about an hour before. The child was so still, they said, that a great moth had settled on his forehead and only fluttered away when they lifted up the body. It was absolutely illogical; but it was this odd 'coincidence' of the moth in my lamp and the moth on the dead boy's forehead that first set me on the track. I can't say that it guided me in any real sense; it was more like a great flare of red paint on a wall; it rang up my attention, if I may say so; it was a sort of shock like a bang on the big drum. No doubt Merritt was talking great nonsense that evening so far as his particular instance went; the flashes of light from the farm had nothing to do with the wreck of the boat. But his general principle was sound; when you hear a gun go off and see a man fall it is idle to talk of 'a mere coincidence.' I think a very interesting book might be written on this question: I would call it 'A Grammar of Coincidence.'

"But as you will remember, from having read my notes on the matter, I was called in about ten days later to see a man named Cradock, who had been found in a field near his farm quite dead. This also was at night. His wife found him, and there were some very queer things in her story. She said that the hedge of the field looked as if it were changed; she began to be afraid that she had lost her way and got into the wrong field. Then she said the hedge was lighted up as if there were a lot of glow-worms in it, and when she peered over the stile there seemed to be some kind of glimmering upon the ground, and then the glimmering melted away, and she found her husband's body near where this light had been. Now this man Cradock had been suffocated just as the little boy Roberts had been suffocated, and as that man in the Midlands who took a short cut one night had been suffocated. Then I remembered that poor Johnnie Roberts had called out about 'something shiny' over the stile just before he played truant. Then, on my part, I had to contribute the very remarkable sight I witnessed here, as I looked down over the garden; the appearance as of a spreading tree where I knew there was no such tree, and then the shining and burning of lights and moving colors. Like the poor child and Mrs. Cradock, I had seen something shiny, just as some man in Stratfordshire had seen a dark cloud with points of fire in it floating over the trees. And Mrs. Cradock thought that the shape of the trees in the hedge had changed.

"My mind almost uttered the word that was wanted; but you see the difficulties. This set of circumstances could not, so far as I could see, have any relation with the other circumstances of the Terror. How could I connect all this with the bombs and machine-guns of the Midlands, with the armed men who kept watch about the munition shops by day and night. Then there was the long list of people here who had fallen over the cliffs or into the quarry; there were the cases of the men stifled in the slime of the marshes; there was the affair of the family murdered in front of their cottage on the Highway; there was the capsized Mary Ann. I could not see any thread that could bring all these incidents together; they seemed to me to be hopelessly disconnected. I could not make out any relation between the agency that beat out the brains of the Williams's and the agency, that overturned the boat. I don't know, but I think it's very likely if nothing more had happened that I should have put the whole thing down as an unaccountable series of crimes and accidents which chanced to occur in Meirion in the summer of 1915. Well, of course, that would have been an impossible standpoint in view of certain incidents in Merritt's story. Still, if one is confronted by the insoluble, one lets it go at last. If the mystery is inexplicable, one pretends that there isn't any mystery. That is the justification for what is called free thinking.

"Then came that extraordinary business of Treff Loyne. I couldn't put that on one side. I couldn't pretend that nothing strange or out of the way had happened. There was no getting over it or getting round it. I had seen with my eyes that there was a mystery, and a most horrible mystery. I have forgotten my logic, but one might say that Treff Loyne demonstrated the existence of a mystery in the figure of Death.

"I took it all home, as I have told you, and sat down for the evening before it. It appalled me, not only by its horror, but here again by the discrepancy between its terms. Old Griffith, so far as I could judge, had been killed by the thrust of a pike or perhaps of a sharpened stake: how could one relate this to the burning tree that had floated over the ridge of the barn. It was as if I said to you: 'here is a man drowned, and here is a man burned alive: show that each death was caused by the same agency!' And the moment that I left this particular case of Treff Loyne, and tried to get some light on it from other instances of the Terror, I would think of the man in the midlands who heard the feet of a thousand men rustling in the wood, and their voices as if dead men sat up in their bones and talked. And then I would say to myself, 'and how about that boat overturned in a calm sea?' There seemed no end to it, no hope of any solution.

"It was, I believe, a sudden leap of the mind that liberated me from the tangle. It was quite beyond logic. I went back to that evening when Merritt was boring me with his flashlights, to the moth in the candle, and to the moth on the forehead of poor Johnnie Roberts. There was no sense in it; but I suddenly determined that the child and Joseph Cradock the farmer, and that unnamed Stratfordshire man, all found at night, all asphyxiated, had been choked by vast swarms of moths. I don't pretend even now that this is demonstrated, but I'm sure it's true.

"Now suppose you encounter a swarm of these creatures in the dark. Suppose the smaller ones fly up your nostrils. You will gasp for breath and open your mouth. Then, suppose some hundreds of them fly into your mouth, into your gullet, into your windpipe, what will happen to you? You will be dead in a very short time, choked, asphyxiated."

"But the moths would be dead too. They would be found in the bodies."

"The moths? Do you know that it is extremely difficult to kill a moth with cyanide of potassium? Take a frog, kill it, open its stomach. There you will find its dinner of moths and small beetles, and the 'dinner' will shake itself and walk off cheerily, to resume an entirely active existence. No; that is no difficulty.

"Well, now I came to this. I was shutting out all the other cases. I was confining myself to those that came under the one formula. I got to the assumption or conclusion, whichever you like, that certain people had been asphyxiated by the action of moths. I had accounted for that extraordinary appearance of burning or colored lights that I had witnessed myself, when I saw the growth of that strange tree in my garden. That was clearly the cloud with points of fire in it that the Stratfordshire man took for a new and terrible kind of poison gas, that was the shiny something that poor little Johnnie Roberts had seen over the stile, that was the glimmering light that had led Mrs. Cradock to her husband's dead body, that was the assemblage of terrible eyes that had watched over Treff Loyne by night. Once on the right track I understood all this, for coming into this room in the dark, I have been amazed by the wonderful burning and the strange fiery colors of the eyes of a single moth, as it crept up the pane of glass, outside. Imagine the effect of myriads of such eyes, of the movement of these lights and fires in a vast swarm of moths, each insect being in constant motion while it kept its place in the mass: I felt that all this was clear and certain.

"Then the next step. Of course, we know nothing really about moths; rather, we know nothing of moth reality. For all I know there may be hundreds of books which treat of moth and nothing but moth. But these are scientific books, and science only deals with surfaces; it has nothing to do with realities—it is impertinent if it attempts to do with realities. To take a very minor matter; we don't even know why the moth desires the flame. But we do know what the moth does not do; it does not gather itself into swarms with the object of destroying human life. But here, by the hypothesis, were cases in which the moth had done this very thing; the moth race had entered, it seemed, into a malignant conspiracy against the human race. It was quite impossible, no doubt—that is to say, it had never happened before—but I could see no escape from this conclusion.

"These insects, then, were definitely hostile to man; and then I stopped, for I could not see the next step, obvious though it seems to me now. I believe that the soldiers' scraps of talk on the way to Treff Loyne and back flung the next plank over the gulf. They had spoken of 'rat poison,' of no rat being able to spike a man through the heart; and then, suddenly, I saw my way clear. If the moths were infected with hatred of men, and possessed the design and the power of combining against him;

why not suppose this hatred, this design, this power shared by other non-human creatures.

"The secret of the Terror might be condensed into a sentence: the animals had revolted against men.

"Now, the puzzle became easy enough; one had only to classify. Take the cases of the people who met their deaths by falling over cliffs or over the edge of quarries. We think of sheep as timid creatures, who always ran away. But suppose sheep that don't run away; and, after all, in reason why should they run away? Quarry or no quarry, cliff or no cliff; what would happen to you if a hundred sheep ran after you instead of running from you? There would be no help for it; they would have you down and beat you to death or stifle you. Then suppose man, woman, or child near a cliff's edge or a quarry-side, and a sudden rush of sheep. Clearly there is no help; there is nothing for it but to go over. There can be no doubt that that, is what happened in all these cases.

"And again; you know the country and you know how a herd of cattle will sometimes pursue people through the fields in a solemn, stolid sort of way. They behave as if they wanted to close in on you. Townspeople sometimes get frightened and scream and run; you or I would take no notice, or at the utmost, wave our sticks at the herd, which will stop dead or lumber off. But suppose they don't lumber off. The mildest old cow, remember, is stronger than any man. What can one man or half a dozen men do against half a hundred of these beasts no longer restrained by that mysterious inhibition, which has made for ages the strong the humble slaves of the weak? But if you are botanizing in the marsh, like that poor fellow who was staying at Porth, and forty or fifty young cattle gradually close round you, and refuse to move when you shout and wave your stick, but get closer and closer instead, and get you into the slime. Again, where is your help? If you haven't got an automatic pistol, you must go down and stay down, while the beasts lie quietly on you for five minutes. It was a quicker death for poor Griffith of Treff Loyne—one of his own beasts gored him to death with one sharp thrust of its horn into his heart. And from that morning those within the house were closely besieged by their own cattle and horses and sheep; and when those unhappy people within opened a window to call for help or to catch a few drops of rain water to relieve their burning thirst, the cloud waited for them with its myriad eyes of fire. Can you wonder that Secretan's statement reads in places like mania? You perceive the horrible position of those people in Treff Loyne; not only did they see death advancing on them, but advancing with incredible steps, as if one were to die not only in nightmare but by

206

nightmare. But no one in his wildest, most fiery dreams had ever imagined such a fate. I am not astonished that Secretan at one moment suspected the evidence of his own senses, at another surmised that the world's end had come."

"And how about the Williams's who were murdered on the Highway near here?"

"The horses were the murderers; the horses that afterwards stampeded the camp below. By some means which is still obscure to me they lured that family into the road and beat their brains out; their shod hoofs were the instruments of execution. And, as for the Mary Ann, the boat that was capsized, I have no doubt that it was overturned by a sudden rush of the porpoises that were gamboling about in the water of Larnac Bay. A porpoise is a heavy beast—half a dozen of them could easily upset a light rowing-boat. The munition works? Their enemy was rats. I believe that it has been calculated that in 'greater London' the number of rats is about equal to the number of human beings, that is, there are about seven millions of them. The proportion would be about the same in all the great centers of population; and the rat, moreover, is, on occasion, migratory in its habits. You can understand now that story of the Semiramis, beating about the mouth of the Thames, and at last cast away by Arcachon, her only crew dry heaps of bones. The rat is an expert boarder of ships. And so one can understand the tale told by the frightened man who took the path by the wood that led up from the new munition works. He thought he heard a thousand men treading softly through the wood and chattering to one another in some horrible tongue; what he did hear was the marshaling of an army of rats—their array before the battle.

"And conceive the terror of such an attack. Even one rat in a fury is said to be an ugly customer to meet; conceive then, the irruption of these terrible, swarming myriads, rushing upon the helpless, unprepared, astonished workers in the munition shops."

-oOo-

There can be no doubt, I think, that Dr. Lewis was entirely justified in these extraordinary conclusions. As I say, I had arrived at pretty much the same end, by different ways; but this rather as to the general situation, while Lewis had made his own particular study of those circumstances of the Terror that were within his immediate purview, as a physician in large practice in the southern part of Meirion. Of some of the cases which he reviewed he had, no doubt, no immediate or first-hand knowledge; but he judged these instances by their similarity to the facts which had come under his personal notice. He spoke of the affairs of the quarry at Llanfihangel on the analogy of the people who were found dead at the bottom of the cliffs near Porth, and he was no doubt justified in doing so. He told me that, thinking the whole matter over, he was hardly more astonished by the Terror in itself than by the strange way in which he had arrived at his conclusions.

"You know," he said, "those certain evidences of animal malevolence which we knew of, the bees that stung the child to death, the trusted sheepdog's turning savage, and so forth. Well, I got no light whatever from all this; it suggested nothing to me—simply because I had not got that 'idea' which Coleridge rightly holds necessary in all inquiry; facts qua facts, as we said, mean nothing and, come to nothing. You do not believe, therefore you cannot see.

"And then, when the truth at last appeared it was through the whimsical 'coincidence' as we call such signs, of the moth in my lamp and the moth on the dead child's forehead. This, I think, is very extraordinary."

"And there seems to have been one beast that remained faithful; the dog at Treff Loyne. That is strange."

"That remains a mystery."

-oOo-

It would not be wise, even now, to describe too closely the terrible scenes that were to be seen in the munition areas of the north and the midlands during the black months of the Terror. Out of the factories issued at black midnight the shrouded dead in their coffins, and their very kinsfolk did not know how they had come by their deaths. All the towns were full of houses of mourning, were full of dark and terrible rumors; incredible, as the incredible reality. There were things done and suffered that perhaps never will be brought to light, memories and secret traditions of these things will be whispered in families, delivered from father to son, growing wilder with the passage of the years, but never growing wilder than the truth.

It is enough to say that the cause of the Allies was for awhile in deadly peril. The men at the front called in their extremity for guns and shells. No one told them what was happening in the places where these munitions were made.

At first the position was nothing less than desperate; men in high places were almost ready to cry "mercy" to the enemy. But, after the first panic, measures were taken such as those described by Merritt in his account of the matter. The workers were armed with special weapons, guards were mounted, machine-guns were placed in position, bombs and liquid flame were ready against the obscene hordes of the enemy, and the "burning clouds" found a fire fiercer than their own. Many deaths occurred amongst the airmen; but they, too, were given special guns, arms that scattered shot broadcast, and so drove away the dark flights that threatened the airplanes.

And, then, in the winter of 1915-16, the Terror ended suddenly as it had begun. Once more a sheep was a frightened beast that ran instinctively from a little child; the cattle were again solemn, stupid creatures, void of harm; the spirit and the convention of malignant design passed out of the hearts of all the animals. The chains that they had cast off for awhile were thrown again about them.

And, finally, there comes the inevitable "why?" Why did the beasts who had been humbly and patiently subject to man, or affrighted by his presence, suddenly know their strength and learn how to league together, and declare bitter war against their ancient master?

It is a most difficult and obscure question. I give what explanation I have to give with very great diffidence, and an eminent disposition to be corrected, if a clearer light can be found.

Some friends of mine, for whose judgment I have very great respect, are inclined to think that there was a certain contagion of hate. They hold that the fury of the whole world at war, the great passion of death that seems driving all humanity to destruction, infected at last these lower creatures, and in place of their native instinct of submission, gave them rage and wrath and ravening.

This may be the explanation. I cannot say that it is not so, because I do not profess to understand the working of the universe. But I confess that the theory strikes me as fanciful. There may be a contagion of hate as there is a contagion of smallpox; I do not know, but I hardly believe it.

In my opinion, and it is only an opinion, the source of the great revolt of the beasts is to be sought in a much subtler region of inquiry. I believe that the subjects revolted because the king abdicated. Man has dominated the beasts throughout the ages, the spiritual has reigned over the rational through the peculiar quality and grace of spirituality that men possess, that makes a man to be that which he is. And when he maintained this power and grace, I think it is pretty clear that between him and the animals there was a certain treaty and alliance. There was supremacy on the one hand, and submission on the other; but at the same time there was between the two that cordiality which exists between lords and subjects in a well-organized state. I know a socialist who maintains that Chaucer's "Canterbury Tales" give a picture of true democracy. I do not know about that, but I see that knight and miller were able to get on quite pleasantly together, just because the knight knew that he was a knight and the miller knew that he was a miller. If the knight had had conscientious objections to his knightly grade, while the miller saw no reason why he should not be a knight, I am sure that their intercourse would have been difficult, unpleasant, and perhaps murderous.

So with man. I believe in the strength and truth of tradition. A learned man said to me a few weeks ago: "When I have to choose between the evidence of tradition and the evidence of a document, I always believe the evidence of tradition. Documents may be falsified, and often are falsified; tradition is never falsified." This is true; and, therefore, I think, one may put trust in the vast body of folklore which asserts that there was once a worthy and friendly alliance between man and the beasts. Our popular tale of Dick Whittington and his Cat no doubt represents the adaptation of a very ancient legend to a comparatively modern personage, but we may go back into the ages and find the popular tradition asserting that not only are the animals the subjects, but also the friends of man.

All that was in virtue of that singular spiritual element in man which the rational animals do not possess. Spiritual does not mean respectable, it does not even mean moral, it does not mean "good" in the ordinary acceptation of the word. It signifies the royal prerogative of man, differentiating him from the beasts.

For long ages he has been putting off this royal robe, he has been wiping the balm of consecration from his own breast. He has declared, again and again, that he is not spiritual, but rational, that is, the equal of the beasts over whom he was once sovereign. He has vowed that he is not Orpheus but Caliban.

But the beasts also have within them something which corresponds to the spiritual quality in men—we are content to call it instinct. They perceived that the throne was vacant—not even friendship was possible between them and the self-deposed monarch. If he were not king he was a sham, an imposter, a thing to be destroyed.

Hence, I think, the Terror. They have risen once—they may rise again.

THE END